MURDER IN
CONEY ISLAND

MURDER IN CONEY ISLAND

MICHAEL JAHN

THOMAS DUNNE BOOKS / ST. MARTIN'S MINOTAUR ⚓ NEW YORK

A THOMAS DUNNE BOOK.
An imprint of St. Martin's Press.

www.stmartins.com

Library of Congress Cataloging-in-Publication Data

Jahn, Michael.
    Murder in Coney Island: a Bill Donovan mystery / Michael Jahn—
    1st ed.
      p.cm.
    ISBN 0-312-30801-9
    1. Donovan, Bill (Fictitious character)—Fiction. 2. Police—New York (State)—New York—Fiction. 3. Coney Island (New York, N.Y.)—Fiction. 4. New York (N.Y.)—Fiction.
I. Title.

PS3560.A35M876 2003
813'.54—dc21

2002191966

First Edition: August 2003

10 9 8 7 6 5 4 3 2 1

In memory of John Loughlin

1. A BRONZE STATUE OF A BALLPARK.

To Donovan's admittedly eccentric New York City taste, the sound was as rock solid and reassuring as that made by the number 1 Seventh Avenue local as it rumbled downtown. It was a friendly and familiar throb, far away and filtered through the music of a dozen radios, each playing a different station: a hundred conversations in as many languages, and children laughing and playing around blankets and parents and giant multicolored umbrellas and in and out of the blue-white surf. Down the beach a bit, a handful of seagulls fought over a bag of Fritos that bobbed around in that surf. Donovan could hear the surf, too, sort of; a comfy old fluffed-up pillow that smoothed the roughness out of the crowd that packed the Coney Island beach that third Sunday in June.

And Donovan heard what had become his favorite word—"Daddy." He heard it over and over, as his son, now three, built a Mega Bloc tower atop the red-and-black-patterned Indian blanket the Donovans had stretched beneath the shade of an immense umbrella. The captain sat in what Daniel's physical therapists told him was the "Y position," with one cheek on the blanket and legs angled off to the other side. Bad for your knees, the Y position was, but easy on the lower back.

Marcy was stretched out on her chaise longue, a white linen cover-up over her powder blue tank suit, reading case law. She had recently graduated from Columbia Law and was studying for the New York State bar exam, with plans to become a public defender. She had sold her Broadway restaurant, the time pressure of becoming an attorney while caring for her extraordinary child having grown too great. So after ten years and a farewell party that was a celebration of all things West Side as well as a fond adieu to the era when a West Side address symbolized the artistically inclined, Marcy's Home Cooking became a Starbucks.

Today, to help snap her husband out of the sullen funk he had been in for much of the last nine months, since the attack on the World Trade Center and the beginning of the war on worldwide terrorism, she had brought him to Coney Island. His mood had been steeped in powerlessness in the face of being left out of the massive investigation. Also, he was beginning to suspect that he had grown soft with age, a suspicion augmented by Moskowitz's endless teasing to that effect. This jaunt to New York's bizarre Riviera, she was sure, would cheer him up.

Donovan got up, emitting a slight grumble as his knees unkinked.

"Honey?" Marcy asked, looking over the top of her sunglasses.

"Daniel and I are going for a swim," he replied, stripping off his blue-and-white NYPD T-shirt and dropping it onto the blanket atop his copy of the Sunday *Times*.

"Yeah, yeah, Daddy!" Daniel said, reaching a small hand up to give his father a high five.

"Did you put on your sunblock this morning?" she asked.

He nodded. "Of course."

"You have to do that every day. You know what the doctor said."

"I know what he said."

"Be careful with Daniel," Marcy said.

Donovan nodded a second time, then bent at the knees and went low, scooping up his son in both arms. The boy's arm went eagerly around his father's neck, and the child smiled gleefully as he was carried down the beach, around countless families camped upon as many blankets, and into the surf ankle high. Then Donovan put the boy down, arranged the tiny legs in front of him, and sat down alongside. Donovan asked, "How does it feel?"

"It tickles my tummy," Daniel said, half laughing, as an incoming gush of white foamy water splashed up to his belly button.

"Is the water too cold on your legs?"

Daniel looked at his father, then laughed and said, "I like it on my tummy."

"You can't feel the water on your legs, can you?" Donovan said.

The boy shook his head, looking momentarily embarrassed, then smiled again and asked, "Are *your* legs cold, Daddy?"

"I'm never cold when I'm sitting next to you," Donovan said.

"Can you catch me a sand crab?" Daniel asked.

"I'll try," Donovan replied, then plunged both hands

into the sand beneath the surf in pursuit of the harmless but hyperactive little things that his son thought so funny when they tried to burrow between his fingers. After a minute or two he found one and dropped the handful of sand containing the critter into Daniel's cupped hands.

As the boy squealed in delight—a little boy who was happy and nearly oblivious to the part of his body that, for no reason the world's top experts could discern, didn't work—the captain misted over a little. Then, to avert a tear, he turned his attention to the surf and beyond, where a party fishing boat, the *Viking V*, out of nearby Sheepshead Bay, blew the whistle that warned its deck load of anglers to pull in their lines.

"I guess the fish aren't biting," he said.

"Will the sand crab bite me, Daddy?" Daniel asked.

"Nothing will ever hurt you, not now, not ever," Donovan told the boy.

An hour later, with the boy napping happily in the arms of his nanny, Donovan's cousin Mary, the captain announced that he was going off in pursuit of hot dogs. A Sunday at Coney Island would be nothing without a Nathan's dog and a cold drink. Following a brief discussion with Marcy of the amount of fat in his diet, Donovan buckled on his fanny pack, slipped his feet into his ancient and crumbling Docksiders, and headed off in the direction of the Boardwalk. He picked his way through a sea of blankets, loungers, umbrellas, and splayed limbs, pausing often to wait his turn to use a narrow walkway between two sun-worshiping families.

Midway between the surf and the Boardwalk on a summer Sunday, the noise of the various radio stations merged into one. The languages spoken over the airwaves or on the blankets became a single language, and it reminded him of the one spoken on the streets of futuristic Los Angeles in *Blade Runner*—a muddle of tongues that sounded part Spanish, part Mandarin, and part smoky syllables voiced in joy or anger.

Donovan bypassed the packed Nathan's Famous takeout counter on the Boardwalk and, unable to find the hot dog cart he had noticed that morning while looking for a parking spot, walked inland two blocks to the original Nathan's. The corner of Surf and Stillwell, where Nathan's had stood since 1916, was thronged. The lines for the multiple sidewalk counters ran out to the curb and then some. The gleam of the stainless steel counters offset the garish yellow-and-red signs above, which towered two stories in spots and advertised hot dogs, hamburgers, fries . . . all the sorts of things that sent a mist of smells—fat, garlic, meat, potatoes, salt—onto the Coney Island beach on a summer weekend.

Donovan scowled at the lines for a moment before trudging to the end of one and beginning, he hoped, a wait of only fifteen or twenty minutes' duration. The smell of mustard and sauerkraut drew him, but when after ten minutes in line he moved only two paces, Donovan found himself glad to be distracted by approaching sirens.

Those sounds came from down Surf Avenue a bit. A major east-west boulevard paralleling the Boardwalk and the ocean, Surf Avenue was home to some of the island's oldest stores. These were shops that seemed unchanged from shortly after World War II, when returning GIs picked up their families and moved to the suburbs and Coney Island began a long decline that bottomed out during the 1960s with the addition of massive low-income housing projects and had only recently been arrested. When first one, then two, then six squad cars converged on a block of Surf Avenue, Donovan looked at the hot dog stand, thought of the heartburn, and left the line to amble down to the crime scene.

Conspicuously untouched by the renovation occurring elsewhere in Coney Island, the block held small stores gone decrepit with the passage of years. Millions of hands, feet, and pennies had coursed through the laundromat, the thrift shop, the plumber's shop, the small-appliance store—which, judging from its graying cobwebbed window, appeared to sell only fans—and the candy store/newsstand known as Surf Avenue News, where it remained possible to buy "penny candy" (but at a dime each). Donovan was very protective of colorful and ethnic neighborhoods and held long-running suspicions about the city's periodic attempts to "clean them up." A few years back, while investigating several murders in Times Square, the captain had seen firsthand what he called the "Disneyfication" of the city's classic honky-tonk district. It's nice to have a clean street, he knew, but also good when you can buy lunch for less than twenty dollars. Later, while on a case on the waterfront, he had bemoaned the disappearance of all the places he remembered where a driver could get a flat fixed for a handful of bucks. So when a block of Coney Island that Donovan spotted as being charming and old was suddenly infested with police cars, he took special interest, knowing well that when the police cast their eyes on something the rest of the city bureaucracy often followed.

The uniformed officers were buzzing around Surf Avenue News, which was the corner store. Its windows were dark with the passage of time and the presence of many signs and posters—announcing the daily lottery numbers, the schedule for the junket bus to Atlantic City, the availability of forms to use in applying for permission to have a float in the Mermaid Parade, a photograph of a missing cat and its heartbroken five-year-old owner, and the existence inside of "Brooklyn's biggest collection of Dodgers baseball cards." Donovan smiled at the notion that there had been a theft of a 1955 Duke Snider.

He fished his badge holder out of his fanny pack, hung it over the neck of his T-shirt, and tapped his forefinger against it for the benefit of the patrolman assigned to stop passersby from entering the crime scene. Donovan said, "Bill Donovan, Special Investigations. What's up?"

The young man gawked at the badge as he took a moment, Donovan thought, to identify the name. Regular patrolmen rarely, if ever, encountered an officer above the rank of lieutenant, let alone one of Donovan's eminence.

"Special Investi . . . ? Oh, Captain Donovan! Sorry, sir."

"Don't worry about it."

"I was thrown by your suit, you know?" the young man said, a certain Brooklynish defiance appearing, as if to say, *If you're such a big shot, what are you doing in a bathing suit?*

"I left the jacket and tie in my trunk," Donovan said.

"What we got here, Captain, is a DOA in the basement. The call just came in ten minutes ago."

"What sort of DOA?"

"You know what I know," the patrolman replied. "Hold on, let me get the sarge for you."

Donovan made a don't-bother gesture, but it was too late. Ever alert for the appearance of a gold badge on his crime scenes, the sergeant came over with his hand out-stretched. He squinted at Donovan's badge and said, "Can I help you, Captain?"

"Bill Donovan, Special Investigations. I just happened by."

"Captain Donovan, sure. Manhattan. Last year, that thing on the waterfront. It's a pleasure. What we got here is the owner of this store found a DOA. Here's how it goes. The guy's been open since seven this morning for the Sunday papers and the crowds, you know? But he don't have reason to go down into the basement until fifteen or twenty minutes ago, when he finds the body."

"What's in the basement that he had to go there in the middle of a busy afternoon?" Donovan asked.

"Among other stuff, his famous baseball card collection," the sergeant replied.

"Was the 1955 Duke Snider card stolen?"

The sergeant said, "Jeez, I hope not."

"Who's the stiff?" Donovan asked.

Another voice came into the conversation, a high-pitched and nervous one, saying, "It's *him!* It would be *him!*"

Donovan saw a gaunt man of sixty or so, who was sweating profusely despite wearing only Bermuda shorts and a thin and inexpensive business shirt—a cotton and nylon blend, mostly nylon, such as a low-level manager might buy—over an athletic tee. The man was bald save for twin tufts of graying black hair, patches the size and approximate shape of hot dog rolls, one over each ear. Sweat rolled down off his forehead and under his glasses, forcing him to keep poking a finger up there to keep the sweat out of his eyes.

"Who are you?" Donovan asked.

"Harry Caplan, who do you think?" the man said.

"My mistake. I'm Bill Donovan, chief of special investigations for the City of New York. Tell me, Mr. Caplan, how are you involved in this? This is your store, right?"

"Of *course* it's my store. Who else would it belong to? And it was my father's before me."

"He must be very proud of you," Donovan said drily. "Now, who is the dead man?"

"*Him!* James Victor."

"I got no idea who that is," the sergeant said.

Donovan said, "Do you mean the real estate developer? The guy who's tearing down the old buildings and putting up new office space and condos?"

"Yeah, yeah, him," Caplan said, his face suddenly eager with the knowledge that he was being understood.

"How'd a Manhattan cop like you know who Victor is?" the sergeant asked.

"I have a special place in my heart for men who tear down neighborhoods where ordinary people live in order to build upper-income condos," Donovan said.

"I hear you," the sergeant nodded.

Caplan said, "I never spoke to the man, at least not in person. I never *would* talk to him. He's a monster who destroys people's lives. He's a *gonif*. Do you know Yiddish, Captain?"

"My wife is half Jewish, and besides, like Lenny Bruce

said, 'in New York you're Jewish even if you're goyish.' In other words, I speak Yinglish," Donovan said. "What was the *gonif* doing in your basement?"

"I got no idea. I was suing him, so my lawyer said to never talk to the man in case I ran into him. Which wasn't likely, because he hung out at Trump Plaza."

"And you hang out in the Russian Baths in Brighton Beach," Donovan said.

Caplan smiled and raised a finger. "Very good. Close, anyway. I hang out at the Coney Island Jewish Community Center, where the committee meets each Thursday night for tea and cake."

"The committee," Donovan said.

"The Coney Island Committee for Common Sense," Caplan replied. "We're a coalition of small business owners, nonprofits, churches, my temple, and ordinary people. We pressure the police to fight crime in Coney Island."

"Crime is down here," Donovan said agreeably.

"Notwithstanding that a terrorist was killed near Nathan's the other night."

There *had* been a death a week and a half earlier: a thirty-two-year-old Yemeni, a resident of Flatbush, killed in a showndown with FBI agents who sought him for questioning in connection with the previous year's attack on the World Trade Center. "Like I said, crime is down," Donovan said. "You should be proud of yourself."

Caplan nodded, then added, "We're bringing suit against Victor to stop him from destroying the character of Coney Island. This block, for example."

The arrival of other police vehicles distracted Donovan momentarily. Those cars and vans, all bearing the markings of Brooklyn South Command, essentially filled the block.

"He wanted to tear down the whole block?" the captain asked.

"Yes, and to replace it with a twenty-story high-rise tower with ocean view apartments. Guess how much they would sell for?"

Donovan shrugged and said, "Top end—one mil."

Caplan said, "One point two. In Coney Island! And the tenants who would be displaced, what would happen to them?"

"I remember when Robert Moses was tearing up neighborhoods to build parkways, someone asked him where people would go to live, and he said, 'There's lots of trailers down South.' "

"*Gonif,*" Caplan snarled. Then he added, "I rent out the second floor, right above my store? It's a two-bedroom apartment."

"A thousand a month," Donovan said.

"Eight fifty. I wish I could get a thousand, but let's be real—my tenants are poor. I mean, let's face it, they live above a candy store," Caplan said.

"A candy store with a body in the basement," Donovan added.

Unwilling to let go of his point, Caplan said, "My tenants—the husband supplements his pension by using a metal detector to find coins in the sand. These are the salt of the earth, these people here in Coney Island who Victor . . . God give his soul eternal unrest . . . was trying to throw out onto the street."

"When did you find the body?"

"I guess it's been half an hour. I had to go down there to get something . . ."

"What?"

"Last week's Sunday *Times Magazine*. Charley, my upstairs tenant, does the crossword puzzle, but he didn't get last week's paper, so I locked the front door and went downstairs to get a copy I saved for him. See, he comes by every Sunday about this time."

"Why'd you lock the front door?" Donovan asked.

"So I didn't have to ask my huge professional staff to watch the shop for me," Caplan replied.

"You work alone."

"Just me and the ghosts in there every day. Anyway, I flip on the basement light and go down the stairs. And there he is, the *gonif* himself, laying in . . . what do you call it, 'a pool of blood?' . . . right between the shelves where I keep my Dodgers cards. I hurried back upstairs and called nine-one-one."

"Any idea how he got down there?" Donovan asked.

"It wasn't after buying a box of Cracker Jack, I can tell you that," Caplan said.

"I want to see the body," Donovan replied.

After introducing himself to and exerting his authority over a brace of local lieutenants who arrived before he could get in the door, Donovan stepped inside Surf Avenue News. The store was so narrow that two people would find it awkward passing between the racks of magazines on the left and the counter and shelves on the right. The ceiling was high enough so that it was rarely cleaned, and as a result the stamped tin that covered it was outlined in dust and cobwebs. Front to back, the store was deep;

it seemed to narrow off into a dark nothingness broken only by the light inside a refrigerated case that contained not only Coke and Pepsi but Jamaican ginger beer, Malta malt beverage, Dr. Brown's Cel-Ray Soda, Yoo-hoo, chocolate and strawberry milk, grape soda, and plain and raspberry-flavored seltzer.

The counter held the cash register and cigarettes, cigars, pipe and chewing tobacco, rolling paper, butane lighters, snuff, ginseng, chocolate-covered cherries, cellophane packets of vitamins and "fat-burning" herbs, Blistex, eyeglass repair kits, pocket Kleenex packets, and black plastic combs. Behind Caplan's stool was a wall full of cough and cold remedies, sunblock and suntan lotions, Solarcaine, condoms, and batteries. A display of foil packets labeled HORNY GOAT WEED also decorated the wall.

Donovan walked past racks of magazines plain and racy (the latter with strategically placed brown paper on their covers) and stacks of thick Sunday newspapers, skirted a stand holding a coffee machine, and walked by several displays of salty snacks. He turned sideways to squeeze by a basic foods section . . . bread, peanut butter, grape jam, and—Donovan smiled at the sight of something he had rarely glimpsed since his bachelor drinking days ended—tins of Dinty Moore Beef Stew and Hormel Corned Beef Hash. Next to those staples, a small housewares section offered duct tape, sewing kits, black cotton work gloves, electrical fuses, regular and Phillips screwdrivers, small hammers, and assortments of nails and screws.

"Down here," Caplan said, leading the way to a small door that was adjacent to the refrigerated beverage case. It opened with a creak, allowing entrance to a short hallway piled high with boxes of paper towels, Comet cleanser, Kleenex, Raisin Bran Crunch, and gummy worms. A box that once held Cheez Whiz was labeled HOUSEWARES.

A narrow white door opened onto a tiny bathroom, just a sink and a toilet that smelled overpoweringly of pine-scented cleaner. Across the hall, another door revealed a stairway, wooden and creaky. On both sides of the downward passage useful items were suspended from nails. Among them were a hammer, a monkey wrench, a roll of duct tape, a staple gun, a length of telephone wire, a pair of suspenders, a Dodgers baseball cap, and a clipboard that Caplan tapped with two fingertips. "This is my inventory of baseball cards," he explained. "I keep it here with the stuff I might need to reach quickly without locking the front door."

"Do you sell these cards or what?" Donovan asked.

"Me, *sell!* No, never. What, are you crazy? Sell *Dodgers* stuff?"

"I'm a Yankees fan," Donovan replied, adding, with a tone suggesting that the explanation was necessary, "Sorry, friend. Such people exist."

"Not in Brooklyn. Where do you live, in the city?"

Smiling faintly, Donovan said, "I get a kick out of Brooklyn guys who don't believe they live in New York City. 'Oh, I have to go to *the city* today.' Where do you think you live?"

"In a better place, and you should know that. Here, watch your step so you don't break your neck, Mr. Yankees Fan."

"What's out that door over there?" Donovan asked, nodding out back.

14

"The alley, what do you think?"

"Did you keep *that* door locked, too, or just the front?"

"I never bother to lock that door," Caplan said. "Nobody ever uses it except me."

"Except maybe today," Donovan said.

Donovan followed Caplan down into a subterranean world even more crowded than the one above.

"I'm sorry the basement is so dirty," Caplan said. "If I knew that I would be having a celebrity corpse, I would have had the floor cleaned more than once every forty years."

Crates and racks were everywhere. This and that were piled here and there, with no labels to distinguish one stack from another. Two dehumidifiers whirred low, managing, Donovan supposed, to keep the mold inevitable to basements, especially those near the seashore, away from the baseball cards. Unlike the other stuff kept down below, the collection was clearly marked. Contained in what seemed to be ten thousand glassine envelopes hung in glass cases, it was heralded by a neon-colored sign reading

BROOKLYN'S BIGGEST
COLLECTION OF DODGERS CARDS

Three uniformed officers—two sergeants and a patrolman—stood around scrupulously not looking at the body, which lay face up in front of the famous baseball card collection.

"I'm not looking at that again," Caplan said, twisting to let the captain pass on the narrow stairway.

The trio of officers looked up and saw Donovan,

who, following a brief conversation that was more about power than evidence, chased them off. Caplan again twisted his body to let others by. Donovan stepped up near the corpse, glancing at it and its surroundings. The victim was darkly handsome and fit, with triceps that suggested a gym membership. He appeared to be in his forties and was casually but expensively dressed. The man's red polo shirt was a brand that Donovan had seen at Lord & Taylor for $120. His gray slacks looked custom made. Certainly the man had invested a hundred dollars in his belt and several times that in his shoes. To the belt was clipped a cell phone that Donovan knew to run at least five hundred dollars.

The captain crouched to examine a bloody lump of metal that lay in the shadow near the victim's left foot. "Does this belong to you?" Donovan asked Caplan.

"I can't see in the dark, but if that's what he was hit with," Caplan announced, "I don't want to look at it."

"Who says he was hit with anything?" Donovan asked.

"Oops," Caplan replied. "Am I in trouble here?"

"Finding a murder victim in your basement generally entails a certain amount of inconvenience," Donovan replied. "Especially since you hated the sonofabitch."

"I didn't *hate* the man," Caplan said.

"Too late to back out now," Donovan replied.

"Besides, killing him might not stop the demolition. He has a wife who I hear is worse than he is, if you can imagine."

"And she inherits the empire?"

"Your guess is as good as mine," Caplan replied.

"This is getting interesting," Donovan said.

He unzipped his fanny pack, poked around for a pencil, then used it to lift up the bloody lump so he could get a better look. He put it back down and stood up. "Do you keep any Dodgers memorabilia other than cards?" Donovan asked.

"Such as what?" the store owner replied, a twitch of nervous caution in his voice.

"Such as a solid bronze statue of Ebbets Field," Donovan said.

"Oy vey iz mir," Caplan said, then sat down on the stairs, fanning himself with his left hand.

2. "IF YOU BOLTED A SOLID ROCKET BOOSTER TO THE ASS END OF THE Q TRAIN IT WOULDN'T GET YOU TO MIDTOWN IN FORTY-FIVE MINUTES."

Finding a guy who was beaten to death in the basement of a candy store is your idea of fun in the sun at Coney Island, right?" Sergeant Brian Moskowitz said.

"The sun is no good for you anyway," Donovan said.

"You yanked me out of my barbecue," Mosko continued.

"Before or after you got to the Junior's Cheesecake?"

"After," Mosko admitted, looking down sheepishly but, in so doing, only drawing attention to the pectoral muscles bulging beneath a T-shirt that read

**REAL MEN DON'T WASTE
HORMONES GROWING HAIR**

The sergeant—who had a steadily advancing bald spot—pulled a clipboard from his car and found a pen in the pocket of the driver's door. "You owe me big-time," he continued.

"For what, for finding a case that's a ten-minute drive from your house?" Donovan replied.

"That ten minutes is when there's no traffic on the Belt, which means we're talking about four in the morning. Anyway, thanks. Who's dead?"

"James Victor, the developer who was trying to get these stores torn down so he could replace them with high-income housing," Donovan said. "The idea being that seaside condos forty-five minutes from midtown Manhattan by subway would sell big."

"If you bolted a solid rocket booster to the ass end of the Q train it wouldn't get you to midtown in forty-five minutes," Mosko maintained.

"I yield to your greater experience with all things Brooklyn," Donovan replied as his family drove up in "Barney." That was what Daniel called his father's new car, a deep purple Chrysler 300M for which he'd traded in his Taurus.

"Here's your clothes, honey," Marcy called out, lowering the window and handing her husband his gym bag.

Daniel waved furiously, laughing, "Daddy's working!"

"We'll play Mega Blocs when I get home," Donovan said, waving back.

"God, you're cute when you go into Daddy mode," Mosko said.

"Brian, you be sure to drive my husband home," Marcy said.

"Hey, what about the advantage of this case being ten

minutes from my house?" Mosko protested.

Marcy shrugged, and Donovan said, "I'll take the subway."

"He'll take the subway," Mosko added. "We're only forty-five minutes from midtown by subway."

Marcy stuck her head out the window to be kissed, and Donovan complied, blushing slightly when a few cops standing nearby applauded.

"Don't be late," Marcy added, then drove off.

"I'm going downstairs to change," Donovan said.

"I want to see the body," Mosko added, trailing along.

Howard Bonaci and his forensics team had just arrived as well. They were setting up their equipment around the body when Donovan and Moskowitz squeezed by. Donovan watched as Mosko lingered to inspect the corpse, donning vinyl gloves to go over the body and extricate the wallet.

"This is one of the better-off corpses I've seen in a while," Donovan said.

"No shit," Mosko replied, flipping through the wallet. "The bum must have a thousand bucks in here."

"The price of hot dogs keeps going up," Donovan said.

"I can tell you one thing, robbery wasn't the motive."

"What else is in there?"

Mosko read off the contents: "Driver's license. Lives on Ocean Parkway near Kings Highway."

"Not exactly Brooklyn's low-rent district," Donovan said.

"Yeah. We have fences to keep guys like this out. What else is in the wallet? Okay, gym membership: Downtown Athletic Club."

"Where they give out the Heisman Trophy," Donovan said.

Mosko nodded. "He couldn't have been beaten to death with *that* and save the memory of Ebbets Field. What else? Platinum card. Gold card. Debit card. Food Emporium check-cashing card."

"I suppose a library card is too much to hope for," Donovan said.

Mosko continued: "Half a dozen of his own business cards. An ATM machine receipt dated today. Wait. There's a name written on it, 'Lisa,' and a time, seven-thirty."

"I wonder who Lisa is," Donovan said.

He walked to the front end of the basement and set his gym bag atop a box proclaimed to contain sixty-four snack-size bags of Mesquite BBQ potato chips. Moving quickly—before anyone noticed what he was up to, he hoped—he changed from bathing suit to khakis and slipped his Docksiders back on, skipping the socks. By the time Bonaci came over to give him a hard time about disrobing with others around, the captain was pulling his belt in a notch.

"Whatsa matter, the Y ain't open today?" Bonaci asked.

"How long has Victor been dead?" Donovan growled.

"Jeez, I just got to the party myself. But I would guess no more than three hours."

"Around noon," Donovan replied, after checking his watch.

"Noon to one. But I'll know more later on today. Better yet, tomorrow."

"How do you think it happened?" Donovan asked.

"First impression? The victim, Victor, was standing

looking at the baseball cards . . . hey, who could blame him? There's a 1955 Duke Snider in there."

"No shit?" Donovan said idly.

"And the perp clocked him on the back of the head with the statue. Hey, I never seen a bronze statue of Ebbets Field before. Do you think it's worth anything?"

"Don't know. Did you look at the fingers on his left hand?"

Bonaci nodded. "He must have grabbed at the wound before he died. Nothing bleeds like a scalp wound."

"Come here," Donovan said, leading the way back to the body, pausing only long enough to say, "Excuse me, gentlemen," and wave the forensics technicians out of his way. He pointed out some trails of blood on the glass front of the display case, easy to see once you were looking for them, but otherwise lost against the colorful array of memorabilia. The streaks started two feet or so above the floor and ended when the display case did, six inches up from the concrete. Bonaci bent to look.

Donovan said, "I think the guy was clobbered and fell on his face. Look at his nose."

"Looks like he went a round with Tyson," Bonaci agreed.

"Then he rolled over to the right . . ."

"Immobilizing his right arm . . ."

"Grabbing at his wound with his left hand, and then reached up for a handhold on the display case."

"Either that or he saw the Duke Snider card and wanted to take it with him to heaven," Bonaci said.

"Guys who evict poor people from their homes are bound elsewhere," Donovan said. "Anyway, his hand is slippery with blood, and he can't find anything to grab onto."

"The perp clocks him again, this time on the left temple," Bonaci said, pointing at the spot in question.

"Victor dies," Donovan concluded.

"I believe you basically got it," Bonaci said, straightening up.

"Leaving behind only a trail of blood on the glass and a bounty of ill will. Is there any idea what he was looking for?"

Bonaci shrugged. "I know he was carrying *this*."

Bonaci held up an evidence bag containing a very large screwdriver. Donovan took the bag and spent a moment staring at the screwdriver. Then he handed the bag back.

"Did he spend any time down here before he got killed?" Donovan asked.

The response was the same. Bonaci added, "If you let me get to work . . ."

"Sorry," Donovan said and backed away.

He could hear feet clomping around in the store above as he did what he could to survey the crime scene, given the number of police personnel in the small space. Behind the stairs was an oil burner that seemed barely adequate for the store and the apartment above. There was also an array of aging pipes, mostly the lead kind that were magnets for dirt, not the gleaming white polyvinyl chloride pipes of present-day plumbing. Two fifty-gallon oil drums placidly accumulated dust and grime in a corner, though one appeared to have been sat on recently. Two or three short lengths of copper pipe rested atop one of them.

There was no way out of the basement other than the

stairs, at least not in the back. Donovan skirted the body and the technicians attending it and made his way to the front of the basement. There, a set of very old and very rusted iron stairs—wide, for use by workmen carrying boxes and other supplies—led up at a shallow angle to a pair of doors set flush with the pavement. A feature of older New York City shopping blocks, these doors swung straight up and away from one another and, if dropped back into place, landed with a crash that was sure to rattle dishes into the next block. Even when padlocked down, the doors were good places for kids to practice vertical leaps, and city kids of the sort Donovan was half a century before knew all the noisiest ones.

The doors that Donovan found himself looking up at, however, appeared to be as little used as the iron stairs below. They were dark brown with rust, and the hinges gave no indication of recent use. Using a Maglite to look closer, Donovan found rust flakes that had fallen onto the stair steps. He, for one, was unwilling to try the steps by stepping on them, so he found an old broom and pushed upward against the doors. They didn't budge, and another rainfall of rust came down. A few flakes landed on his forehead and stuck in the sunblock. He brushed them off with the side of his hand.

As he turned away, he heard a familiar "Hey, yo!" and the heavy footfalls of Brian Moskowitz. "The vic didn't get down here that way, Cap," Mosko said.

"I didn't think so."

"It's padlocked from the outside, and Caplan says he lost the key in the 1970s. He says those doors haven't been used in at least that long."

"Anyway, those doors are set right near the front door

to the shop," Donovan said. "And the shop is two blocks from the beach at Coney Island on a summer Sunday, when . . ."

"The Charge of the Light Brigade would pale beside the hot dog line at Nathan's," Mosko added.

"I already punked out of standing in it," Donovan said.

"I'll bet you punked out of parking on the street, too," Mosko said.

"We used a lot. Why?"

" 'Cause we found Victor's car parked by a hydrant on Neptune a block over," Mosko said. "It's a black Porsche."

Donovan nodded.

"Regarding the foot traffic, plenty of people were coming in the door and would have seen something," Mosko said. "And you can sort of see these doors . . ." Mosko took the broom from his boss and poked them from underneath, as Donovan had done. That sent down another shower of rust flakes, this time on the two of them.

"Thank you," Donovan said, brushing rust out of his hair.

". . . from behind the cash register," Mosko continued. "I mean, if the perp was small enough to hide behind the Atlantic City bus schedule, and if ten people were demanding lottery tickets, maybe he could open the doors and slip down into the basement unnoticed."

"Lottery sales are low on Sundays," Donovan said.

"But if Caplan is an alert kind of guy he would have seen those doors opening himself."

"Caplan appears to be plenty alert," Donovan agreed.

"So how could the victim get into this place?"

Mosko replied, "The back door leading to the alley."

Donovan wanted to check it, so the two men went up the stairs, brushing by Caplan. He was perched on the top step watching morosely as the forensics technicians pored over the corpse of his enemy.

"Twenty-five hundred dollars I was offered for that statue of Ebbets Field," Caplan said, his chin in his hands.

"As a used murder weapon it will be worth a fortune on eBay," Donovan said.

That appeared to cheer Caplan up somewhat, and he stood and stepped back onto the main floor of his candy store.

"Will I get the statue back?" he asked.

"Eventually, if you didn't kill Victor," Donovan said.

"Of *course* I didn't kill him! How can you think such a thing?"

"It's what the city pays him to do," Mosko said.

"I'm kind of developmentally arrested that way," Donovan said. "There's a dead body and the guy standing nearby hates him, I can't help thinking there's a connection. I'm going to therapy to work this out."

Caplan smiled. Donovan was sure it was a fatalistic sort of smile. Caplan said, "You're fooling around with me, but I understand."

"Your understanding is nice, but at the moment I'm more interested in your fingerprints," Mosko said.

"What for?"

"To check against the statue," Mosko replied.

"What do you think, my fingerprints *aren't* on the statue?" Caplan exclaimed. "Didn't I say that I was offered money for the thing? It's *mine!*"

"We need to see if your fingerprints are *over* or *under* the blood," Donovan said.

"Did you touch it after Victor was killed?" Mosko asked.

"I didn't know it was the murder weapon until you told me," Caplan said.

"I think that's a no," Donovan said.

"I haven't seen it in three or four months," Caplan added.

"Where did you keep it?" Mosko asked.

"In a cardboard box set atop a plastic milk carton at the bottom of the stairs."

"An open or closed box?" Donovan asked.

"Open."

Donovan nodded. "Who knew it was in the box?" he asked.

"Just me," Caplan replied.

"Give additional thought to that, would you?" Donovan said.

"Why?"

"You're digging a nice little hole for yourself to drop into, that's why," Mosko replied.

"You could see it atop the other stuff in the box as you were going downstairs," Caplan said. "I *liked* to have it within sight. It was *Ebbets Field!* And until today no one but me went down there. Maybe someone was stealing it and Victor interrupted him." Caplan's tone was that of someone trying to be helpful.

"Oh, so now Victor is your security guard?" Mosko said.

Donovan touched Caplan on the arm reassuringly,

then said, "Go sit down and have a nice cup of tea and think about who might have known that statue was in that box."

"I think you're right," Caplan replied. "I think I'll have a couple of Tums, too."

"I'm going to look around out back," Donovan said.

"And I'm going downstairs to make sure we dust that box for prints," Mosko said, heading back down to the basement.

Donovan pushed open the back door to find himself in the sharply angled shadows of late afternoon. He stood in the doorway and looked around. The alley would be wide enough for a small car, were it not cluttered with trash receptacles and trash of all sorts—galvanized iron and plastic garbage cans, cardboard boxes into which other cardboard boxes had been neatly folded and tied with twine, and shopping carts that had strayed from the local C-Town market and had become carriers of the random garbage of old stores. Stuff that the merchants on the block had been unable to sell or unwilling to throw out lay everywhere. Donovan saw large toys, their primary-colored plastic faded to pastel with the years and the assaults of the noonday, beachside sun, propped against walls next to twenty-year-old furniture that probably could sell for *something* were it not for the many scratches and the odd wobbly leg. Behind the appliance store sat a gigantic freestanding fan, at least ten feet tall with a business end three feet wide, that before the dawn of rust might have stirred the air at Grand Central Station.

At the far end of the alley, Donovan saw beachgoers trudging away from the surf and sand toward cars and buses and trains, kids in tow, folding chairs over arms, the weight of salty exhaustion heavy upon them. At the nearby end, where Caplan's was the corner store, the only foot traffic was on the opposite side of the side street. And those people were less interested in getting home than in gawking at the yellow crime scene tape that surrounded Surf Avenue News.

Carefully stepping around the cobblestone immediately behind the back door, then walking gingerly along a path he presumed would avoid areas where the feet of stalking or fleeing suspects would likely fall, Donovan poked around the piles on both sides of the door. Finally he selected a red tubular trash receptacle, the kind with a domed top and a swinging trash door stamped with the word PUSH.

He lifted the top off and peered inside. This was, he found quickly, the trash can that Caplan himself used. It was full of small-business paperwork—receipts, ledgers, envelopes, coupons, and junk mail. Several envelopes were addressed to

> Surf Ave News
> Harry Caplan, prop.
> 62145 Surf Avenue
> Coney Island, NY 11224

Atop the pile was a black cotton work glove of the sort Caplan sold, right handed and covered with blood. Donovan used his Maglite to peer at it from several angles but avoided touching the thing. Then he punched some numbers on his cell phone. When Mosko answered he said, "I found the glove the murderer used. Seal off this alley at both entrances and make sure our cops don't stomp all over any footprints with their hobnailed boots . . . Yeah, that's right, and tell Caplan to take another couple of Tums."

3. "YOU'RE WITH HARRY, YOU GET OUTTA HERE WITH YOUR MONEY."

You mean that the murderer stole a glove from me and used it to hold the murder weapon?" Caplan exclaimed.

"Are you missing any?" Donovan asked.

"Let's see. I'm pretty sure I had four pair hanging on the rack this morning."

Caplan led Donovan and Moskowitz to the "housewares section" of his store and jabbed a twiglike finger at the display, over and over. "Four . . . I told you, four."

Donovan looked around, craning to see the cash register at the front of the store. "Do you get a lot of theft from back here?" he asked.

"Kids steal candy. That's why I keep all the stealable items behind the counter. Back here, where I can't see what's going on, I keep things like big boxes of cereal. Nobody steals Quaker Oats."

"Or cheap cotton gloves?" Donovan asked.

"That would be a first," Caplan replied.

"I suppose it would be possible to steal a pair of gloves from this rack without you noticing," Donovan said.

"You bet. Around lunchtime, which is when you told me Victor might have been killed, I had three or four people at the counter at all times. The only busier time is the day before a big lottery drawing."

Donovan said, "I hate the tyranny of lottery. You want to buy a newspaper and you have to stand in line behind six sweaty, overweight losers . . . the same guys who spend their days in Off-Track Betting parlors . . . who smell like cigarettes and liquor and hold everyone up while they fumble through the pieces of paper in their shirt pockets looking for their lucky numbers."

Caplan nodded. "At lunchtime anyone could have walked off with a pair of gloves from way in the back of the store," he said.

"But it doesn't make sense for the killer to take the chance of opening the back door and stepping into the store at all," Donovan said. "Is there a supply of the gloves out back?"

"Yes!" Caplan said excitedly. He took them back through the door that led to the basement, the john, and the alley. Caplan fumbled around his cache of boxes and found the box labeled HOUSEWARES. It stood open and within a pace or two of the basement door. "Here," he said. "In here." He pointed at the box, then peered into the top. Gleefully, he said, "There was a pair of gloves on top of the stuff in there this morning. Look! They're gone."

"So you say," Mosko said.

Donovan also looked inside the box and quickly catalogued a handful of screwdrivers, several fuses, and a good supply of duct tape. He said, "It's possible that the killer followed Victor into the back of your store planning on grabbing something and killing him."

"Yes!" Caplan agreed.

"I would have nabbed the duct tape," Mosko said. "A guy can't have too much duct tape."

"Especially when he's got an aboveground pool," Donovan said. "Look, I think the killer saw the gloves sitting there and picked them up to hide his fingerprints."

Looking at the storekeeper, Mosko said, "It's also possible that you saw Victor sneaking down into your basement and did the job yourself, wearing your own gloves."

"Did you think of someone you might have told where you kept the statue of Ebbets Field?" Donovan asked.

"No," Caplan said sadly.

"Then I'm afraid you're falling prey to the horses factor," Donovan said.

"What's that?"

"Advice that all medical school students get. It goes, 'When you hear hoofbeats, think of horses, not zebras.' The idea being that, upon seeing a sniffle, you should suspect that the patient has a cold, not Upper Zambezi River Fever."

"You're the obvious suspect," Mosko translated.

"Am I . . . am I under arrest?" Caplan asked.

"No," Donovan and Mosko said, more or less at the same time.

Caplan looked relieved but quizzical.

"I don't like the obvious," Donovan said.

"It makes his teeth itch," Mosko added.

"I can understand that you might have a motive for killing Victor," Donovan said. "What I don't understand is what Victor was doing in your basement."

"I didn't invite him," Caplan said.

"If *I* were planning on killing my enemy, I sure wouldn't invite him in to look at my baseball cards and then bash his brains in using one of my prize statues while wearing a pair of my own gloves," Donovan said.

"And then call the cops to show them the body," Caplan said quickly.

"So I have to wonder, what in hell was Victor doing down in this basement? What did he want?" Donovan said.

"It's this sort of stuff that gets the captain's juices flowing," Mosko said.

Caplan wasn't forthcoming with an answer to Donovan's question, so he posed it again. "What was down there that James Victor might want?"

"You may as well ask me how to achieve world peace," Caplan said.

"And want badly enough to come here on his own," Donovan added.

"As opposed to hiring somebody to do it for him," Mosko added.

"From the little that I've read about Victor in the papers, he was a boardroom kind of guy," Donovan continued. "He got an idea, he told someone to handle it for him. I don't recall seeing anything about hands-on. So whatever he was looking for when he made his fatal appearance in the basement of Surf Avenue News, it was either personal . . ."

"Like I told you before," Caplan said, "I never met the man or talked to him. There can't possibly be anything down there personal to him."

". . . and/or so sensitive he couldn't trust anyone else to go and get it," Donovan concluded.

"The only stuff down there is your store stuff?" Mosko asked.

Caplan bobbed his head up and down.

Donovan ruminated for a moment. He was thinking, but also distracted by the comings and goings of forensics technicians moving between the store and the alley.

"And when your dad owned the store, the only things he kept down there were store stuff?" Mosko asked.

"Just things related to the store," Caplan said. Then he added, "Well, not counting my Radio Flyer wagon, my bike, my tube."

"Your tube?" Mosko asked.

"My inner tube. For swimming."

Donovan's attention returned. He smiled and said, "Sergeant Moskowitz is thirty-something. He has never in this lifetime set eyes on an inner tube."

The wondrous look of illumination glowed on Mosko's round face, oddly cherubic for someone so muscle-bound. He said, "Oh, like in tires from the old days when guys drove cars with AM radios."

"You got it," Donovan said.

"I seen them in pictures. You had one?"

"To use in the surf," Caplan said.

"And apart from your childhood stuff, everything stored in the basement was stock for the store," Donovan said.

"That's it."

"What was the store before your father owned it?" Donovan asked.

"A haberdasher. But you're talking the time of the Great War now."

Mosko said, "The Great War. The Great War?"

"World War I," Donovan replied. "When guys drove

cars that didn't have radios at all. But they had inner tubes."

"Oh."

"When was the last time anyone other than you was in the basement?" Donovan asked.

Caplan thought, then said, "The electric and gas meters are out back, so that would be the boiler repairman."

"When was that?"

"January or February. When else would the boiler break down?"

"And before then?" Donovan asked.

"Oh, I don't know," Caplan replied.

"You had plumbing work done."

"How do you know that?"

"Most of your pipes are the original stuff put in when the building went up," Donovan said. "But there are a few pieces of newer pipe laying around."

"That would have been three or four years ago," Caplan replied. "They put in a new main. Do you have any idea how much that cost me?"

Donovan asked, "When you sued Victor, it was over what issue? Demolition of the block? Tell me again."

"What else would I sue him for, his taste in women?" Caplan asked.

"Why do you mention that?" Donovan asked.

"The man is married to someone who makes Lady Macbeth look like Mother Teresa, that's all," Caplan replied. "Not that I've ever met Mother Teresa, either."

"You don't like Victor's widow," Mosko said.

Caplan nodded. "Personally, I would rather sleep with road kill."

Smiling, Donovan said, "And the name of this delightful creature is . . ."

"Chloe," Caplan said, oozing disdain.

"I must make her acquaintance," Donovan replied.

The captain was distracted once again, this time by the sound of angry voices out in the front of the store. "Whazzat?" he asked, prompting Mosko to open the door a crack and peek.

"Press," the sergeant replied quickly. "The uniforms are trying to get rid of a TV crew."

"The name of the victim must have gotten out," Donovan said.

Rising to a higher level of indignation than Donovan had seen that day, the store owner said, "What, they have my name? I ask because *I am the victim here!*"

"I always thought of you that way," Donovan replied, just enough irony in his voice to make the suspect feel unsure.

"I am going to get blamed because this monster James Victor managed to get killed in my basement."

"*Gonif,*" Donovan replied.

"Probably while trying to steal my 1955 Duke Snider," Caplan continued.

"Probably," Donovan said agreeably. He turned to his associate and suggested that he go out and apply his legendary forcefulness to helping the uniformed officers deal with the presence of the press. Once Mosko was on his way, Donovan said to Caplan, "You know, I think we've come as far as we can on round one. Why don't we let the forensics technicians work? They'll do as much as they can with the body, then we'll haul it off to the morgue and seal the basement until tomorrow, when I'll want more work done."

"Whatever," the store owner replied.

Donovan continued, "When I drifted off the beach and in the direction that took me into your life, Mr. Caplan, my original goal was to buy a hot dog. There was a hot dog wagon on Stillwell Avenue, but he seems to have split."

"Sidewalk vendors are a blight," Caplan spat. "They pay no taxes and they take your customers. We complained about him. We being the committee."

"I went to Nathan's, but the line was so long I allowed myself to be distracted by sirens, and here I am," Donovan said.

Caplan lit up, clearly welcoming the chance to get away from the oppressiveness of having forensics technicians work over and around the body in the basement. He took a pinch of Donovan's shirt and pulled it in the direction of the back door. "I have a friend over at Nathan's," he said.

"I was kind of hoping you did," Donovan replied, matching the store owner's smile.

"You come with me and you don't have to stand in line."

That's what the captain did. The two men followed Bonaci's instructions on where to step so as to avoid potential evidence and slipped down the alley. As they walked behind the other stores on the block, a back door was conspicuously ajar. It was the one behind the appliance store. Donovan was sure that someone was peeping through the crack, and indeed a man stepped halfway out. Like Caplan he was sixtyish and a bit stooped, but unlike the owner of Surf Avenue News he was brawny and black, with a thick mustache that covered his upper lip and offset a mostly bald head.

Nervously, he said, "Harry?"

"You were expecting Prince Charles?" Caplan replied, without breaking stride.

"What happened?"

"Somebody killed James Victor in my basement."

The questioner sucked in his breath. Donovan could hear it. Then the man asked, "Are you being arrested?"

Caplan shook his head and continued on down the alley, shooting over his shoulder, "With any luck I'm being bought a hot dog."

"Don't go anywhere," Donovan said to the man. As he kept walking, the captain phoned Mosko with orders to send a detective to interview him.

When they got to Nathan's the lines remained long, perhaps even longer than before. The reason, Donovan could see, was the arrival of fans for the Brooklyn Cyclones' pending twi-night doubleheader. The New York–Penn League baseball club was a farm team of the New York Mets, and its arrival at spanking-new KeySpan Park had been immensely successful. The Cyclones revived memories of Brooklyn's Ebbets Field and the beloved Dodgers, who natives swore "tore the heart out" of the borough when they decamped for Los Angeles in 1957. The Cyclones also were seen as being key to the revival of Coney Island, in consequence of which developers such as the late James Victor suddenly were willing to sink fortunes into upscale housing.

Right on the Boardwalk in the shadow of the Parachute Drop, KeySpan Park on game day was a whirlwind of families and fans from all over the region. The Cyclones and their stadium had generated so much media attention that no one seemed to notice that this minor league club was *very* minor league. The players traveled by bus, not limo or plane, and went up against such opponents as the Batavia Muckdogs and the Mahoning Valley Scrappers. Nevertheless, in the late afternoon sun, as Donovan and Caplan walked amidst the happy crowds converging on the ballpark, the Cyclones might have been the World Champion New York Yankees. Their presence lit up the ghostly memories of arcades and freak shows and seemed nearly to erase the decades when the neighborhood was known mainly for the excellent stab-and-gunshot-wound trauma unit at Coney Island Hospital.

Even Caplan smiled. "These Cyclones are a good thing, a great thing," he said.

"Except that they encourage developers," Donovan replied.

Caplan smiled in a knowing sort of way and said, "Ah, when it's baseball in Brooklyn you can sort of forgive."

A few minutes later and true to his word, Caplan had led Donovan into the special "line" at an obscure corner of the Nathan's Famous counter. Donovan watched as Caplan's long history and obvious fame in the neighborhood immediately got them four hot dogs and two cups of Coke. When Donovan put a twenty on the counter, it was pushed back across the stainless steel toward him, along with a guttural "You're with Harry, you get outta here with your money."

He smiled with a memory. *Try to pay for an apple at the fruit stand on the corner of Broadway and 110th.*

4. "WANNA SEE A BROOKLYN U-TURN?" MOSKO ASKED.

We need a van," Donovan said as he lifted his son out of his wheelchair and into the booster seat in the back of Barney.

"What's a van, Daddy?" Daniel asked.

"It's like a small truck."

"Can we get a van?" the boy asked excitedly. "I want a van."

"With side doors and a lift for your wheelchair," Donovan said.

"I want a van," he said again.

"Where do you get one?" Marcy asked.

"There are places around, mostly out of the city. I think there's a dealer in White Plains that handles custom medical vans. I think Howard got the forensics van there."

"The van would have a lift?"

"Like they have on city buses that are wheelchair accessible," Donovan said. "You press a button and this shelf comes out from under the van and down onto the curb. You wheel the chair onto it, then push another button and the shelf lifts up to the level of the van. Then you wheel the chair inside and lock it in place."

"Would you like that, Daniel?" Marcy asked.

He bobbed his head up and down.

"We can have a VCR built in, too," Donovan added.

"I want a *van*," Daniel said.

Donovan snapped the seat belt over his son and

around the booster seat, pausing to get a kiss on the cheek and give one back in return. Then he closed the curbside back door and folded Daniel's wheelchair into the trunk. When Donovan closed the trunk, he told his wife, "I'll ask Howard where he got the van and check it out today. I think the basic model is about fifty grand."

"Where will we park it?" Marcy asked.

"You don't care, right?" he asked.

"I don't care what?"

"What it costs."

"If you have to ask, you can't afford it," Marcy replied. "This is for our baby."

"I'm not sure that I'll ever get used to having money," Donovan said.

"So where will we *keep* the van?" she asked.

"The garage on Eighty-seventh."

"Get a red one," Marcy said. Then she put her arms around her husband's neck and gave him a hug and a kiss. "I love the way you take care of Daniel."

"I love you," he told her.

As she walked around to the driver's side, she said, "We have physical therapy at ten and swimming at eleven. Then Mary is taking him to his art class while I study."

"Call me on the Bat Phone if you need me," he said, patting the cell phone on his belt.

"Make sure that the van has a cell phone cradle and a laptop holder," she said.

"Yes, honey," he replied, then stood there waving at Daniel until his family pulled away from the curb and into the northbound traffic on Riverside Drive.

"Here's your coffee, honey," Mosko said, handing

Donovan his Starbucks—Ethiopia Sidamo mixed with French-roast decaf.

"*Grassy-ass,*" Donovan replied, taking the cup.

"*De nada.* I'm pretty sure that Howard got the van on Queens Boulevard in Forest Hills. I'll ask."

"I can buy my own van," Donovan said. "How much do I owe you for the coffee?"

"If you have to ask, you can't afford it," Mosko replied.

Donovan said, "Fuck you."

"Your whole Robin Hood image of yourself is being messed up by being rich, isn't it?"

"I'm not rich," Donovan snapped.

"Oh, *no.* You can just whip out the plastic and charge a fifty-thousand-dollar van."

"The fact that my wife brought a couple of bucks into the marriage means nothing to me," Donovan said.

Mosko giggled.

Donovan stuck two dollar bills into his friend's pocket. "Where do we stand on this fine Monday morning?" he asked, looking around in a peaceful sort of way at the distinguished old trees lining Riverside Drive and the noble lines of the Soldiers and Sailors Monument. Beyond, the morning light rippled off the Hudson all the way over to the Jersey shore. At that moment, the problems of the world seemed very far away, and Donovan realized that one of the reasons he loved Manhattan was that it *was* an island. The smell of salt water and the kiss of a sea breeze on the cheek were never far away.

"Where we stand is that Victor was killed between noon and one, probably right around twelve-thirty," Mosko said. "Just like Howard thought yesterday."

"When Caplan says his store was as busy as it gets other than days before big lotteries," Donovan said.

"The statue of Ebbets Field *was* the murder weapon," Mosko continued. "The blood on it was Victor's. As we suspected, Caplan's fingerprints are all over the thing—but *under* the blood, as we also suspected."

"Anyone else's prints on there?" Donovan asked.

"One unknown, also under the blood," Mosko said. "We're running it through more databases, though."

"Was the glove I found a match?"

"You got it, boss. It was an exact match. There are fibers from the glove on the murder weapon, and the blood on the glove is Victor's. The glove was from the store, and brand new. It even had one of those little plastic wires . . . you know, the ones with the T-bar at the end . . . still stuck in it."

Donovan walked up to Mosko's car and let himself into the passenger's side. When the sergeant got behind the wheel, Donovan asked, "Was there any evidence left by the perp?"

"Not that we can tell on first glance," Mosko replied.

"You're following somebody into a building meaning to kill him. You grab a glove out of a box along the way and pull it on. You don't pay such close attention to minimizing evidence."

"Such as by wearing surgical gloves."

"If you had surgical gloves on, you wouldn't need the cotton glove," Donovan said. "Have the boys look more closely."

"They're doing that," Mosko said. "Don't you think they're doing that?"

"Did we find the mate to the glove?"

"Yeah. Tossed into a trash receptacle right where the alley meets the side street. The killer came out of the store, ripped off the right glove, and tossed it where you found it. Then he hung a right and ran to the corner and tossed the left glove. Right-handed killer. Right-hand turn. Disappeared into foot traffic."

"You presume," Donovan said.

"What else would he have done? Get beamed up onto the *Enterprise?*"

"Escaped in a car," the captain replied.

"The counterman at the pizza place didn't see a car," Mosko said.

"It was lunchtime, and he was watching the street the entire while," Donovan said.

"Whatever. Look, I stand by my analysis. Anyway, the left-hand glove had blood on it where you would expect from pulling off the right-hand glove."

Donovan nodded. "I want to go to Brooklyn," the captain said.

"I never fuckin' thought I'd hear you say that," Mosko exclaimed, starting the engine and checking the mirrors. The sergeant's flame-red Corvette roared to life, the chassis swaying slightly side-to-side with the engine. "Wanna see a Brooklyn U-turn?" Mosko asked.

"No!" Donovan shouted, to no avail as Mosko gunned the engine and popped the clutch and tugged the wheel to the left. Leaving a patch of rubber that began in the gutter, the 'Vette spun into a 180-degree turn that began in the parking spot on the northbound side of Riverside Drive and didn't end until the car was racing south.

"Jesus, Mary, and Joseph!" Donovan swore.

"Don't let the Jewish relatives hear you say that," Mosko replied, smiling wickedly.

"No wonder Brooklyn guys scare the shit out of everyone else. Come on, man, I'm thinking about my reputation in the community," Donovan said as he glanced out the window to catch a glimpse of his doorman running out onto the sidewalk to see who the jackass was.

"So am I," Mosko said, smiling again.

Settling down to just ten miles per hour over the speed limit, Mosko drove down to Seventy-ninth Street and took the on-ramp to the West Side Highway south. It was a brilliant, bright day, and the sharp sunlight of morning etched fine shadows of skyline across Riverside Park and the highway and out over the several dozen yachts that swayed at their moorings near the Seventy-ninth Street Boat Basin. The morning rush was mostly over, in consequence of which Donovan and Moskowitz were only held up a few minutes at the bottleneck alongside the U.S.S. *Intrepid* Sea-Air-Space Museum. As usual, three lanes of traffic—one of them illegal—were making simultaneous left-hand turns onto Forty-second Street. The Corvette broke free in the single remaining downtown lane only to get into a brief tangle with shuttle buses departing the Thirty-eighth Street NY Waterway ferry terminal. The number of commuters taking ferries had risen dramatically after the terrorist destruction of the World Trade Center the previous September, because many normally imperturbable Manhattan workers had developed a fear of attack-vulnerable bridges and tunnels. A regular fleet of ferries now chugged across the broad and churning river, just like at the end of the nineteenth century.

As Mosko drove through the financial district en route to the Brooklyn Bridge, they glanced over at the parade of trucks still rumbling in and out of the World Trade Center rubble nine months after the attack. With a sigh rather louder than the normal one he used to punctuate dramatic proclamations, Donovan said, "They'll never get all the way to the bottom of that investigation. The truth is way buried."

"The mayor is an asshole for keeping you out of it," Mosko replied.

"For keeping *us* out of it."

"Ah, y'know, fuck 'em. I don't want to work with feds anyway. Too many goddam suits. I'd have to dress up." To accent his remark, Mosko plucked at the skin-tight fabric of his T-shirt, which read

I LOST IT AT THE MERMAID PARADE

"The World Trade Center case amounts to chainsaw surgery," Donovan replied. "You and I wield scalpels. What can *we* do concerning international terrorism?" He turned his eyes forward toward the bridge to New York City's most outrageous borough.

"Truth is," Mosko went on, "it's the feds who kept you . . . I mean, us . . . out of the investigation. They're still pissed at you for letting that guy go. What the hell was his name?"

"Mojadidi," Donovan added.

"I mean, the bum went back to Afghanistan to fight the Taliban. So fuckin' what if he took a shot at you before you got to know each other? He missed."

Donovan nodded. "And he made it up to me. I'm

prepared to forgive those who miss the target and atone."

"Let's hope his aim improved once he got home."

About three years ago—as Marcy was lying in the hospital preparing to give birth to Daniel, in fact—Donovan had become involved in a case in which one player was an Afghan freedom fighter named Yama Mojadidi, the leader of a mujahideen guerrilla brigade, who was in New York City just long enough to settle an issue with someone. After a few rounds with Donovan, in which the Afghan first tried to wring the captain's neck and then saved it, Mojadidi was deported back to Afghanistan, where he intended to lead his men against the Taliban.

"He should have gone back with a damn nuclear device," Donovan said. "Maybe we could have been spared this. Okay, my friend. I got a proposition for you."

"What?" Mosko asked, turning the car eastward off Centre Street. The Corvette rumbled onto the potholed Brooklyn Bridge on-ramp and began shaking violently. Donovan recalled a several-years-old car commercial in which the Brooklyn Bridge addressed a luxury auto that was racing across it, growling, "I got your fancy suspension *right here!*"

"Get us to Coney Island in one piece and at lunchtime I'll take you to Roll-N-Roaster for cheese fries."

"You got it," Mosko said, taking the deal as a challenge and downshifting into second, making the engine scream even louder than the noise from the potholes.

Half an hour later they had made their way down the utilitarian Brooklyn-Queens and Prospect expressways and were driving along Ocean Parkway, a six-lane highway. Brooklyn's Champs Elysées, it traversed an area in which the monumental homes of wealthy, mostly Jewish residents mixed with high-rise apartment buildings and synagogues alternately immense and rich or tiny and poor, many of the latter reflecting the small Hasidic sects that flourished in Brooklyn. Ocean Parkway dead-ended in Brighton Beach, Coney Island's neighbor lately famous as "Little Odessa by the Sea," home of immigrants from the former Soviet Union, including the increasingly wealthy and bold Russian mafia. A swing off to the right took the Corvette down Surf Avenue to Coney Island and, before too long, Caplan's corner store.

The blue barricades and yellow crime scene tape were gone from the sidewalk, but the area had changed unmistakably. The concrete was scrubbed, and the windows were sparkling from Windex. It looked to Donovan as if the notices had been taken off the inside of the windows and put back, this time in perfect alignment with the window edges and each other, using fresh Scotch tape. The store was open for business, and after Mosko pulled to the curb in front of it Caplan came running out.

"You're back! You're back!" he exclaimed.

"You should become a detective," Donovan said, climbing out of the 'Vette and shaking his legs loose.

"I have a fresh pot of coffee."

"Half decaf, half regular, one Sweet'N Low," Donovan said.

"And you, Detective . . . *Moskowitz*, is it?" Caplan asked, twirling the last name around to indicate bonding on the Jewish issue.

"From Canarsie," Mosko added. "How are you today?"

"I'm as good as can be for a man who's being accused of murder," Caplan said.

"If you had been accused, you would have spent the night in jail," Donovan said.

"*Suspected*, then."

"Everyone's suspected," Donovan said. "Don't you watch *Law & Order?*"

"This whole business is killing my wife," Caplan went on. "She's so worried about me she could *plotz*."

"Can your wife account for her whereabouts between noon and one o'clock yesterday?" Mosko asked.

"That was cruel," Donovan said, as Caplan appeared more stricken than usual.

"Hey, I was just telling the man to tell his wife that things could be worse," Mosko replied.

"Is that when Victor was definitely killed?" Caplan asked.

Donovan said that it was.

"Well, I was behind the register. That's all I can tell you."

"Do you remember who came in?" Mosko asked.

Caplan tossed his hands up and said, "Oh, I couldn't possibly tell you. All my regulars. Jimmy from the appliance shop. You met him yesterday. He always comes in at noon for a can of grape soda and a bag of Mesquite BBQ potato chips. The guy from the car service stopped by like he always does. Double-parked right in front and came in for a coffee and a cinnamon bun. The manager of Nathan's. You're not going to believe this."

"Believe what?" Donovan asked.

"Guess what his name is?"

"Nathan," Donovan said.

"How'd you know that?"

"I guessed. No relation to Nathan Handwerker, right?"

Caplan replied, "None. *My* Nathan is African American, like Jimmy."

Mosko said, "You see, Mr. Caplan, this is why you can't mess with the captain. Most detectives will say, 'Nathan's was founded by a guy named Nathan.' But Captain Donovan knows the man's actual name, and it was like a thousand years ago, right?"

"I surfed into the Coney Island Web site last night," Donovan explained.

"He does a lot of that," Mosko explained.

"I surf into the water sometimes, me and my inner tube," Caplan said.

"As my wife would say, did you put on your sunblock?" Donovan asked.

"Always."

Donovan urged Caplan back into his store, where an agitated customer awaited. The man was fortyish and overweight, with a belly that poured over cheap cotton pants and a vinyl belt. An assortment of papers and Bic pens was shoved into the breast pocket of his white shirt.

"The Lotto jackpot is ten million for tomorrow night," Caplan said. "The lines are beginning to form. Can I give you a ticket?"

"That's *our* job, isn't it?" Donovan said, plucking a bag of gummy worms from a metal rack and leaving a dollar bill on the counter.

Now on the other side, Caplan took the dollar and said, "You should be careful with those. There could be traces of peanuts in there."

"I'm only allergic to murderers," Donovan said. "So far, you haven't set off a reaction in me. But we'll see how things go."

"Make yourself at home," Caplan said.

Donovan led Moskowitz through the store and out into the back hallway. After opening the back door and looking up and down the alley to find that it hadn't changed overnight, he opened the door to the basement stairs. He flicked on the light switch, and the dark shadows gave way to the sharply defined shapes of several lifetimes spent collecting junk.

"If you want to know all about Coney Island, you should talk to my Uncle Stanley," Mosko said.

"I would except that I don't want to be constantly subjected to sales pitches," Donovan said.

"Ah, he'll turn it off for you. I'll give you his cell number."

Donovan stepped down the stairs gingerly, as would a solitary intruder trying to evade detection while descending into a dank unknown. At the same time, he motioned to Mosko to hold back.

"Whatsa matter?" Mosko asked.

"I want to do this myself," Donovan replied.

"I'm impressed—looking for a van *and* going down the stairs by yourself, all in the same day."

Donovan reached behind his back and made a rude gesture.

"I want to hear something," he said.

As he suspected, when he put his weight on the third step from the bottom it made an audible creak.

"Whoa," Mosko said. "How come we didn't notice that yesterday?"

"Because yesterday the joint was full of cops tramping around with their big flat feet," Donovan replied.

"If Victor was down there already . . ."

"Which he was . . ."

"Looking for God-knows-what . . ."

"He would have heard that creak and whipped his head around," Donovan said.

"Go all the way down," Mosko said.

Donovan did so. Not more than a pace or two from the foot of the stairs, he found the feet of the chalk outline that marked where Victor fell.

"Nice chalk outline," Donovan said. "Amazing how well defined it is, given that Caplan says the floor hasn't been washed since Ike was in the White House."

"Some guys are better at cleaning up than some others," Mosko said. "On top of that, you have the sanctuary factor."

"What's that?"

"The basement is a guy's sanctuary," Mosko explained.

"Other than spending summers at my aunt's house on the North Fork when I was a kid, I've lived my entire life in apartments. But I hear you. The basement is . . ."

"Glorious." Mosko went on. "A guy can keep it, basically, like . . ."

"The Black Hole of Calcutta comes to mind," Donovan said.

"Yeah, that. You can keep all your shit there, including—I mean, *especially* the stuff that makes your wife want to run into the bushes and puke. Old beer cans."

"Pepperoni from the Stone Age."

"Old tobacco tins filled with rusty nails. Twenty years'

worth of sneakers. Your first license plate. The street sign you stole from the corner of Broad and Beaver in the financial district."

"All the items guaranteed to keep your wife out of the basement," Donovan said.

"You bet. And lots of tools. You just leave 'em where the fuck you like," Mosko said. "All you need is a beverage refrigerator and a twelve-inch black-and-white TV set good enough to get ball games."

"Uhm hmm," Donovan said, distracted by the idea of putting his feet where he imagined that Victor was standing the day before when he had apparently been looking at the baseball cards.

5. UNDER THE BOARDWALK WITH CHARLEY THE PLUMBER.

Whatcha got?" Mosko asked.

"I'm Victor, and I just got into the basement and I'm gawking at the cards. The rest of the place is in darkness, these are lit up."

"Okay, I'm the killer, and I'm coming down the stairs." Mosko did so, and when he got to the third step from the bottom it obliged with a squeak that made Donovan flinch, no matter that he expected it.

He said, "I hear the creak. I start to turn to my left." He did so.

Mosko said, "I reach down for the first convenient bludgeon." His hand went into the cardboard box in which Caplan said he kept the statue. "I wrap my hands around the center field bleachers at Ebbets Field and hoist it."

"I'm still turning," Donovan said.

"And I clock you on the left side of your head," Mosko said, pretending to do it.

Donovan reached up and touched an imaginary wound.

Mosko thought for a moment and said, "There's something wrong with this picture."

"Yeah, Victor was hit first on the back of the head," Donovan said.

"If he had heard someone on the steps behind him, he would have turned to look. Victor is sneaking into the basement. He ain't no pro at breaking and entering. He's got to be nervous and on guard."

"Right," Donovan replied, looking around. Indeed, from where he was standing there seemed to be nothing in the basement but boxes. The corner where the boiler and plumbing sat was reachable only after walking down a corridor between piles of boxes, all of them sitting atop wooden shipping pallets. Able to see the entire length of the basement for the first time, Donovan scanned the floor, then the overhead pipes and other conduits, then the boxes.

"Did Howard find anything on the victim's shoes to suggest he roamed around the basement any?" Donovan asked.

Mosko shook his head. "There's an oily patch up near the front of the store, but Victor didn't step in it. Or anything else down here, so far as we can tell. His shoes have soles that pick up shit. You ever have shoes like that?"

Donovan nodded. "It's why I'm deeply suspicious of dog walkers," he said.

"Yeah, gotcha. And remember yesterday when we got those rust flakes in our hair?" Mosko asked.

"Vividly."

"Well, they're all over the floor up in front but not on Victor's shoes."

"What *is* on his shoes?"

"Glad you asked," Mosko replied, setting his laptop atop a pile of boxes adjacent to Brooklyn's biggest collection of Dodgers cards and booting it up. "What *was* on his shoes? Let's start with sand from the alley. We *are* near the beach, and there's a fair amount of sand everywhere on the pavement. I don't know if you noticed."

Donovan had noticed.

"There's also fresh wax—as in from a hardwood floor."

"Office-cleaning places wax the floors on weekends," Donovan said.

Mosko nodded. "Yesterday being Sunday counts as the weekend."

"He went to his office before being killed," Donovan said.

"Yep."

"Where's Victor's office?"

Mosko scrolled down some pages, peered at the screen, and said, "Back in the city."

" 'Back in the city.' You Brooklyn guys crack me up. Okay, I'll bite . . . *where* in the city?"

"Broadway near Trinity Church," Mosko replied.

"Close to Ground Zero. And the joint is still standing?"

"I hear it's got a few dents from the events of nine-eleven-oh-one, but it's still there," Mosko said. "We'll find out when we go over there this afternoon. I made us an appointment."

"You did."

"Lady Macbeth wants to talk to you," Mosko said with a smile.

"The widow."

"The *black* widow, from what I hear."

Donovan put his hands on his hips and said, "We're into role-playing today. I'm Victor, and a minute and a half ago I was beaten to death with a statue of Ebbets Field. Now you're telling me that my grieving widow is at my office and not home crying?"

Mosko shrugged. "I get the impression that crying ain't in her playbook, boss," he said.

Donovan made a clearing-the-throat sort of sound.

Mosko continued, "Hey, she's right up your alley. You're attracted to these strong women."

"*They* find *me*," Donovan said, again looking around the basement, as if in search of a change of subject.

"They smell a patsy."

"Wrong. All their lives they've had to put up with patsies. Now their forward sensors pick up someone who's not afraid of strong women, and it piques their curiosity."

"We're unafraid because we both have industrial-strength Irish moms," Mosko said.

The captain clapped his hands together and said, "If Victor came down here with someone, he might have had his back turned. We need to know who he hung with."

"Mrs. V. should be able to help us."

"And we also need some really hard evidence concerning who's been in this basement in the past week," Donovan said.

Looking again at his laptop, Mosko replied, "Caplan said nobody but him until yesterday."

"He runs this store all by himself? No help?"

"He said not."

"What, he locks the front door if he has to take a leak?" Donovan asked.

"I guess so," Mosko replied. "He's got one of those flip-over signs on a chain hanging on the front door. Did you see it?"

Donovan shook his head.

"There are dancing musical notes and the words BACH SOON. OFFENBACH SOONER."

"One has to admire a man with classical tastes," Donovan said.

"Caplan works from seven to seven," Mosko said. "During the week he catches both rush hours and the lunch crowd. He closes from one-thirty to two-thirty to go eat. On Sunday he's only open from seven to four to sell Sunday papers and that Solarcaine and hand out business cards for his brother-in-law Marty, the dermatologist."

"What about Saturdays?" Donovan asked.

"He's *closed*, man," Mosko said, his tone indicating that it should be obvious. "You know, *Shabbat shalom*."

"Oh, right."

"Don't Marcy and you . . . ?"

"She's only fifty percent Jewish, and I'm a hundred percent indifferent to religion," Donovan said.

"I was just asking."

"Don't. So Caplan locks the front door to inspect the

plumbing and eat. Doesn't Mrs. C. ever set foot in the basement?"

"He says she'd die first," Mosko said. "Like I told you, a properly tended basement will repel women."

"What about the upstairs tenant?" Donovan asked.

"Charley Hennigan," Mosko replied.

"And *his* wife? They never come down here?"

"Presumably they come in the front door to buy Cheerios," Mosko said. "As for going into the store off-hours or down into the basement, Caplan says they don't have a key."

"But Caplan leaves the alley door open," Donovan said. "Hennigan would know that."

Mosko acknowledged that his boss was right.

"We need to talk to him," Donovan said.

"I'll see where the bum is," Mosko replied.

"Caplan told us he discovered the body while coming down here to get a copy of the previous Sunday's *Times Magazine* for Charley, who does the crossword puzzle."

"That's what Caplan said," Mosko agreed.

"He closed the door and turned away customers to do this?" Donovan asked.

"He also took a leak."

"Why, at three on a busy Sunday afternoon, does Hennigan need a copy of the *previous* Sunday's crossword puzzle?"

"Caplan says he always comes by in midafternoon on Sundays," Mosko said.

"Where was he?" Donovan asked. "I don't recall any-one saying that he showed up."

"Good question," Mosko replied.

"Besides, yesterday's new puzzle wasn't enough to

keep him occupied? These things can take three or four days to finish."

"Let's ask," Mosko replied.

"And I don't see a stack of old newspapers down here," Donovan continued.

"Meaning?"

"Meaning that if Caplan is saving last week's paper for the guy upstairs, there are a lot of places in the store itself. He *does* sell newspapers and magazines there. And I don't know if you noticed the small selection of magazines in the can."

Mosko nodded. "I remember them now."

"I'm just wondering why Caplan came down here when he did. Where was Hennigan, if Caplan had to go get his paper at that moment? Do you see where I'm going with this?"

Mosko said, "There are lots of holes in Caplan's story. In my opinion, he ain't the bumbling Woody Allen schnook he makes himself out to be."

"There's something else down here," Donovan said, looking around once again. "There's something down here that Victor was looking for, and maybe it's something that Caplan isn't telling us about."

Donovan dropped down to a squatting position. While Mosko sat at the bottom of the stairs and read the morning reports coming into his laptop via cell modem, Donovan ran his palms over the concrete beneath the cases holding the baseball card collection. Then he did the same under each of the wooden pallets holding up boxes elsewhere.

He scrutinized the dirt on the floor at various spots. He ran his fingertips over the tops of all the boxes he could reach, checking the levels of dust. Then he walked down to the basement nook filled with infrastructure stuff—the boiler, the gas main, and assorted plumbing. Donovan checked dust and dirt levels there, too, and pulled out his Maglite and squatted to investigate the underside of the boiler and the pipes. His knees complaining slightly, he got up and snagged a piece of copper pipe from among the several fragments sitting on a nearby oil drum. Then the captain squatted down again and held the fragment of pipe next to the pipe that plunged through the concrete, exiting the basement. Finally, Donovan ran his fingers over a several-square-foot section of floor surrounding the copper pipe, where the concrete was relatively new but still covered with a layer of grime comparable to that elsewhere.

Donovan stood and tossed the fragment of pipe onto the floor. It made a resounding clank before rolling under the boiler.

Mosko looked up. "Whazzat?" he asked.

"Caplan had some plumbing work done within the past few years," Donovan said.

"He told us the old pipe to the main cracked and had to be replaced."

"Must have cost him," Donovan said.

"Ain't that the truth. I wonder who he used. I need some work done, too."

"Don't tell me there are no plumbers in your family." Donovan idly tilted the two oil barrels up to peer under them and found nothing.

"There ain't no Jewish plumbers, boss," Mosko said, shaking his head.

"What do folks do in Israel, get themselves dry-cleaned?"

"That's different."

"I know a family of Jewish plumbers in the Bronx," Donovan said. He wiped his hands on his pants and walked back to where Mosko was sitting.

"I live in Canarsie. The Bronx could be the far side of the moon."

"In places, it is," Donovan said. "What about on your mom's side, the Irish side? No plumbers there?"

"*Nada* but carpenters. Them plus one priest. He's the only one in the family who gets down on his knees, so I'm gonna have to outsource the plumbing."

Smiling, Donovan said, "Find out what plumber Caplan used. Also, I want a team in here to inventory every single item in these boxes."

Mosko finished typing a note into his computer, then said, "Everything? In all these boxes?"

"Don't skip so much as a gum ball," Donovan said.

"You got it."

"Furthermore, nothing gets moved out of here except as evidence."

"Absolutely not," Mosko replied, making another note.

"Victor was a very wealthy man who developed a sufficient interest in Caplan's basement to risk coming down here, either by himself or, I suppose, with the guy . . ."

"Or girl . . ."

"Who killed him," Donovan said. "Apparently, this interest developed suddenly, although it might be argued that Victor's attempt to buy the whole block was round one. Anyway, I need to know what he was looking for. The answer could be in one of these boxes."

"We'll inventory it," Mosko said.

Donovan thought for a moment, one of his don't-go-away, there-may-be-more moments that Mosko often filled by drumming his fingertips on the laptop. When the tap-tapping reached the captain's consciousness, he said, "Go up and see if Caplan knows where Hennigan is. I want to spend a few minutes down here alone."

"Searching for a tremor in the Force?" Mosko asked.

"And while you're at it, get some guys to make calls. Yesterday there was a hot dog vendor parked on Stillwell near the Boardwalk in the morning. But he split by three or so."

Mosko said, "You want lunch already?"

"I just want to know, okay? I want to know why a rich real estate developer breaks into the basement of a dime-a-dozen candy store in Coney Island and gets himself killed for the effort. I want to know why Charley Hennigan suddenly needs a copy of last week's paper. I want to know why a hot dog vendor takes off in the middle of one of the busiest summer Sundays."

"When Clan Donovan was in need of dogs," Mosko added.

Slightly annoyed, Donovan said, "Okay, you got me. I want to arrest the sonofabitch for not being there when I suddenly found myself in need of salt and cholesterol. Now would you please do it?'

"Whatever," Mosko said.

"Check the license bureau to see who has that spot. Check the Brooklyn catering garages to see where the guy might keep his cart."

"Yadda, yadda, yadda."

"But mostly, locate Hennigan," Donovan said.

Any beach is very sad and a little desolate on the morning after a big summer Sunday. The Coney Island beach was especially so, because there was little natural beauty to give it appeal in the absence of throngs of happy people. No palms swayed in a tropical breeze. No colorful native outriggers plied crystal blue waters. And there was a complete lack of verdant thatched huts beneath which nut-brown maidens in grass apparel served elaborate cocktails in halved coconut shells. In tacit recognition of the natural drabness of the geography, the Coney Island Aquarium was filled with local species—brown on the top, white on the bottom, and, for the most part, lazy or bored.

The occasional elderly couple ambled along the Boardwalk, while on the beach there were no swimmers and only an occasional sunbather. A handful of city park workers roamed the sand, using sharp-tipped poles to pluck candy wrappers from the beach and deposit them in large shoulder bags.

Off in the distance to the east, a lone speck of a man stood at the high tide mark, the ridge of sand and seaweed carved by the ocean as surf reached its farthest up the beach. As Donovan and Mosko walked along the hard sand toward that figure, the captain said, "This is like the scene in *Lawrence of Arabia* where Omar Sharif and his camel grow out of the horizon."

"Except there ain't no camels in Coney Island," Mosko said.

"There *used* to be a squad of mounted Algerian swordsmen at Dreamland," Donovan said.

"That was down near the edge of Brighton Beach, right?" Mosko asked.

Donovan said that it was just off to the left, and his friend looked in that direction.

"There also was a tribe of wild men from Borneo, a horde of Somali warriors, and a bunch of Ubangi women whose lips had been stretched grotesquely, all up there on Surf Avenue," Donovan said.

"You got this off the Web?"

Donovan shook his head. "From your Uncle Stanley. I worked out a consultant arrangement with him."

"How much is the City of New York paying him?"

"Fifty bucks a phone call plus his cell charges," Donovan replied.

"Not bad. Uncle Stanley tells me that Coney Island is coming back economically and soon will be full of rich white people."

"That's what the Chamber of Commerce, the Brooklyn Cyclones, and guys like the late James Victor would have us believe," Donovan said.

"Charley Hennigan, on the other hand . . ."

"That guy down the beach . . ."

"Is a throwback," Mosko said.

"In what way?"

"Caplan told me he's a beach scavenger," Mosko said. "Hennigan goes up and down the beach every morning with a metal detector, looking for coins."

"And doing this he makes enough money to pay the eight-fifty rent?" Donovan asked.

Mosko shook his head. "Mrs. Hennigan works at Coney Island Hospital."

"Doing what?"

"ER nurse. Trauma specialist. You, know, deals with the Friday knife-and-gun club."

"Curiouser and curiouser," Donovan said.

"Yeah, I thought you would have that reaction," Mosko said. "But she's getting on in years and sits at a console taking radio calls incoming from ambulances."

"That can't pay too badly."

"It's only a part-time gig to supplement Social Security. They need the coins Hennigan finds on the beach."

"Some way to live," Donovan said.

Mosko nodded.

"This is the soft white underbelly of resort life—the guys who have to prospect for crumbs. I suppose that when the resort in question is somewhere near Bali, the indignity goes down a little easier. Where was Mrs. Hennigan yesterday at noon?"

"How should I know? Let's ask her husband."

Donovan said, "Hold up. I have something in my shoe."

Steadying himself with one hand on his friend's shoulder, Donovan pulled off one of his Docksiders and shook sand and pebbles out of it.

"We ain't dressed for a romp on the sand, boss," Mosko said.

"What comes to mind is the famous photograph of Nixon walking on the beach in a business suit," Donovan replied.

The captain's own outfit that day was what he had come to call his uniform: good khakis worn with Docksiders and a deep blue, button-down oxford shirt. Depending on the occasion, he added a navy blazer or a suede jacket. Mosko, for the most part, wore sneakers, jeans, T-shirts famously decorated with colorful sayings, and a black Flying Tigers World War II fighter-pilot jacket.

The far-off figure seemed less so and, moreover, seemed to have become aware of the two fully dressed men walking down the beach toward him.

"I think we've come up as a blip on his radar," Mosko said.

The two detectives were about a hundred yards from the man at that point. He had stopped the pendulum motion of the metal detector and was using it to lean on as he stared at them. Then he took off the headphones that fed beeps into his ears when the detector swept over something metal.

"Bright boy," Donovan said. "He's figured out that the Marines are landing."

Hennigan looked behind him—nervously, Donovan thought.

"No, there's just the two of us," Mosko said, as if speaking to the man across the yards of sand. "There's no one behind you."

Donovan and Mosko had come to within fifty yards. Hennigan had become obviously alarmed and was looking around in all directions.

"Do you get a sense he has something to hide?" Donovan asked.

"Just a little," Mosko replied.

Donovan smiled and waved at the man in a disarming sort of way and called, "Hey, Charley!"

Hennigan grabbed up his detector and took off at his version of a run up the beach in the direction of the Boardwalk.

"Did you expect this?" Mosko asked.

"Not for a nanosecond," Donovan replied.

They began running themselves, angling across the soft sand in an attempt to cut off the fleeing old man.

"I don't know where this old guy thinks he's going," Mosko said, jogging alongside Donovan as Hennigan struggled against the soft sand and the years. He was in his seventies and, as older people so often do, wearing corduroys even in the summer to warm the veins in his spindly legs. The heavy pants and the tightly held metal detector made running in the sand very difficult at best.

"This is ridiculous," Donovan said as Hennigan ran into the shadows under the Boardwalk.

Mosko had run ahead. He caught Hennigan by the back of his flannel shirt and pulled him to a halt. "Where the fuck do you think you're going?" he said to the panting old man as he patted him down.

"You're not Steve McQueen, and that was absolutely the worst escape attempt I have seen in thirty-plus years on the force," Donovan said when he caught up.

"Who are you?" Hennigan asked, his sad old eyes flicking jerkily from one detective to the other.

Donovan introduced his partner and himself. "We're investigating the murder of James Victor," he said.

"Victor! The monster who was going to make us homeless!"

"You've been talking to your landlord again," Donovan said. "Not a good idea even at the best of times."

"The man who killed Victor should get a medal," Hennigan insisted.

"Where were you yesterday between noon and one?" Donovan asked.

"You think I killed the monster?"

"Yeah, frankly, we do," Mosko said.

"We might never have gotten this idea if you hadn't run away," Donovan added.

"Most white folks who haven't done a crime don't run away from the police," Mosko said.

The old man hesitated, still trying to catch his breath. He hadn't shaved in a few days, and his beard was mostly gray with a few flecks of the original red. The hair atop his head also was gray with traces of red, and the ancient red flannel shirt, faded by years in the salt air and sun, seemed to Donovan to indicate an attempt to match shirt and hair. To Donovan, that meant that the old man had cared about something at one point.

"The captain asked you where you were yesterday between noon and one," Mosko said.

"I was *here*," Hennigan replied, as if they should have known that.

"Here?" Donovan asked. "Under the Boardwalk?"

The old song of that name popped unavoidably into Donovan's head. He even found himself humming a few bars . . . quietly, so Mosko couldn't hear . . . and looking up at the slats of sunlight that poured down between the boards in the Boardwalk. Oblivious to the scene below, a solitary man—a heavyset one, from the sound of the footfalls—clumped across the Boardwalk from one of the food stands and helped himself to a vacant bench. He sat with a creak and a thump.

"This is my secret place," Hennigan said.

"Not any more," Mosko replied.

"I come here all the time."

"Kind of a clubhouse, is it?" Donovan asked, looking

at the assortment of yard- and garage-sale furniture jammed against the back wall deeply in the shadows, folded up and stored for when needed. There was a ten-dollar chaise, two five-dollar chairs, a plastic milk carton useful as a table, and a plastic tarpaulin that covered something. As they spoke, Donovan poked under the tarp and found assorted old Tupperware and a brown blanket. The milk carton held a small stack of *New York Times Magazine*s and a pencil sharpener.

"This is my place," Hennigan insisted.

"It's his basement, boss," Mosko added, pleased with his analogy.

"I live above the candy store, but when my wife throws me out I come here. The cleaning crews know me and make sure my stuff is safe."

"And I'll bet *they* come here, too, during the day when they want to get out of the sun, hide from their bosses, and take a nap," Donovan said.

"How did you know?" Hennigan asked, his eyes softening and widening.

"I've been in city parks before. I know how the game is played. When was the last time your wife threw you out?"

"Saturday night," Hennigan replied.

"What happened?" Mosko asked.

"How long have you been married, Sergeant?"

"Ten years this month."

"Happy anniversary," the old man said.

Donovan smiled and put the tarp back in place. "What happened Saturday night?" he asked.

"We had a fight over money. We have a lot of medical bills, and I can't work no more."

"What did you do for a living?" Mosko asked.

"I was a plumber. That was my shop right down the block from Harry's store. But I got arthritis real bad in my hands and had to stop working. I sold the shop." Hennigan held up knuckles swollen to the size of chestnuts. "I got no strength," he said.

"How long has this been going on?" Donovan asked.

"Since before *he* was married," Hennigan replied, waving a wounded paw at Mosko.

"So your wife threw you out," Donovan continued.

Hennigan nodded. "She told me to run into the surf and drown."

"Sounds like a great relationship," Mosko said.

"She's a good woman, fellas. She just doesn't know where the money will come from. Like I told you before, we got a lot of medical bills."

"Because of your hands?" Donovan said.

"Mainly it's Margaret," Hennigan replied, shaking his head.

"That's your wife's name?" Mosko asked.

Hennigan nodded. "Margaret Ann."

"Pretty name," Donovan said. "What's the matter with her?"

"You're not going to believe it," the old man replied.

"As long as it doesn't involve extraterrestrials we might," Mosko said.

"Margaret was number twenty-two," Hennigan said grimly.

"Twenty-two," Mosko replied.

Seeing that what was obvious and immediate to him was something other than that to them, he said, "You know, from last year. Anthrax."

Both detectives straightened up and stood taller, their eyes ablaze. Donovan wasn't sure, but he thought he heard the man on the bench above them shift his weight and shuffle his feet. Maybe the man up there was looking down at them through the slats, Donovan speculated.

"What kind?" Donovan asked tersely.

"The kind in the lungs," Hennigan replied.

"When and how did she get it?"

"October last year. A month after the World Trade Center attack."

"I didn't hear of anyone working at Coney Island Hospital getting anthrax," Mosko said. "My cousin from Bensonhurst works there, and believe me the subject would have come up over Christmas dinner."

The old man shook his head. "She was a postal worker then. She sorted mail at the Morgan Mail Facility in the city. She got anthrax and was in the hospital . . . in Coney Island Hospital . . . for two months. My wife nearly died on me, Captain."

"How is she now?" Donovan asked.

Hennigan held his palm out parallel to the ground and waggled it. "They say she's cured, but I know better. She's got no wind and no strength. Getting up in the morning can make her tired. By nighttime she's weak and miserable and just wants to be left alone."

"So she throws you out, and you go because she needs to be alone," Mosko said.

Hennigan bobbed his head up and down, eyes glistening.

"How'd she wind up working at Coney Island Hospital?" Donovan asked.

"She can't stand up for more than a minute, so she

couldn't go back to work at the post office. She took disability, but it don't pay that much and we can't live on it. The insurance gave her a hard time about some of the medical bills. But the hospital took pity on her and gave her a part-time job."

Donovan sighed and glanced up toward the heavens, in this case the underside of the Boardwalk. He was sure that the man above was listening in. Anthrax, Donovan supposed, was a conversation topic guaranteed to draw eavesdroppers.

Hennigan wiped some sand off a sleeve and then used the cuff to try his tears.

Donovan said, "She kicked you out on Saturday night and you came here."

Hennigan nodded. "I like to sleep under the stars," he said. "Well, under the Boardwalk under the stars. It gets a little cold sometimes, but I have my blanket."

"And you stayed until when?" Donovan asked.

"At eight or nine in the morning I got up and went to buy a cup of coffee and a muffin from Harry," Hennigan replied. "I got Sunday's paper—just the magazine, you know. The rest is too heavy to carry. I don't read the news . . . too much misery in the world."

"So I hear," Donovan replied.

"But I like to do the crossword puzzle," Hennigan said, smiling for the first time in the encounter.

"So does the captain," Mosko said.

Hennigan's smile got bigger. "Did you do yesterday's?" he asked.

Donovan nodded. "While sitting on a blanket down by Stillwell," he replied.

"That was fun! Puns and wordplay! I love that!"

"So does he," Mosko said.

Hennigan focused on Donovan and said, "There was one I couldn't get for the life of me. Tell me you got twenty-three across. The clue was 'Fishy Texas city.' "

"Porpoise Christi," Donovan replied.

Hennigan laughed out loud and raised his right arm high, in a gesture of vicarious triumph.

Abruptly, Donovan stuck out his palm and, "Gimme five!"

Hennigan gave him five.

"Harder," Donovan snapped.

Hennigan looked a bit quizzical but complied. The result was a tiny slapping sound.

"My Aunt Tillie hits harder than that," Donovan said. "Hit me as hard as you can."

Challenged, Hennigan did so. The result was a slap that raised no eyebrows.

"That's the best you can do?" Donovan said.

"Yes."

"That was about a three on the Richter scale of eight," Donovan said. "Do you have arthritis in your shoulder, too?"

"No, but I got a rotator cuff injury that still makes me weak after a year."

"How'd you get that?" Mosko asked.

"Fell off the Boardwalk. I mean, down the stairs." He added a shrug and said, "It happens."

"Where were you treated for it?" Donovan asked.

"At Coney Island Hospital. My arm was in a sling for a month. Boy, was my wife pissed! I couldn't use my metal detector to sweep the beach, and we need the income."

"How much do you pull in with that thing?" Donovan asked.

"After a big Sunday, oh, forty or fifty bucks. I got really big pockets in these old pants." He stuck his hands into his pockets and wiggled them. The jiggling noise was impressive.

"Is that why you ran away from us?" Donovan asked.

The old man nodded, then said, "I was afraid you would rob me of *this*." He poked two fingers into his shirt pocket and, despite a complete lack of cooperation from his knuckles as illustrated by some quiet cussing, extricated a small gold coin. "I just found it," he said. "A gold coin! Okay, so it's a little one. I never found a gold coin before."

Hennigan dropped the coin into Donovan's hand. The captain held it up into one of the shafts of sunlight streaming down through the Boardwalk and gave it a look. The coin was tiny—not even the size of a thumbnail—but shining brilliantly, with an American Indian on one side and an eagle on the other. Beneath the bird was the legend "2½ DOLLARS."

"Nice," Donovan said.

"I'll bet it's worth a lot."

"About a hundred and ten bucks," Donovan replied.

"How'd you know *that?*" Mosko asked.

"My mother has one. Got it from *her* mother. Keeps it in a small embroidered purse in her jewelry box. I looked up the value for her once."

Hennigan was disappointed, but only for a moment. "Hey, there are whole weeks that I don't find that much. This has got to be my lucky day."

"It will prove to be luckier if you can think of someone who saw you here yesterday between noon and one," Donovan replied.

At that moment, a heavy foot stomped on the wood of the Boardwalk above and a deep, whiskey-and-tobacco-fired voice boomed, "*I* did."

6. A MAN WITH A TERRIBLE SECRET.

Everyone looked up.

"We got company," Mosko said.

"We have had for some time," Donovan replied.

"*I* saw the man," the voice repeated, adding the hint of a laugh.

"Are we in Coney Island or did we drift over the border into Brighton Beach?" Donovan asked.

"We're in Brighton Beach."

"Damn. I should have known he'd be around. Okay, Charley, you're off the hook for the murder of James Victor—at least until I find that you've been lying."

"I've been telling the truth," Hennigan insisted.

"I've got to run," Donovan said.

"Hey, thanks."

Leaving Mosko behind to clear up the details, Donovan hurried back into the sunlight and looked up at the figure now standing at the rail, holding up a paper coffee cup as if it were a ceremonial offering.

"*Nazdrovya*, Captain Donovan!" the man bellowed.

"Georgi, you old commie thug!" Donovan shouted back. "What the hell are you doing spying on me?"

Georgi Mdivani was a longtime Soviet Communist

Party apparatchik who once ran a tractor factory that had been moved from Russia to Pamiristan, a Central Asian province on the far side of the Urals, to get it away from Nazi bombing during World War II. After the Soviet Union collapsed, Mdivani was named cultural attaché by the fledgling government of Pamiristan and sent to the United Nations, where he promptly fell into one of Donovan's cases and became a friend. Now he was the owner of the Gemini, a prosperous nightclub in Brighton Beach. He also hovered on the periphery of the notorious Russian mafia by virtue of once, and perhaps still, running a small but highly illegal sports betting operation.

Mdivani was sixtyish, barrel chested, and prone to gold chains and shirts open to the waist in summer and Israeli Defense Force sweaters—the brown ones with leather shoulder patches—the rest of the year. He was fond of vodka and mentholated cigarettes. Spying, however, was not on his menu. "You are making a joke," he shouted. "Spying is for those afraid to confront the truth."

"I would have thought that one of your mafia pals would have killed you by now," Donovan shouted.

"I am not mafia. I keep telling you that. I am a hard-working businessman who is simply trying to get by."

"Yeah, yeah," Donovan said. "I'll tell you what, though—when you *do* get bumped off, I promise a fine funeral for the man who did it."

"I will accept that with gratitude," Mdivani replied. "Come on up and share a drink with me."

Donovan looked around and found the nearest stair. It was twenty or thirty yards down the beach. He ran through the sand and bounded up the wooden steps. Then he jogged down the Boardwalk and into a bear hug from this old friend with the knack of turning up in the captain's murder investigations.

"What's in that cup?" Donovan asked, regarding the paper container with a sort of amused suspicion. "Let me see, I still have memory left in the old CPU—triple espresso, half a pound of sugar, and a shot of *wodka*."

"*Two* shots of *wodka*," Mdivani replied. "I'm getting older and need the extra to inoculate me against the injustices of this vast and cruel world."

"What are you doing here?" Donovan asked.

"What do you mean? This is my bench." He kicked it to make the point. "Don't you remember? We sat on this very bench three or four years ago to speak of life and love and all those fine things."

"And to arrange the surrender of Valery Koslov," Donovan said.

"Ah yes. Another customer lost to American prosecutorial zeal. So be it."

"Is this the same bench?" Donovan asked, looking around. "It's easy to lose your bearings when you're walking on the sand."

"This is my bench. Come, sit on my bench and tell Georgi your troubles."

Mdivani sat with a thud and a sigh, and Donovan took a seat next to him.

"Did you really see that man yesterday between noon and one?" Donovan asked.

"Yes."

"With all the crowd?"

"Let me just say that it behooves a man of my standing in the community to know who may be sneaking up on him. Especially when they're carrying long metal objects."

"You're afraid of being killed," Donovan translated.

Mdivani waved off the suggestion. "Ah, people approach me all the time to give them jobs or lend them money."

"Is that it?" Donovan replied.

"Would I lie to you? Don't say a word!" Mdivani held his hand up to ward off a reply.

Donovan smiled.

"This old man with the metal detector? Sure, I saw him come out from under the Boardwalk and buy a cup of coffee at lunchtime. And then go back again into the shade." Mdivani gestured over his shoulder at a tiny bagel-and-knish shop built into the side of an old brick building across the Boardwalk. "Who were you thinking he killed yesterday instead of eating lunch like a gentleman?" Mdivani asked.

"Nobody, if what you say is true."

"I am always glad to help an innocent man establish his innocence. What is this about anthrax? Is that why you're here?"

"That man's wife was one of the postal workers who got anthrax last year," Donovan said.

"Is she still alive?" Mdivani asked.

"Yes."

"Are you looking for the terrorist who gave it to her? Are you on the World Trade Center case?"

"Not me," Donovan replied.

Mdivani nodded in a knowing sort of way. "Too many FBI, eh?"

"Too many this, too many that. Too many black

Grand Cherokees with D.C. plates cluttering up the streets of New York. And I don't know if you noticed, but ordinary folk didn't stop killing one another in this town. Murder investigation is what I do. War I leave to others. This is not the first time in my life I have had to say that."

"So then, why *are* you in Brighton Beach?"

"I'm actually in Coney Island, investigating the murder of James Victor," Donovan said.

"Ah!" Mdivani replied. "I should have expected you and put out the welcome mat."

"I was planning on dropping by for some of your chicken Kiev," Donovan said. "The recipe with a stick of butter in each piece of chicken."

"And you still must do so. Come by the club. But as for James Victor, I know nothing. The man is a complete blank to me. All I know is that he was a wealthy American who puts up buildings."

"Come on now," Donovan admonished.

Mdivani set his cup down on the bench so he could better toss up both hands.

"The man came in my club a few times, that is all. He had the chicken Kiev, now that you mention it. I greeted the man, as I do with all my guests, and shook his hand and kissed the hand of his young lady friend." Mdivani paused as a grin made an appearance on the captain's face. Then the Georgian shared the smile. He said, "Oh, I see. Victor had a wife, no?"

"Yes."

"His age? Forty or more?"

Donovan nodded. "Chloe," he added.

"Chloe? What sort of a name is that? It sounds like a

disease you get on your feet." Mdivani looked down past his bull-like torso and waggled his feet.

"I think it's an old English name," Donovan said.

"Well then, he did not come in with Chloe. He came in with someone much younger, and I can tell you her name—Lisa."

"I was wondering. I knew there was a Lisa in his life."

"And I can tell you her last name *and* where to find her," Mdivani said triumphantly. He picked up the cup and offered a toast. "To young women," he said, taking a sip and sighing.

"Nazdrovya," Donovan replied.

"You should have some of this," the Georgian said, offering Donovan the cup.

"Not today."

"How long is it now since you had a drink?"

"Twelve years," Donovan said.

"Saint Peter will pin a medal on you as you go through the pearly gates. Well, you are looking for Lisa Fine. Do you know of her?"

"Should I?"

"She is a celebrity in Coney Island," Mdivani explained. "She is a movie star. Well, as much of a movie star as we get these days. She appeared in a movie with . . . what is the name of the new martial arts guy?"

"Not my area of expertise," Donovan said. "Ask my wife."

"The Italian martial arts guy. Two years ago the movie came out. *Something Something Conquest* was the title."

"I must have missed that one," Donovan said.

"It's in all the video stores around here."

"I'll bet."

"She wore a black spandex outfit and carried an AK-47. Good movie to watch with the boys. Not so good to watch with the wife."

"Especially if your wife's name reminds you of a foot disease," Donovan added.

"Very true. This Lisa Fine also starred in a show that was on TV very briefly last year. Wore a tiny pair of shorts and flew a hang glider that was armed with a missile launcher."

"Damn! I seem to be missing out on a whole chunk of life," Donovan said. "I take it she's pretty."

Mdivani rolled his eyes.

"That good?"

"She's a knockout, my friend. The face of an angel and a bottom that any red-blooded male would proudly wear as a hat. Which makes me wonder why Victor seemed embarrassed when I came up to them to say hello. Such men like to be seen with their pretty mistresses."

"What do you mean, 'such men'?" Donovan asked.

"Oh, I don't know . . . rich men at midlife with their twenty-five-year-old girlfriends. I'll tell you, though— there is something wrong with James Victor."

"Apart from being dead."

"You are right. That *did* add to his list of woes."

"What did you see in him that was off kilter?" Donovan asked.

Mdivani shrugged and tossed up a hand, the one not holding the cup. "I can't put it into words. He appeared to be . . . I guess you might say a man with a terrible secret."

"Not at all what you would expect of a middle-aged

guy out on the town with his bombshell mistress," Donovan said.

"Hardly."

"Is there any chance that *she* was the dark secret?"

"That was not my impression," Mdivani said. "In my club a man can be as free as he chooses and not have to worry that his secret will get out. No tabloid photographers wait in ambush on Brighton Beach Avenue."

"I'm glad to hear that," Donovan said.

"So, I do not know what lurked in James Victor's heart. Whatever woe it was, she didn't share it. She seemed very happy—a pretty lady in love with a successful man. He was not bad looking, you know . . ."

Mdivani's voice trailed off, and he began making a gesture—grabbing the air, or at straws. Then he shrugged and said, "There was just something about him that was wrong." The Georgian slapped Donovan on the knee and said, "You will figure out what and tell me over dinner at my place. You will bring your gorgeous wife and your son."

"I promise to do that," Donovan replied.

"Anyway, if you want to find this girl, she works at the Coney Island Council on the Arts. It is over there by KeySpan Park, above the Chase bank. You will find it easily."

"What does she do there?" Donovan asked.

"The sort of thing you would expect from a local celebrity," Mdivani said. "She cuts ribbons at supermarket openings and has her picture taken with the borough president while he digs the ceremonial first shovelful of dirt at new building construction."

"No doubt where Victor met her," Donovan said.

"I imagine that is so."

Mdivani drained his cup, lifted up the plastic lid, and gazed balefully into the emptiness. "Here is an injustice not even you can rectify," he said.

"Speaking about construction, what do you think about Victor's plan to buy some old stores on Surf a few blocks this side of Nathan's, tear them down, and put up luxury housing?"

Mdivani laughed, and it was a hearty laugh. "Now you have gone from the sublime to the ridiculous. Real estate! Of all the questions to put to a man who, as you say, is an old commie thug! In Russia the ancien régime has been dead for only a dozen years or so. I am of the generation of Soviet officials who grew up believing that private property was a crime. Real estate! Hah! Of this I truly know nothing."

"I am waiting for an answer," Donovan insisted.

"All I can offer is the observation that, while a man is entitled to engage in pointless behavior, when it becomes *so expensive* . . ."

"Exactly my point," Donovan said.

"There are much better blocks to purchase and destroy. At that location, half the luxury apartments would overlook the subway tracks. Not very attractive considering the top dollar Victor would need to recoup his investment. I would build closer to KeySpan Park, where the apartments that didn't have a view of the ocean would overlook the stadium. But what do I know, a man who once ran a tractor factory in Pamiristan?"

"What you suggest is what I would do," Donovan said.

"But what do either of us know, a nightclub owner

and a policeman. There, I answered your question. You have done it again."

"Done what?" Donovan asked.

"What you do so well. Squeeze blood from a stone. Get a man to give you information that he didn't know he possessed."

"Is that what I do?" Donovan asked.

Mdivani nodded. "That and get me to verify the thought that you already have in your head. What is this all about? Who killed Victor?"

"I have no idea at this point."

"I am grateful for not being asked for my alibi," Mdivani said.

"Why bother?" Donovan replied. "You would have a handful."

"A man can never have too many alibis. How is your boy?"

"Good. He's very bright and lots of fun."

"That is good. A man can never have too many sons, either. Will he follow in your footsteps?"

"His life is his to lead, but if he wants to go into criminal investigation I will be glad to help. And speaking of criminals, do you ever hear from your old buddies in Pamiristan?"

Mdivani waved off the suggestion. "Who would want to? The Russians who remained in that godforsaken pile of rocks are useless. They are slugs. The ones who looted the joint and ran are now mafiosi. Why don't you go and arrest them?"

"Are they around?" Donovan asked, involuntarily glancing to the right and the left to see only innocuous-looking strollers on the Boardwalk.

"They are in Moscow and Odessa," Mdivani said. "I don't think that any have come to the land of the free and the home of the brave. Surely I would have heard."

"They would have come around looking for a job," Donovan said.

"More likely a handout. Hey, whatever happened to that Bamiyani you knew?"

"Who?" Donovan said.

"The Afghan. From Bamiyan Province north of Kabul. The guy who shot at you in the underground garage."

"Oh, Mojadidi. He went back to the old country to fight the Taliban. I keep waiting for him to turn up on CNN, being interviewed by Christiane Amanpour. Maybe he's dead."

"You are the most tolerant man I have ever met," Mdivani said.

"He missed," Donovan replied.

"Someone shoots at me . . ." Mdivani made a wringing-the-neck gesture.

The two men were interrupted by the arrival of Brian Moskowitz, who came up the stairs and walked down the Boardwalk with a smile that grew with each step. As he neared the bench he fished a ten-dollar bill from a pocket, pushed it at Mdivani, and said, "Ten bucks on the Yanks tonight."

"I am out of that business," Mdivani said hurriedly.

"Yeah, you are," Mosko replied.

"You are looking fit, Detective Moskowitz," Mdivani said, reaching up to rap his knuckles on Mosko's pectorals.

"You too, pal."

"I'm done here," Donovan said.

． ． ．

The house was a summer house once, tiny and bright and adorable and fit. Used only three, perhaps four months of the year, it stayed young for many years. That was in the 1940s and 1950s, when people could afford a lovely little summer place along New York City's miles of beach. Then came middle age and housing senescence—rooms were tacked on, shingles molted and nailed back up, and the open front porch was glassed in. A furnace was installed so that the new owners, facing more perilous financial times, could make it their sole residence. In all, the house looked aging and very lived in but still comfy.

It sat halfway down a block composed entirely of converted summer homes, smack up against one another, separated at most by driveways. When Donovan and Moskowitz pulled up in the red Corvette, it was early afternoon and the sun no longer shone on the red ceramic pot of geraniums that sat alongside the white front door.

"This must be it," Donovan said, crumpling the paper wrapper from his Roll-N-Roaster roast beef sandwich and pushing it into the emptiness of his coffee container. Then he deposited the thing on the floor mat, Mosko's eyes following the motion like an owl eyeballing a field mouse.

"You're gonna throw that out later, right?" Mosko asked.

"Yep."

"This is where her boss said we could find her."

"Not my idea of the young starlet's residence," Donovan said.

"It was where she grew up," Mosko said.

"Moving back in with the folks also doesn't fit my

picture of what such a woman would do a year after appearing in a TV show," Donovan said. "No matter if it was only a summer replacement series about an armored hang glider. On the other hand, maybe she's bright enough to have figured out that her Hollywood career is unlikely to parallel Julia Roberts's and is carving out a secure little niche for herself at the old homestead. You know, spokesperson for the local council on the arts . . ."

"And rich man's mistress," Mosko said.

"She may have been thinking rich man's *wife*," Donovan replied.

"Let's find out."

They got out of the car and walked up the short flagstone path to the front door, Donovan taking vague note of being watched by a stocky man in his mid-twenties who was bringing in the garbage cans three doors down. The man had a fair amount of muscle that he displayed under an athletic T-shirt.

Mosko caught the man's eye and gave him a kind of raised-fist, one-muscleman-to-another wave. The fellow looked away and disappeared behind a house not unlike the one they approached.

Donovan pressed the doorbell, his shield hanging from his jacket's breast pocket. After half a minute, the door opened.

The young woman may have been pretty, may have been a knockout, but not on that day. She wore a plain old gray sweatsuit, and her curly blond hair—dyed, the captain noticed—was pulled into a ponytail that puffed only a bit more than her eyes. She had been crying, crying a lot, and made no attempt to hide the fact. Tear trails crossed cheeks swollen half again their size, and her lower lip quivered as she looked into Donovan's soft brown eyes and said, "Yes?"

"Miss Fine? I'm Bill Donovan of the New York Police Department. This is Brian Moskowitz." Then Donovan's voiced dropped into the velvet register. "I'm so sorry for your loss."

She sort of sucked in her breath, catching herself as one does at the end of a diving board before succumbing to gravity. Her lip quivered even more, then she let out a wail of grief and fell into the captain's arms. He hugged her as she sobbed herself out, pulling at him as hard as Daniel did during his monster hugs.

When she calmed down a bit and relaxed her grip, Mosko said, "Where are your folks?"

"They're in Israel," she replied.

"There's nobody here who can stay with you?" Donovan asked.

She shook her head. "I just moved back to Coney Island from Hollywood . . . well, Studio City . . . a year and a half ago. All my good friends are out there."

"What about high school friends?" Mosko asked.

She laughed, a bit sadly, Donovan thought, and said, "No. I wasn't popular in high school. I had no friends." She went to wipe her nose and eyes on her sleeve, then caught herself and said, "God, I need some tissues."

"Can we come in?" Donovan asked.

She looked around, maybe a little thrown by the afternoon's turn of events but somehow resigned to the notion of having events run her. She said, "Sure . . . oh, the place is a wreck. I better get my act together and clean it up before my parents come home."

Donovan smiled warmly and said, "I'm sure they'll understand given the circumstances."

"They don't know about James and me. They'd *kill me* if they did, for getting involved with a married man. How did you guys know?"

"We're detectives," Mosko replied. "It's what we do."

Donovan edged her toward the door, putting his big hand on her shoulder and urging her inside. She said, "Come in."

"Thanks."

They followed her into a living room that was tiny but cozy, with an immense overstuffed couch, lacquered end tables and coffee table, and a large TV. The top of the TV and the mantel above a nonworking fireplace were decorated with silver-framed photographs of Lisa. The pictures were stills from her movies, signed pictures of her leading men, and, prominently, an eight-by-ten of her strapped into her hang glider. Next to it stood a young man with frosted blond hair. Donovan wandered over and looked at the photo.

"That's Matilda," she said, plopping down onto the couch and burying her face in her hands, the better to try to rub away the swelling. Most of the top of the coffee table was covered with wadded-up tissues.

"Say again?"

"Matilda is the name of my hang glider," she replied, talking into her hands. Then she looked up and said, "Did you see my show, *Ladyhawk?*"

"Sorry," Donovan replied, shaking his head.

When she looked over at Mosko, he too shook his head.

"Okay, you're New Yorkers and don't watch commercial television," she said. "I understand. It's on cable Tuesdays at ten if you want to check out a rerun. And I'm going back in the fall for three or four months to shoot a full-length feature for the video market. I'm being strapped back into Matilda and going to war against terrorists." She looked up, gave a little laugh, and whisked the tissues off a stapled-together collection of papers three quarters of an inch thick that Donovan recognized as a script. "Want to read it?"

"I'm not a drama critic," Donovan replied.

"It's a living," she said. Then she added, "I have a big kung fu scene in this movie, and I'm totally unprepared. I had hoped to work on my moves this summer, but my sensei died."

"Can we talk about James?" Donovan asked.

"Sure," she replied with a sigh.

"Is it okay if I look around while you guys talk?" Mosko asked.

"If you don't mind the mess."

"No problem to me."

"I was planning on getting an apartment here—James was saving me one in the new building. But now I don't know if I'm staying in Coney Island."

"Don't want to stay with the parents, I guess," Donovan said.

"They're sweet and I love them," Lisa replied. "But, you know, my Barbie dolls are still in my room."

"Gotcha. My mom is eighty-five and is still hanging on to my Captain Video Decoder Ring. How long have your parents been in Israel?"

"Two weeks. I sent them there as an anniversary present—their thirty-fifth. They'll be back after the Fourth of July."

"And you said they don't know about James," Donovan said.

"God, no. I have enough to deal with." She sort of smiled, then said, "Even though I've made movies and am pretty independent, who needs the aggravation of having your parents do the I-told-you-so bit?"

Donovan said that he understood. "Who *did* know?" he asked.

"I told a friend . . . a girlfriend, in L.A. And I told Scott . . . my stunt coordinator . . . that's him next to me in the photo on top of the TV . . . who I sort of see but who is mainly my buddy. He's in L.A., too."

"Did James's wife know?"

Lisa looked down at her hands and shook her head. "No," she said. "He said he would tell her when the time was right."

"So he promised you he would divorce her, right?" Donovan said.

The girl nodded. She said, "We were in love. And he wanted to have a son. It was important to him."

"I understand. His wife couldn't have children?"

"There was some medical reason why she couldn't, but I don't know what it was," Lisa said.

"Did James ask you to marry him?" Donovan asked.

Lisa bobbed her head up and down.

"What kind of apartment was he getting you?"

"A two bedroom with a terrace overlooking the beach," she replied. "Of course, that would be in a year or more, when the building was put up."

"And that's where the two of you would live?" Donovan asked.

"No. That would be temporary until the divorce was final. Then we'd see who got the house. If she didn't, we'd live there. Otherwise we'd take one of the penthouses in the Coney Island building."

"Are the plans nice?" Donovan asked.

"The apartments were beautiful! Three bedrooms with a huge terrace. Where do you live? In a house?"

He shook his head. "Riverside Drive," he replied.

"I've never been in an apartment there," Lisa replied. "But I've heard they're big."

"I have three bedrooms, two baths, a formal dining room, and a maid's room."

"Wow!"

"The place has been in my family a long time. But there's no terrace. I'd like a terrace or a garden someday."

"I'd love to be able to walk outdoors and see the ocean," Lisa said, a bit wistfully. "Well, there's always the Pacific. If the movie is a hit, maybe I can afford something in Santa Monica."

"We've been talking about moving to a place where you can do something like that," Donovan said. "My young son would like to be able to go outdoors. Speaking of him, he's crazy about things that fly and would love to have a picture of Matilda. Do you mind if I borrow that one and have it copied?"

"Be my guest," she replied. Then she added, "If you move, you'll give up the deal you have now?"

"I have someone else in the family who could take it over," Donovan replied. "Did you ever meet Mrs. Victor?"

Lisa made a face. "Once. Before James and I were involved she came with him to a jazz night the Council on the Arts ran on the Boardwalk."

"Who played?"

"Herbie Hancock."

"Not too shabby," Donovan replied. "What was your impression of her?"

"Cold as ice?" Lisa replied. "She didn't smile once the entire evening."

"Did the two of you ever talk?"

"James introduced me to her. She had the tightest lips I have ever seen. You know, even when she was *trying* to smile she couldn't smile."

"Some people are just like that," Donovan replied. "Are you *sure* she didn't know?"

"There was nothing to know *then*," Lisa insisted. "He was her faithful husband, and the only guy in my life was Scott, my buddy who I mentioned. He worked on the set . . . did stunts and strapped me into Matilda every day."

"Scott who?"

"Jamison. Lives in Studio City. He's kind of my personal trainer, too. A really sweet guy. But like I said, mostly a friend."

"He's in L.A. now?"

"Yes. I talked to him on the phone yesterday afternoon right after James left me here alone to go run an errand," Lisa said. "I would ask him to fly here and stay with me, but he hates New York and refuses to set foot in the city."

Mosko had finished poking around the house and came back just in time to hear those words. Donovan looked over at him, and the sergeant said, *"Nada."*

"Sit down," Lisa said, and he did so, beside her. Emerging from her depression, she gently pulled back his jacket and stared at his pectorals. "Are those real or a prop?" she asked.

"What are you *doing?*" he asked.

"Staring at your chest," she said, as if talking to an imbecile.

"Can I get a little quid pro quo going here?" he replied.

"Rent the movie," she replied playfully. "There's a shower scene."

"You got it," Mosko said, smiling back.

Donovan said, "You mentioned that James was here yesterday and . . ."

"Yeah, he came over. We were supposed to send out for Chinese."

"When?"

"Eleven-thirty, noon. He didn't even sit down. James had a problem with sitting down. He was a workaholic who was out of the office a lot, working on stuff. But this time he had something *really important* he had to do and was really worked up about it."

"Excited?" Donovan asked.

She shook her head. "More like determined. More like 'I got this thing that's been eating away at me and I got to take care of it.' "

"Had he been upset?" Donovan asked.

"For the past two weeks he was like a different person," Lisa said. "James was normally a pretty upbeat guy. But two weeks ago . . ."

"What day?" Donovan asked. "Exactly."

"Thursday. Two weeks ago this coming Thursday."

"June sixth," Donovan said.

"What happened then?" Mosko asked.

"James got into this *dark* mood. I don't know what came over him. He seemed to be obsessed with something."

"Did you ask him what?" Mosko replied.

"I do nude shower scenes and fly a hang glider that shoots missiles," the girl replied. "I'm not shy."

"What did he say?" Donovan asked, smiling faintly.

"He said he couldn't tell me but it had nothing to do with me. But of course I thought it did. You know how women are."

Both Donovan and Mosko rolled their eyes simultaneously.

"You felt like it was you who was being rejected," Donovan said. "Nude shower scenes notwithstanding."

She nodded and for a moment lapsed back into a funk. She leaned forward and buried her face in her hands and, one more time, rubbed her eyes. Lisa was silent for a time, and when she lifted her head the tears had returned.

Donovan reached out and touched her knee, and she shook off the tears.

"I thought he was about to dump me," she admitted. "I had worked myself up to believe that he couldn't ask his wife for a divorce and was going to back out of the relationship with me. I tried to stay upbeat . . . but, you know."

"It's hard," Donovan said.

"Then all of a sudden . . . yesterday . . . he gets this weird thing with the screwdriver. Takes one of my Dad's big screwdrivers . . ."

"With an orange-and-white handle," Donovan said.

"We found it," Mosko added.

She nodded, and added, "Then he goes off on an errand he says will fix everything. Will patch up the mood he's been in for two weeks. I tried to get him to tell me what the hell he was doing. He *never* did anything himself, I mean never did anything mechanical. Always got someone else to do it for him. I'm surprised he even knew what a screwdriver *is*."

Donovan said, "So James takes the screwdriver and gets into his Porsche and drives down Surf Avenue. This was around noon or a little after, right?"

"Yes."

"And that was the last you saw of him?"

She nodded, looking down. "He apologized for having been into his own thoughts lately and left. I never saw him again." Lisa was silent for a full minute, then abruptly expelled a burst of air, slapped herself on the knees, and sat back on the couch and crossed her legs. She said, "So that's the end of the romance."

"What did you do after he left?" Mosko asked.

"Hung out. Tried to work out by myself in the living room, but you really can't do kung fu alone."

"And nobody saw you, right?"

"Not unless you count Eddie," she said.

"That would be the guy three doors down," Donovan said.

"Yeah. He's had the hots for me since seventh grade. He's kind of sweet and dumb. He always seems to be there when I walk into or out of the house."

Donovan gestured to Mosko to have someone talk to Eddie. Mosko nodded.

"James and I were going to go out last night," she continued. "He wanted to celebrate what he called 'the end of the ordeal.' "

"What he was looking for with the screwdriver," Donovan said.

She bobbed her head up and down. "The screwdriver thing was weird," she said, "but he was a gentle man. Who would want to kill him?"

"Anyone come to mind?" Donovan asked.

"I guess his wife if he was going to leave her," she said. "*Me* if he *wasn't* going to leave her." Lisa looked up, forced a smile, and said, "Just kidding, guys."

"Uhm hmm," Donovan replied.

"That's about it that I know of. What was he doing in the basement of that candy store?"

"Ever been in there?" Donovan said.

"Sure. Lots of times. None of them since high school."

"Where were James and you going at seven-thirty last night?" Donovan asked. "Back to the Gemini?"

"You *know* about that?" she asked. "It was our favorite place. You really can go in there and no one will ever know . . ." She smiled at her own words.

Donovan completed the thought. "And no one will ever know unless he happens to be friends with the owner of the club."

"*That's* how you knew about us," she said.

Donovan nodded.

"You even know what time we were going there."

"James wrote it on an ATM receipt."

"God, you know *everything*," Lisa said. "I think I'll go back to L.A. Would you guys like a Coke or anything?"

Donovan said, "Thanks, but we just came from Roll-N-Roaster."

She smiled, warming, a glimpse of memory apparent, and said, "Oh, I *love* Roll-N-Roaster. That was my whole teenage life! Can we go back? I haven't eaten since yesterday. God, I would *kill* for some cheese fries."

"Sure," Mosko said.

Lisa was getting excited. "I'll take my cell phone and make reservations on the next flight to the Coast. So, I tried to make a life for myself back in Coney Island and it didn't work out. At least I gave it a shot."

"Can you hold off on going back to L.A.?" Donovan asked. "I'd like you to stick around for a few days."

"I can't be alone right now," she said.

Donovan stood and said, "Do you guys want to compare notes on how you wasted your youths in Roll-N-Roaster for a while? I need to make a call."

"Sure," she said.

Mosko said to his boss, "I know what you have in mind, and are you sure that it's a good idea?"

"I'm sure," Donovan said and walked out into the front yard. As he brought his cell phone to his lips, he noticed that Eddie down the block had found another excuse . . . doing the edging on his tiny front lawn . . . to keep an eye on the Fine house.

7. A SIXTEEN-ACRE MOONSCAPE LIT BY INDUSTRIAL LAMPS.

Donovan went back inside a few minutes later to find his friend and the B-movie star discussing the finer points of ab control.

Donovan said, "Okay, here's the deal. Lisa, you need to be with someone, and I need you to stick around a while. You can stay with me. I have a big place, and my wife, Marcy, is . . ."

"Superwoman, basically," Mosko interjected.

". . . a black belt in kung fu. She's studying for the bar exam and needs someone to beat up on every morning to loosen herself up. The two of you can work out together, and I'll know you're safe while I sort out whatever happened to your boyfriend in the basement of Surf Avenue News."

The girl smiled. It was an astonished sort of smile. She said, "I'm really, I don't know, amazed. I don't really know you."

"Play your cards right and you could wind up on the cover of *Perfect*," Mosko said.

"What?"

"The captain's mother-in-law owns that rag."

"Well, I . . . I *was* on the cover of *Maxim*; in a leather bikini. But *Perfect* is, wow, like *Vogue* or *Elle* or something. Okay, sure. I'll go to your place. I want to find out who killed James, too."

"That's good," Donovan said.

"But what do you mean when you say you want to make sure I'll be safe?" Lisa asked.

"I'm not sure why I said that," Donovan replied.

"But go with it anyhow," Mosko advised.

"There's something lurking in the darkness here, and while I don't know what it is yet, I can assure you that it hasn't gone away."

"You don't think that the man who killed James could come after *me?*" she said.

"Just come stay with me for a few days," Donovan said.

"You'll be in illustrious company," Mosko said. "The only other one to get this invitation was Katy Lucca."

Lisa's eyes seemed to light from within. "I studied all her movies!" she said. "What happened to her, she went to jail for trying to kill a cop?"

Mosko smiled and jabbed a finger in the direction of his boss.

"It was *you?*" Lisa asked Donovan.

"The Captain is a nice guy and has a great place," Mosko said. "Don't commit no felonies and you'll be cool. Just remember that his wife has more degrees of black belt than you."

"I don't even have a *brown* belt," Lisa said ruefully.

"You'll be staying on the studio couch in my study, same as Katy did."

Donovan felt foolish about having said "Katy did." He smiled goofily like Kevin Costner does and tried to wave the phrase away from his mouth. Then he said, "Get your things together. Throw some stuff into a suitcase, and we'll take off."

"Okay," she replied.

Donovan added a kicker. "I forgot to mention—Marcy liked your movie."

"She *did?*"

Mosko said, "Mrs. D. watches martial arts movies? When? Before or after studying for the bar, child care, working out, and taking care of *you?*"

Ignoring that, Donovan said, "She asked if you do all your own stunts."

Smiling sheepishly, Lisa said, "All but the flying kick. I'm afraid of landing hard and bruising my ass."

"Marc will take over the job of bruising your ass," Mosko said.

"God, I can't want to meet her. What does she look like?"

"Halle Berry," Mosko replied.

"Sort of," Donovan added, modestly.

"Wow! She's black?"

"Multiracial," Donovan said.

"You really *aren't* the average cop, are you?" Lisa said, looking into Donovan's eyes deeply.

"*He* ain't exactly Fred Flatfoot," Donovan replied, nodding at his friend.

"*You're* the bone crusher," Lisa said to Mosko.

"When he has to be, and he's *very good* at it," Donovan said. "But most of the time he's my director of ops and communications wiz."

"All *right*," she said. "I'll go get some stuff."

"We'll run over to Roll-N-Roaster. I could use another cup of coffee. Then Brian will take you to my place. On the way he'll drop me off in the financial district. I'm going to pay a call on Mrs. Victor."

Lisa made a face, as a teenager might.

"Problem is," Donovan went on, "my friend here is

driving, and I don't know if you noticed, but he has a Corvette."

She hadn't noticed but said, "So what? You drive and I'll sit on his lap."

"No way, José, is he driving my car," Mosko said, his temper rising quickly from absolute zero to moderate outrage.

Feeling offense, Lisa said, "Hey, worse things could happen to you than having me in your lap. I haven't been doing any flying kicks lately. I have a nice butt."

"Nix on anyone but me driving my car," Mosko insisted. "No one treats my car with respect like me."

"He parks catty-corner in lots so no one can park near enough to open their doors into his paint job," Donovan explained.

"Yeah, and I *still* haven't gotten him to pick up the garbage he left on the floor," Mosko added.

"You guys sound like fun. So does Marcy. Let me go get packed."

With that, she went out of the room. A few seconds later, footsteps went up the stairs.

"What, are you out of your mind?" Mosko asked.

Donovan shrugged. "Maybe," he replied.

"You're taking a fucking suspect home to stay with you and your family. *Again!* The last time you did this, the woman was setting you up to be killed."

"Look, I can handle myself. Marcy certainly can handle herself. We both have guns. We'll be okay."

"Miss Direct-to-Video here could easily have killed Victor. She was afraid he was dumping her."

"I know," Donovan replied.

"She's strong enough. She has no alibi."

"Which reminds me, while she's packing, run down the block and say hello to Nosy Norris. He's out edging his lawn so he can maintain line-of-sight to this house. Find out if he saw her leave the house yesterday. And while you're at it, scare the shit out of him. I want him to keep away from her."

Rolling his eyes, Mosko said, "You're adopting another potential murderer. You always take a liking to one of the players and go the extra mile."

"Keep your friends close, keep your enemies closer," Donovan replied.

The captain was early for his appointment with Chloe Victor, so after Mosko dropped him off at the corner of Broadway and Trinity he wandered a few blocks over to what remained of the World Trade Center. The fires that provided lower Manhattan with a creepy glow for months were gone, leaving a sixteen-acre moonscape prowled over by construction workers on foot and operating various equipment. Their movements sent up occasional clouds of gray from the rubble left behind September 11, 2001, when the twin towers collapsed into a heart-wrenching funeral pyre of steel, concrete, plaster, and human remains.

Donovan watched the hundreds of workers and the dozens of trucks, vans, and other support vehicles swarming around Ground Zero. The huge yellow cranes looked like immense steel praying mantises. At the perimeter, New Yorkers and tourists trudged slowly up and down ramps built specially for viewing. This was the first time in memory that New Yorkers and tourists had done *anything* together. They viewed the remains like the mourners who lined up to view JFK's casket, then trudged off, changed and sad. Small tears appeared in Donovan's eyes, and he turned away.

The offices of Victor Coney Island Properties were on the seventeenth floor of a new glass-and-steel tower not far from the intersection of Wall and Broadway. Though it had been cleaned up, perhaps several times, since September 11, the facade still seemed to be recuperating. Traces of the gray dust that covered all of lower Manhattan remained in joints and cracks across the entrance, and some windows looked vaguely pitted, as if they had survived a sandstorm.

Donovan showed his badge to get through the increased security now evident in every Manhattan building tall enough or important enough to be a terrorist target. When he got to the seventeenth floor, the elevator door opened into a dark blue-gray reception area dominated by a large Formica island behind which a smartly dressed receptionist commanded a phone complex, monitor, and "guest" sign-in book.

After signing simply "Donovan, NYPD" and waiting for approval from the inner sanctum, he was shown down a light gray corridor decorated with blue framed architectural renderings of assorted Victor Coney Island Properties holdings. Among them was a rendering of "Proposed Surf Avenue Condominiums & Spa," which had an estimated completion date five years in the future.

As he walked through a medium-sized common area of cubicles and filing cabinets, Donovan noticed his arrival being met with stares that the office workers were unable to suppress. One young woman elbowed a young man in the ribs and whispered in his ear. Donovan imagined a comment along the lines of "This is where the bitch gets hauled off in chains."

Chloe Victor stood behind what was clearly her late husband's desk. The way she stood—in front of an executive chair that had been pushed back, looking down at papers—suggested to the captain that she was reluctant to be seen occupying her husband's throne while his body remained warm.

She wore a dark gray suit over a white blouse and a black bow tie. A small red, white, and blue ribbon, commemorating the destruction of the World Trade Center, was pinned to her lapel. The woman's blond hair was short and appeared molded to her head. A pair of diamond earrings peeked around austere cheekbones. If she had been mourning, she was a better actress than Lisa Fine and showed nothing.

"Captain Donovan," she said, smiling quickly and walking around the desk to shake his hand. "Thank you for coming."

"I'm so sorry about your loss," he said.

She looked down at the floor, then up again at him, and replied with a grim smile, "Yes, thank you. Do you know who killed my husband?"

"Not yet. I was hoping you could help me."

"How can I help find who killed James?"

"I was wondering if that's what you're doing now," Donovan said.

She looked around at the expansive desk, which seemed only a bit smaller than the flight deck of the *Intrepid*. She said, a bit uncertainly, "Ah, no. I was doing something else. You must think it cold of me to be in my husband's office the day after he was killed."

"Not at all. I know a policeman who was killed and the first thing his wife did was go down into the basement where he had his workshop. She wanted to be near his stuff. She sort of browsed around and didn't really do anything. Later the family came over and they had a wake. When a loved one dies, you want to surround yourself with stuff and memories."

"Thank you for understanding," she said.

"I'll bet much of his life was right here," Donovan added.

She nodded. "James worked long hours. He rarely got home before nine. There were breakfast, lunch, and dinner meetings."

"Were you involved in the business?"

"I was office manager."

"Did he let you in on decision making?" Donovan asked.

Chloe looked up at him and smiled, as if in appreciation of having been understood. "Not often enough," she replied. "He was kind of old-fashioned that way. He didn't think that wives should be that much in evidence."

"Just stay here and make sure everyone punches in, right?"

"Along those lines. Plus go to the spa. Entertain clients' wives. Stay young looking." She smiled grimly.

"Sounds exciting," Donovan said.

"Very. Now, there were some things that he wanted to do that were *just wrong!* One of the reasons I'm here today is to put a stop to one of them."

"That would be building condominiums in the wrong part of Coney Island," Donovan ventured.

"Yes!" she exclaimed, as joyously as could be expected

under the circumstances. "How did you know?"

"It seems obvious," Donovan said. "Why build on a block where half the apartments will face the subway tracks? *And* have to go through the hassle of civil proceedings, lawsuits, the fog of city regulations, etc., when there's a much better parcel of *vacant* land right next to KeySpan Park."

"Exactly. Just what I told him."

"And his response was?"

" 'I want the Surf Avenue property. It has long-term potential because it's near the subway. Tenants have to get to work in the city.' "

"Forgetting that people who buy million-dollar condos have cars," Donovan said. "They won't sit on the Q train for forty-five minutes to get to work."

"You are *so* right! I don't know what it was between him and that block. He was obsessed with it."

She lifted a map of Coney Island from the desk and carried it to the large glass-topped conference table that occupied much of the other side of the room. She placed it on the glass and tapped the map with her finger.

"It was personal," Donovan said.

"I suspected so. And he wouldn't talk to me about it, either. He just worried and worried about getting that land . . . especially over the last few weeks."

"Since June sixth," Donovan said.

"*Yes!* I mean, James was after that property for two or three years, but a week and a half or two weeks ago he got really crazy about it. Do you know the significance of that date?"

"I'm working on it," Donovan said.

"Would you let me know when you figure it out?" she asked.

"Absolutely."

Chloe sat at one of the chairs surrounding the conference table and waved Donovan down into another. She said, "You would think, given his obsession with the land, that he was born on it. But of course he wasn't."

"Where *was* he born?" Donovan asked.

"Algiers," she replied.

"Excuse me?"

"Algiers. In Algeria. James was adopted, something he didn't find out until he was in college. His real name is . . ." She fumbled for the name, pulling at imaginary words in the air, then said, "Yusef something. Hold on." She got a medium-sized black bag from atop the desk and returned to the conference table. After poking through an old address book for several moments, she said, "Madjer. Yusef Madjer." She spelled out both names for the captain, then said, "The circumstances of his becoming an orphan had something to do with Algeria fighting for independence from France. Which was before my time, so I don't really understand it."

"This is fascinating," Donovan said.

"*He* was fascinated with it. After college, he spent a few years trying to track down his birth parents, only to find out that they were dead. But he found the orphanage he was placed in and, I imagine, came to some sort of resolution. I know that he lived in Algiers for a year or two absorbing the local culture and politics. You know how some college men get, I guess you would say . . ."

"Radicalized?" Donovan offered.

"Yes, exactly. Anyway, that was just a phase for James.

He snapped out of it and began some kind of consulting business relating to urban development. He came back to America with enough money to start his career, and that brings us up to today."

"James and you were married how long?"

"Almost ten years," she replied, reaching up with the point of her pinkie to wipe what may have been a tear from the corner of one eye.

While she did so, Donovan wandered over to the western window—which took up nearly the entire wall—and gazed out. He turned back to her when she resumed tapping the map.

"Actually," she said, appearing to choke down an unseemly burst of emotion, "I thought that maybe the block was where *she* had something—such as an investment—and buying it at an inflated price was his way of funneling money to her without my knowledge."

"She?" Donovan asked.

"His *girlfriend*, of course," Chloe said.

"That would be . . ."

"Lisa Fine, the actress . . . sort of . . . but I suspect you know that."

"I heard," Donovan replied. "And I spoke with her. She's not aware that you know about the relationship."

"Hah," Chloe replied.

"How *do* you know?" Donovan asked.

"I got an e-mail telling me," she replied.

"Did you keep it?" he asked.

She nodded, then began fishing in her bag for something new to show him. As she did so, she said, "May I get you something? Coffee? Tea? We have a wonderful espresso machine that James brought home from Algiers."

"Espresso with sugar," Donovan replied.

Chloe touched the intercom button on the conference table phone and said, "Carolyn, would you mind getting the captain one espresso with sugar?"

"No problem, Mrs. V." was the reply.

The woman handed Donovan a printout that was folded in half and clearly had been opened and closed many times. It bore smidges of blush and flecks of mascara and emitted a faint scent of White Shoulders perfume. The message had a return address that was no more than a jumble of letters and numbers at a large commercial website. It was addressed to Chloe Victor at her office address and said simply, "Your husband is having an affair with Lisa Fine, the actress. Be warned."

"It's from an anonymous e-mail address," Chloe said.

"There's no such thing," Donovan replied. "Would you mind faxing this to my office for me?"

A bit surprised, she nonetheless said, "No, not at all." Donovan wrote a number on a Post-it note and handed it to her. As she walked behind the desk to the fax machine on the credenza, she said, "I assume you'll keep this matter confidential."

"Of course," Donovan replied, reaching for his cell phone.

"I plan to assume control of the company," she added.

"It looks like you already have."

"And word of this scandal—on top of the murder, of course—would seriously harm my effectiveness. I am in a business that relies heavily on an ability to get along with elected officials, and if they get a whiff of scandal . . ."

Donovan said that he understood, then spoke into his cell. "It's me. I'm faxing over a printout of an e-mail.

Track down the name and address of the sender . . . Yes, now . . . No, Brian isn't with me. He's running an errand . . . I doubt we'll be in today. I'm in a meeting, and when I'm done Brian is picking me up and we're taking a ride out to Queens . . . Yeah, right. To go to a Mets game. Bye."

Chloe returned to the table with the piece of paper. She sat back down and said, "You seem to have an informal relationship with your staff."

"Pretty much," he replied.

"I'm more formal. The fax went through."

Donovan thanked her, then thanked the pretty, brown-haired young woman who brought in the espresso. He took a sip and said, "Very good. Thanks. Now, you got this message about two weeks ago. At least, it came in on June fifth. Did you read it right away?"

"Yes. I don't allow e-mail to build up in my in-box."

"That's smart," Donovan said. "And what was your reaction?"

She thought for a moment, then said, "At first, disbelief. Then the feeling that his recent mood could be explained by a decision to break up with her. My husband was, above all, a practical, career-driven man who was afraid of scandal. My third reaction was that he broke off with her and she killed him."

"That possibility occurred to me," Donovan said.

"Good. Then it doesn't have to be my idea. That would just reinforce my reputation for being a bitch."

Donovan smiled. "Is that your reputation?" he asked.

"The woman who handles employee accountability is often seen that way," she replied.

"You said that James was afraid of scandal," Donovan said.

"Terrified. How he could have an affair in the face of this fear is beyond me."

"Interesting," Donovan said. "And to more than just me. Tell me, do you have any idea who sent that e-mail?"

"None whatsoever," she replied. "But there are several e-mail addresses listed on our corporate website—James's, mine, and two of our property managers."

"We'll find out who sent it," Donovan assured her. "Now, can you think of anyone who might want to kill your husband?"

She shook her head. "Other than the girl or someone in her life, no."

"Such as a jealous would-be suitor?" Donovan asked.

"Precisely. Does she have an excuse for where she was at the time of the murder?"

"None worth a damn," Donovan replied.

"My suggestion is to check to see if she has a financial interest in the Surf Avenue property," Chloe said.

"I intend to do that. And since you brought the subject up, do *you* have an alibi for yesterday at lunchtime?"

"None worth a damn," she replied. "In fact, it's sort of the opposite."

"Where were you?" Donovan asked.

"First I was at home, where James often leaves . . . left . . . me in the morning on Sundays when he ducked into the office to check on things . . . or at least that's what he said he was doing. I sat in the Jacuzzi for a while with music on. I like show tunes and had the CD of *The Producers* running."

"Amazing show," he said. "The movie was the only

instance in my life where I actually, literally, fell onto the floor laughing. The play was even better."

"Then I took a walk," she added.

"Where?"

"Down Ocean Parkway to Coney Island," she sighed. "I walked by the Surf Avenue site. I guess it must have been about one. My understanding is that my husband was lying dead inside the candy store at that point."

Donovan nodded slowly and gently. "What did you do then?" he asked.

"Walked by the *other* site, the better one, next to the ballpark. Then I bought a bottle of water at a deli on Stillwell, walked home, and got back in the Jacuzzi."

"Did anyone see you?" Donovan asked.

"The Spanish man in the deli, which was near the Boardwalk," she said.

"Why did you go into the deli for water?" Donovan asked.

She looked a bit surprised. "I was thirsty," she replied.

"Why not buy the bottle of water from the hot dog vendor who had set up his cart right around there? Those guys sell water, and for a buck, too."

"There was no hot dog vendor," she replied.

"Really."

"None. I'm a woman who sees detail."

"So I gather," he replied.

"You ask interesting questions," she said.

"Including 'Did you confront your husband about the girl?' "

"No," she replied, shaking her head. "On the strength of an anonymous e-mail? It could have come from any-body. Maybe one of those troublemakers on the Coney

Island Committee for Common Sense, the group that's suing us."

"I *will* find out who sent it," Donovan replied.

She continued, "But I knew that something was up. The nights that were later than usual. The sudden 'dinner appointments with clients.' " She smiled bitterly, adding, "And the sudden interest in sex acts he had never expected me to perform. It all added up. Did you ever cheat on your wife, Captain?"

"No. We're very much in love. And she's both a kung fu master *and* a better shot than me."

Chloe smiled, and it was a nicer smile this time. "I was planning to confront him, but someone robbed me of the chance."

Donovan finished his espresso and put the tiny cup down. "One more thing . . ."

"However I can help," she said.

"Why do you imagine he was in the basement of the candy store?" Donovan asked. "His interest was in the entire block."

She tossed her hands up. "I have no clue," she replied.

Donovan stood and stretched, yawning. "Excuse me," he said.

"Long day?"

"Not particularly. Just a perplexing one. Tell me, I find you to be an agreeable person. How'd you get the reputation of being Lady Macbeth?"

"Who said that, the committee?"

He nodded.

"Well, what *would* they say, even though none of them has met me, to their knowledge anyway."

"To their knowledge?" Donovan asked.

"I shouldn't tell you this, but on the walk home I stopped in that candy store and bought strawberry Twizzlers," she said.

Donovan looked at her with a kind of amazement.

"When?" he asked.

"Oh, one-thirty or two, I guess. That man . . . Caplan, is that his name?"

Donovan said that it was.

"He looked right at me and had no idea who I was," she continued, a glimmer of satisfaction showing. "But then, I was just another forty-year-old woman in a gray sweatshirt and shorts out doing a little power walking in an attempt to keep her figure and her husband."

"I'm sorry," Donovan said.

Chloe Victor looked down into her hands for a moment, and Donovan noticed that she was twirling her sizable diamond ring. Then she saw him watching, brushed aside a fleeting embarrassment, stood, and said, "Well, on with life. You can tell Mr. Caplan and the others that their stores and apartments are safe. The Surf Avenue condominium project died with my husband. Lady Macbeth gives her word."

"They will be very happy," Donovan said.

She smiled. "It was an insane notion to build there. When you discover what my husband had in mind and thought it worth getting killed for, please tell me right away."

"I promise. Hey, was James a do-it-yourself kind of guy?"

"Hah," she said, tossing her head back.

"Never used a screwdriver?"

"He didn't even own one. He kept all sorts of handymen on retainer. Why do you ask?"

"He brought one into the basement with him."

"Not a clue," Chloe replied.

Donovan's phone rang. He listened for a moment, then thanked the caller and hung up. He returned his attention to Mrs. Victor, who had gone back behind the desk and, freed from her earlier restraint by having spoken in depth to the captain, sat in the big chair, trying it out. Donovan asked, "Do you know a man named Nicky Dollar?"

She shook her head and asked, "Who's that?"

"Proprietor of Nicky Dollar's Sideshow and Freak Emporium."

"That would be in Coney Island, I imagine," she said.

"It wouldn't be in Beverly Hills," Donovan replied.

"What sort of crowd do you imagine I mingle with?" she asked.

8. FAREWELL, MAYBE, TO THE UPPER WEST SIDE.

Who is Nicky Dollar?" Donovan asked as he skewered a piece of grilled chicken and a slice of onion and dipped them in tzadziki sauce. The scent of the takeout Greek dinner mingled with the aroma of salt air coming off the Hudson and into the Donovans' living room.

The Donovan family and their pretty young guest sat around the huge coffee table eating. Tidied up and appearing to feel a bit better, Lisa Fine sat cross-legged on an ottoman. Daniel had rolled his wheelchair up next to her and smiled while she cut up his chicken for him. In very short order, the boy had become smitten with the blond guest who would sit on the floor and play with him.

Lisa said, "Nicky Dollar is a jerk in Coney Island who has the hots for me."

"What's he like?" Marcy asked.

"Thirty. Fit. Way too slick. Can be charming, but most people think he's a loudmouth. Hey, the guy is a carnival barker."

"Is he a dog?" Daniel asked.

"Actually, he's kind of cute," Lisa replied.

"But does he *bark?*" Daniel asked.

"Only when the moon is full, son," Donovan replied.

"What, Daddy?"

"Daniel, a barker is someone at the circus who talks and tries to get people to go see a special show," Marcy said.

"Oh. Can we go see the show?"

"Not this one, honey. But we'll take you to the Big Apple Circus the next time it comes to Lincoln Center."

"Okay," the little boy replied.

"There's a neat show with seals at the Coney Island Aquarium," Lisa said. "I have a picture of me feeding fish to one of them." She looked down at her hand with evident distaste.

"Can we go see it?" Daniel asked excitedly.

"Sure," Donovan said. "We'll go one Sunday."

"Why do you ask about Nicky Dollar?" Lisa asked.

"He sent what he thought was an anonymous e-mail

to Chloe Victor, telling her about James and you," Donovan said.

Lisa's face drew tight. She said, "The bastard! I'll kill him!"

"He was after you?" Marcy asked.

"Relentlessly. He was even worse than that schmuck Eddie who I went to high school with."

"This must happen a lot," Marcy said.

"*All* the time. But you kind of get used to it. It's part of being a movie actress. Marcy, you're very beautiful."

"Thanks. My husband thinks so, anyway."

"You must get the same thing."

"Not as much as I used to. I take it as a compliment and move on."

"That's the idea," Lisa said. "Eddie, you know, was obsessed with me. I swear he was spying on me to see where I went and who I was with."

"He was," Donovan said. "But he won't anymore."

"Why?"

"Brian scared the living shit out of him," Donovan said.

Marcy said, "You probably see Brian as this big, goofy guy who works for my husband. But Brian can be very intense."

"When he walks into the zoo, the animals hide in the backs of their cages," Donovan said.

"I know some character actors like that," Lisa said. "Some of the guys who play villains can *look* at you and make you wish you were invisible."

"How is Nicky Dollar different from Eddie?" Donovan asked.

"He's older and established. He has a business. He's a

prominent man who plays a big role in the effort the Chamber of Commerce is making to bring back Coney Island. He acts as emcee at a lot of civic events. You know the type."

"Oh, yeah," Donovan said. "The smart-talking guy who calls women 'sugar.' "

"That's him! So he *e-mailed* Chloe Victor about James and me? Why, to break us up?"

"Almost certainly," Donovan said.

"I mean, he was always asking me out, but I always turned him down. He doesn't take no for an answer."

"He probably thought you would see the light eventually," Marcy said.

"As soon as James was out of the way," Donovan added.

"Oh," Lisa said. Then, after another few seconds' thought, she added, "*Oh!* Do you think he *killed* James?"

"Men have killed men over women before," Donovan said.

"My God."

"I'll talk to him tomorrow. Right after I run out to Forest Hills and buy a new van *for you*," Donovan said, reaching across the table and poking Daniel gently on the arm.

"A red one!" the boy said.

"Yep."

"With a VCR."

"Okay."

"So you can roll your chair right into the back and go driving," Marcy said.

"Yeah!"

To Donovan, Marcy said, "I talked to Mom about the

brownstone. The current tenant's lease is up at the end of the month, and they're moving next week. We can have it then."

Donovan looked down at his plate, idly chasing a slice of carrot around as if it were a hockey puck.

"I know this apartment is where you grew up," Marcy continued.

"It's a priceless bargain," Donovan said quietly. "We're paying eight hundred bucks for three bedrooms and two baths with a formal dining room and a maid's room, with a view of the Hudson. Four thousand a month on the open market."

"Lewis can have it. The apartment will stay in the family."

"Can *I* have it?" Lisa asked—only half in jest, Donovan thought.

"If you didn't kill anyone and Lewis asks you to move in with him," Donovan said.

"Who is Lewis?" she asked.

"Lewis is too long a story to go into now," Donovan said. "But he's cute and has a good job."

"Sounds good to me," she replied, then went back to eating.

Marcy said, "We'll have to make the front entrance and the garden door wheelchair friendly. The elevator should be okay as is. I want Daniel to be able to go out in the garden or onto the sidewalk whenever he wants."

"Yeah!" the little boy said.

"You're moving into your own brownstone with an elevator and a garden?" Lisa asked.

"It would seem to be inevitable," Donovan replied.

Laughing, Lisa said, "You're funny."

"He just doesn't want to leave the Upper West Side," Marcy explained.

"It's been fifty-odd years," Donovan said.

"Most of them *very* odd," Marcy replied. "Honey, you have to face it—the West Side today isn't the West Side you remember. It's no longer the community of intellectuals, artists, and blue-collar guys you used to know. Rents are higher here than almost anywhere else in Manhattan . . . higher than in most of the silk-stocking district. It's been thoroughly yuppified, and you *hate* that."

Donovan grumbled. He arranged two green beans as if they were goalposts and tapped a carrot slice through them.

"Where is the brownstone?" Lisa asked.

"In the Village," Marcy replied.

"Oh, in the *Village*," Lisa said to Donovan. "Can I come and stay with you guys sometime?"

Donovan speared the carrot slice with his fork, waved it at her, and said, "If . . ."

"I know, if I didn't kill anyone."

"Right."

"I would never hurt James, even if he was planning on dumping me and staying with his wife. That's what you're thinking, I know it. If he was thinking of dumping me, it would explain the mood he was in for the past few weeks."

"It might," Donovan replied.

"Maybe she confronted him after getting the e-mail . . ."

"She says she didn't."

"Do you believe her?" Lisa asked.

"I don't get the impression she was lying to me. I

don't get the impression that *you're* lying to me. But this is a very complicated investigation, and I've been wrong before."

"Do I look like a killer?"

"No."

"Neither did Katy Lucca," Marcy added.

"I gotta tell you one thing, though," Donovan said. "So far you're the only one I've met who seems strong enough to do it."

"*Chloe* isn't strong?" Lisa objected.

"She's in shape but doesn't strike me as the violent type. I don't think she likes to get her hands dirty."

"She kills him, she inherits his empire," Lisa said.

"True."

"And you told me she admitted being in the candy store yesterday afternoon, buying Twizzlers. *I* was *home*. Eddie told Brian that."

"Eddie would hit the pope in the face with a pie if he thought it would get him on your good side," Donovan said.

"Why would I kill James? Do you think I only *have*, like *one shot* at marrying a rich guy?"

"Is that what you want?" Marcy asked.

"Yesterday it was. I wanted to marry James. Now I think I'm going back to Studio City and finding myself a nice film editor or cameraman or something—a guy with a steady job and long-term potential."

"Very sensible," Donovan said.

"Ladyhawk has a head on her shoulders," Lisa said, smiling and stretching.

"Who's Ladyhawk?" Donovan asked.

"The girl commando with the hang glider," Marcy added.

"Oh. How do you know that?"

"We've been talking about our careers," Marcy said.

"I think it's so neat that you plan to become a public defender," Lisa said. "You'll be a beautiful rich lady who has a famous cop husband and who, nonetheless, defends the poor. I can go to my agent with this plot, if you like."

Donovan muttered an oath.

Lisa continued, "If you pass the bar exam soon, you can defend *me* against *him*," Lisa said, nodding at Donovan.

"There's no defense against Donovan," Marcy said, rising to begin clearing off the table. "He gets you in too many ways. Lisa, I booked workout time for us tomorrow morning at six. Is that too early for you?"

"Sounds perfect," Lisa replied.

"Play Legos with me, Daddy," Daniel said.

"You got it," the captain replied.

The Ford dealership that handled conversion vans was what Donovan wanted. It turned out not to be in Forest Hills, however, but a few miles away in Glen Oaks, a bedroom community of single-family houses and townhouses up against the Nassau County border. Donovan and Mosko spent a morning hour there, then they reemerged into the early sunlight. The rush-hour stream of cars heading west down Union Turnpike toward Manhattan remained strong.

"I never seen anything like that before in my life," Mosko said.

"What, the van?" Donovan asked.

"No. Paying the whole thing up front by check."

"You'd have been less surprised if I had paid cash?"

"Why didn't you?"

"I didn't want them to think I was a big-time drug dealer," Donovan said. "Besides, it's too hard to get that much cash out of an ATM." He cocked his head in the direction of a small bagel shop three doors down. "Let's get something," he said and led the way.

Once back in Mosko's car and heading for the Cross Island Parkway, Mosko said, "You really wanted to walk out with it, didn't you?"

"I promised Daniel I was going to buy a van. When I come home he'll be expecting to see it. I hope Marcy explains that it will take a few days to prep it and install the cell phone and laptop ports."

"You're getting laptop ports in the front *and* back?" Mosko asked.

"I have a feeling that Daniel's future will have a lot to do with computers."

"So the little guy will be able to take his chair on the lift into the van and roll up to the VCR and the laptop? Pretty cool. I would like something like that for my retirement."

"I thought you would," Donovan said.

"I'm pretty sure I saw a satellite dish store back there," Mosko said.

"Maybe later," Donovan replied.

As the Corvette roared down the ramp onto the southbound Cross Island Parkway, Mosko said, "Yesterday and last night the boys went through every single box in the basement of the candy store."

"What did they find?" Donovan asked.

"A whole lotta stock for a candy store and little else. Did you know that jujubes will last, like, forever?"

"Longer than the teeth of most customers," Donovan replied. "I read this interview with Conrad Dobler, you know, the tough-guy football player from the 1970s?"

"I *know* who he is," Mosko said.

"This is the guy who bragged that he hit Merlin Olsen so hard he knocked him right out of the frame on the TV and you had to run into the kitchen to see the end of the play?"

Mosko remembered it.

"A couple of years ago Dobler said words to the effect that you know you're getting old when you have to switch from jujubes to gummy bears."

"You're not getting old," Mosko said.

"Who said anything about me?" Donovan replied.

"Not so long as you can still invite Hollywood babes to your house and they show up. How did the kung fu session go this morning?"

"Marcy womped the shit out of Lisa . . . a kind of warning, I suspect. As I was shaving I heard Lisa groan all the way down the hall, slam the door, and collapse into bed."

"I guess she has bruises on her ass *today*," Mosko said with a smile.

"I wasn't invited to inspect the damage," Donovan said. "But I'll get on it. You said there was *nothing* in the basement beyond candy store stuff?"

"Some *tchotchkes*," Mosko said. "Family photos. Pictures of the store in 1947. Gas and electric bill receipts. A copy of the bill from the plumber who put in that big pipe you were looking at. Caplan's inner tube, deflated.

I'm thinking of getting it fixed for the old guy. There are joints on Coney Island Avenue where you can still get a flat fixed for seven or eight bucks."

Donovan said that he knew. "I'm on Coney Island Avenue a lot. That's where our accountant is."

"You never told me," Mosko said.

"We never got to the subject of accounting, I guess," Donovan said.

"What's his name?"

"Joe Reisman. Coney Island Avenue and Avenue Y. Right across from the Russian-language bank where Mdivani stashes his ill-gotten gains. Joe has a great sense of humor. Has a stuffed gorilla that does the Macarena if you poke it in the belly. Daniel loves the beast. You ought to go to this guy for your taxes. What else did the boys find in the basement?"

"The stuff you expect," Mosko said. "Roach Motels. Mousetraps. Tin cans. Lost socks."

"Nothing that helps us figure out who killed Victor?"

"*Nada.* But it's all stacked out in the alley under guard, like you wanted. Caplan ain't too thrilled."

"We have news that will make him *very happy*," Donovan said.

"Absolutely."

"Did you get the champagne?"

Mosko nodded. "Two bottles. What if Caplan turns out to be the murderer?"

"He can pay me back out of his prison allowance," Donovan said.

"I think it's nice that you take such a personal interest in the lives of our chief suspects, boss. But keep in mind that every so often one of 'em pays you back by trying to kill you."

"Ah, I'll be okay," Donovan said. "Everything's been going my way lately."

"Oh, yeah? Well, things ain't been going *my* way, so please enlighten me on the topic of who may and may not have killed Victor. What's the latest thinking?"

"Lisa Fine," Donovan said.

"Okay. No alibi unless you count Stanley Kowalski down the block. She's the lead suspect in my book, too."

"True if you ignore the fact that someone with her looks and in her industry will have no trouble getting dates," Donovan replied.

"A girl falls in love with a powerful guy, she can fall hard," Mosko replied.

"Causing bruises, which we know she hates. Okay, next is another blonde—Chloe Victor."

"I thought you liked her," Mosko said.

"I liked her more than I expected to, but she's still a chief suspect. She knew he was cheating on her and admits to having been in the candy store not long after the murder. However, she told me that they got married before he was rich and without a prenup. So if Victor planned to divorce her to marry Miss Direct-to-Video, it would cost him half his empire. To my way of thinking, money is less of a motive for her."

"What about Harry Caplan?"

"A *big* suspect," Donovan replied. "His livelihood was directly threatened by a man who had a relentless and counterintuitive drive to take his land. You ever see *Shane?*"

"Only a thousand times," Mosko said.

"Somebody who threatens to get me off *my* ancestral home . . ."

"What, Eighty-ninth and Riverside?"

". . . is in big trouble." Then the captain sighed and said, "Unless, of course, the perp is my wife and the mother of my son who intends to present me with my very own townhouse in the hip part of town."

Mosko smiled, thought for a moment, and said, "Hey, are you gonna have a *basement?*"

"Unh, yeah," Donovan replied.

"Outstanding! So you'll see what I mean about a man's basement being his castle."

"This basement thing is making me crazy," Donovan said. "What in hell was Victor doing down there?"

"It wasn't going through those boxes," Mosko replied.

"Or the baseball card collection?"

Mosko shook his head as he drove the Corvette onto the on-ramp for the Belt Parkway, heading in the direction of Coney Island. "Nope. We turned over every card. There's nothing useful. And my uncle, who as you know is the authority on all things a guy could sell to turn a buck, swears that Caplan's collection is a nice thing to have but nothing you could sell and retire on."

"I guess there are a lot of guys who collect Dodgers stuff," Donovan said.

"No shit, Sherlock. Anyway, you can see for yourself about the collection. It's still down there. Caplan threatened to throw his body in front of the movers if they touched it."

Grinning, Donovan said, "You can't fault the man for tenacity."

"Is Hennigan still on your suspect list?" Mosko asked.

"You bet. It's nice that Georgi alibis him, but keep in mind that Georgi only saw Hennigan buy coffee and scoot back under the Boardwalk. There's nothing to say that he didn't scoot back out and over to the candy store once Georgi finished his *wodka* and left."

"The two of 'em, Caplan and Hennigan . . ."

"Could have done it together," Donovan said. "I'm with you. Irish-Jewish teams abound in history. Most of them in stand-up comedy, but what the hell. Both those guys were threatened with eviction. Hennigan also has an extra motive—a sick wife who can barely work. They *really* have nowhere else to go, and in a condemnation and buyout the rental tenants get nothing."

"Hennigan could have done the murder while Caplan watched the door," Mosko said. "I'm not so sure that your little test of his arm strength meant much."

Donovan shrugged. "It seemed like a good idea at the time," he said.

"Who else we got?" Mosko asked.

"Lisa. Chloe. Eddie . . . did you check his alibi?"

"Working in the yard by himself. Neighbors can't verify."

"Okay, he's on the list, too. Who else? Caplan. Hennigan. That makes five so far. We can make it six when we add the jerk we're meeting at lunchtime."

"Nicky Dollar," Mosko said.

"He could have wanted Victor out of Lisa's life," Donovan said.

"And we *know* he was aggressive enough to do it— he sent that e-mail to Mrs. V. warning her about the affair."

"That gives us six suspects," Donovan said. "Now add a seventh—John or Jane Doe."

"For what?"

"There's more going on here than we've uncovered. Look at it this way. We have a group of suspects, Lisa, Chloe, Eddie, and Dollar, who had a stake in Victor's love life. We also have a second group of suspects . . ."

"Caplan and Hennigan," Mosko said.

". . . who had a stake in the future of the property," Donovan said. "But there's a third group whose motivation is hidden. Did you ever rent *The Third Man* like I keep telling you?"

"I was going to last week, but there was this copy of *Waterworld* . . ."

"*The Road Warrior* with fish," Donovan said.

". . . that I was unable to pass up." Mosko swerved around a sports utility vehicle that was hogging the center lane. "You keep me too busy to sit and watch a movie."

"I'll bet you ran out and got Lisa's, didn't you?"

Smiling sheepishly, Mosko said, "My wife would kill me."

Donovan continued. "This third group is involved in whatever Victor was doing in the freakin' basement."

Mosko tossed his hands up, steering momentarily with his knees. "Any ideas?"

"One, but it's so bizarre that I'll make a howling asshole out of myself if I'm wrong," Donovan said.

"Why not! Come on, I love it when you do that!"

"Let me spend time in the empty basement and think a bit," Donovan said. "In the meantime, can you get me the FBI report on that guy they shot?"

"What guy? Who? The one near Nathan's? Two weeks ago?"

"Yeah, him."

"Sure. What for?"

"It's the only other violent death in Coney Island in the past month," Donovan replied.

"You think there's a connection?" Mosko asked.

"Two men were murdered in Coney Island in the month of June," Donovan said. "I know a lot about one of 'em. I'd like to know a little about the other."

"Fair enough."

The captain finished his coffee as Mosko drove past Kennedy Airport and along the southern coast of the City of New York. Jamaica Bay and the Atlantic Ocean zipped by on one side and the broad expanse of perfect flat land and rows of single-family houses known as Canarsie on the other.

"Home!" Mosko said, saluting his neighborhood as they drove by it. "The home I never see."

"The inflated paycheck that pays for it," Donovan said.

They drove past Canarsie Pier and Starrett City, the housing development known, to the owner's dismay, more for the mountainous, seagull-swarming landfill on the opposite side of the Belt Parkway than for the beauty of its appointments. They drove past the fishing fleet, moored sailboats, and Mosko's beloved Roll-N-Roaster, the locally legendary fast food emporium of Sheepshead Bay. Finally Mosko took the off-ramp to Ocean Parkway. A few minutes later, he parked in front of Surf Avenue News.

Down the side street a bunch of cops guarded the

displaced contents of Caplan's basement. The boxes over-flowed the alley and spilled out onto the sidewalk, giving the impression of a mammoth yard sale that for some reason was under heavy guard.

Carrying his home video camera, Donovan got out of the car, unkinked his legs, and straightened his jacket. Then he said, "Keep the champagne hidden. Talk to the other store owners on this block and get them to close up for a while and come 'round." The captain looked down at his watch and added, "Have them join me in the basement in an hour. I want Caplan and Hennigan there, too."

"You want a crowd for your announcement, huh?"

"Yeah. And I want to talk to one of 'em in particular."

"Which?"

"The guy with the old plumbing store," Donovan said. "Without letting him know that's what I'm doing."

"You're good at that," Mosko said. "I never saw any-one so good at getting suspects to give up the keys to the crown jewels—and smile as they do it."

"Thanks," Donovan said.

As he headed into the store, he heard a wail of despair and saw Caplan hurrying out from behind the counter, the palm of his right hand held against his temple as if to contain the thoughts.

"Oh, my *God*, do you know what's happened?" the man asked. "Did you look out *back?* I've been dispos-sessed."

"Only temporarily," Donovan replied. "We'll put everything back once we're done."

"The police officers are treating me like a second- . . . no, a third-class citizen!"

"An unfortunate consequence of having your archenemy found murdered in your basement," Donovan replied. "This too shall pass. If you're innocent, of course."

"It's like the Nazis are back!"

Stung, Donovan snapped, "The Nazis would have taken you *and* the baseball cards. Calm down."

Caplan was unmollified but at least appeared to stop hyperventilating. He removed the hand from his temple and began fanning himself with it. "My life is a shambles," he said.

Touching the man on the shoulder, Donovan said, "You still ain't doing bad compared to James Victor."

"I guess I should count my blessings," Caplan said. "Problem is, I can count them on the fingers of one hand."

"I sense storm clouds lifting," Donovan said. "In fact, I have news and am asking you and your fellow store owners on the block to join me in the basement in an hour. I hope that's okay with you."

"Oh, *sure!* Why not just take over my life. Get behind the counter and sell cigarettes."

Caplan's tone had taken an angry turn, ignoring the promise of good news. Reacting to the change, Donovan said, "I *wouldn't*."

"Wouldn't what?"

"Sell cigarettes," Donovan said firmly.

Caplan chewed on that for a bit, then said, "Oh, now you think I'm a monster because I sell cigarettes?"

"Not a monster. But you're the prime suspect in a brutal murder, and while I'm in the basement trying to restore civility to this corner of the galaxy, you're up here peddling cancer. Lower the level of moral indignation a peg or two."

After chewing over *that* comment for another few moments, Caplan said, "Do what you want. I have a business to run." He waved Donovan off and went back behind the counter.

9. THE BIGGEST PARAKEETS YOU'VE EVER SEEN.

Donovan walked to the back of the store and went down into the basement, pausing only a bit to chat with the uniformed officers guarding the alley and basement doors.

With the contents of the basement removed, the squeak made by his foot as it landed on the third step from the bottom was wrenching. He grimaced at the sound. Donovan set up his camera on the baseball card case, adjusted it to wide angle and aimed it at the stairs, and pressed the RECORD button. Then he went up and down the stairs several times, until he found the correct spot to step so as to avoid making the squeak. Satisfied, he left the camera running and set about examining the rest of the basement.

Naked, the space seemed much bigger, truly cavernous. The crime scene lights that Bonaci had set up made the rectangular hole in the seaside earth appear like a Broadway stage. Even the assorted conduits carrying water and electricity across the ceiling stood in sharp relief. Momentarily at least, the decades of dust atop them seemed less dense.

Donovan looked in every corner, even under the baseball card collection again and, using his Maglite, on

133

top of the conduits. He peered in and around the circuit breaker box and at every inch of the boiler and electric and gas meters. He revisited the long-unused freight door and stairs and made an inch-by-inch examination of the walls. When Mosko caught up with him, forty-five minutes had passed and the captain was sitting atop a purloined milk crate staring at the plumbing.

Donovan swung his head around at the creak made when his burly associate stepped on the third step from the bottom. "Hey," Donovan said.

Mosko laughed. He said, "You know that thing you say sometimes when you gotta go take a leak?"

"What do I say?"

"I gotta go inspect the plumbing," Mosko replied.

"Is that what I say?" Donovan asked.

"That's what you say, and guess what? Here you are inspecting the plumbing."

"Yeah," Donovan replied, looking back down at the concrete patch surrounding the six-inch pipe.

"Find anything?"

"No. Is the plumbing store guy coming to my party?"

"Yeah. And I found out that other stuff you wanted."

"Let's hear it," Donovan said, swinging around to face his partner.

"Caplan is a real neighborhood guy," Mosko replied, "just like you suspected. He buys his shirts from the man two blocks down. He goes to the dentist above the liquor store on Neptune. He gets his plumbing fixed by the man down the block. Always has."

"Name?"

"Al Resnick," Mosko said.

"A Jewish plumber. Didn't I tell you there were such things outside the Bronx?"

"He's the one who Hennigan used to work for until the arthritis set in. It was Hennigan who did all of Caplan's plumbing work up until he retired."

"Then who did this?" Donovan asked, hooking a thumb in the direction of the new pipe and the concrete patch around it. "Resnick himself?"

"No," Mosko said. "He gave the job to a kid who worked for him at the time."

"Who?"

"He was a little vague. Harry or something."

"Harry or something," Donovan replied.

"Harry, Hatti, Halli, something. Resnick couldn't recall exactly. He said he was having a senior moment. He promised to look it up before he came down here. What *is it* with you and *plumbing?*"

"The cycle of life," Donovan said idly, standing and wiping some dust off his hands with a piece of paper towel. "Yin and yang. 'Let it out and let it in.' Don't you listen to the Beatles?"

Mosko smiled and shook his head.

"*Daniel* listens to the Beatles," Donovan said. "He's got 'Hello Goodbye' memorized. Even hits the notes, something his dad can't do."

"You're not going to treat us to your singing, are you?"

"Not today. Where's the champagne? I'm in a celebratory mood."

"Why?" Mosko asked.

"Another stretch of New York City is being saved from the wrecker's ball," Donovan replied. "Whoever killed James Victor and for whatever reason, he saved the block. Or she. He or she."

"And prevented Chloe Victor from having to share her husband's estate with Lisa Fine," Mosko added.

"That too."

"You hate straightforward cases, don't you? The more possibilities, the better."

"I like to be challenged," Donovan replied.

A short while later, the captain stood behind a card table that Mosko had set up next to the baseball cards and the outline of Victor's body. An officer had put a row of plastic cups, filled with champagne, next to the two bottles.

Donovan heard voices and the scuffling of feet upstairs, and soon the guests came down. The video camera caught them as they trooped down the stairs, their eyes drawn first of all to the tape outline and then to the card table set up for a celebration. Their expressions grew quizzical, and Caplan, last in line, perhaps still stung by the earlier exchange with the captain, said, "We're celebrating what, the end of the world?"

Ignoring that, Donovan said, "To those I haven't had the privilege of meeting, my name is Bill Donovan. I'm a captain in the NYPD and head of the Division of Special Investigations. They send Detective Moskowitz—who is a Brooklyn boy, in the unlikely event you haven't heard—and me out to look into matters that are a little bit more important and, often enough, a lot more complicated than the run-of-the-mill murder where a jealous wife does her philandering husband."

"He's figured out who killed Victor," Hennigan announced.

"Maybe, Charley," Resnick replied.

"Actually, we haven't," Donovan said. "I'm here to

make an announcement. Yesterday I had a long and en-lightening talk with Chloe Victor . . ." Most of those in attendance groaned. ". . . and I learned a few things. One is that she patronizes neighborhood stores. She was in here yesterday, Harry, buying Twizzlers."

"What?" Caplan replied, astonished.

"She says it was around one-thirty or two. She was wearing a gray sweatshirt and shorts."

Caplan said, "I sell a lot of Twizzlers."

"Blond hair," Donovan continued. "Cut short. She's about forty."

"What flavor Twizzlers?"

"Strawberry," Donovan replied.

"Sorry," the store owner said.

Donovan said, "Harry, in New York City most murders are done by a family member. The victim's wife, who you described as a monster, is offering to place herself forty or fifty feet from the body not long after the time of death and, maybe, get you off the hook."

"You could try harder to remember her," Mosko said.

"It was a busy Sunday," Caplan said. "There could have been four or five people in here at any time. But maybe I sort of recall a blond lady coming in after lunch wearing a gray outfit."

"Maybe she was acting as a decoy so Victor could get into the basement and get whatever he was looking for," Resnick, the plumber, offered.

Donovan smiled and said, "I thought of that, and, if so, she was late and it didn't work. She made no impression on Harry whatsoever. But I like the way you think."

Resnick waved off the compliment and, at the same

time, dug a slip of paper out of his shirt pocket. He said, "Detective . . . Moskowitz, is it?"

"You got it" was the reply.

"You're from Canarsie? You still live there?"

"Nowhere else," Mosko said.

"I've known a couple of Moskowitzes from Canarsie."

"There's ten of us," Mosko said. "When my kids are bar mitzvahed we'll have a minyan and can start our own congregation. Congregation Moskowitz. Too bad my mom's Irish and I'm not even considered a Jew."

"Didn't I tell you we specialize in complicated?" Donovan said.

Resnick nodded while Donovan shuffled his feet impatiently.

"Are you related to Stanley Moskowitz?" Resnick asked.

"That's my uncle," Mosko replied.

"He's one of my suppliers."

Donovan said, "He can supply anything but an end to this line of conversation."

"Later," Mosko said to the plumber, who nodded.

"What's the name of the kid who fixed the plumbing over there?" Donovan asked, hooking his thumb in the appropriate direction.

"A couple of years ago?" Resnick asked.

Reading from the slip of paper he pulled from his pocket, Resnick said, "Haji Nehal. He was a Palestinian kid I hired in the spirit of peace. Well, so much for peace. I tried."

"He was a good plumber," Caplan added.

"Was he?" Donovan asked Resnick.

"Oh, sure. Never had a complaint about him. Always cheerful. I was sorry when he left after only a couple of months."

"Where did he go?" Mosko asked.

"Florida. He said he couldn't stand the cold."

"The kid did a good job on Harry's pipes," Hennigan offered.

"I thought you never came down here," Mosko asked.

"Oh, well, you know. From time to time. Harry saves crossword puzzles for me and doesn't always have time to go get them when I come in. So I let myself in the back door. It's never locked, you know."

"It is *now*," Caplan said.

"And I get the puzzles myself," Hennigan added.

"Oh-*kay*," Donovan replied, as Mosko made a note. "So the Palestinian kid was a good plumber. I'm glad to hear it. Anyway, folks, plumbing is not why I invited you down here. Remember that I said my conversation with Chloe Victor was enlightening?"

"Yes," Caplan said, growing interested.

"She turned out to be a pretty okay lady," Donovan said. "Not one who displays a whole lot of emotion, and I realize that's a class D felony in Brooklyn. Maybe that's where her image problem comes from. But it's not really a crime to grieve privately. To get to the point, she swore to me yesterday her belief that the plan to demolish your block and put up an apartment building is completely insane. As the new president of Victor Coney Island Properties, she is canceling it. Your homes and businesses are safe."

A collective whoop went up from the assembly, then

they hugged one another, then one after another shook Donovan's hand.

"This is *true?*" Caplan asked after a time.

"She said it flat out. She was in the office yesterday partly to put a stop to it."

"What if she was lying to you?" Resnick asked.

"Too bad if she was," Mosko said. "She made a commitment to a high-ranking official of the New York City government. The captain stands in for the mayor at ceremonial occasions from time to time. If she went back on her word, your attorney would have a field day. And the press . . ."

"The plan is dead," Donovan said. "She's gonna build her condos on the lot next to KeySpan Park. Have some champagne."

"I *told* you that the lot over by the ballpark is a better location," Resnick said as he joined the others in reaching for cups. "Didn't I tell you that?"

"You told us, you told us," Caplan replied.

"*L'chaim,*" Donovan said, hoisting an imaginary glass in a toast.

"You aren't drinking, Captain?" a newly solicitous Caplan asked.

"Not today."

"Let me get you something from the store. A seltzer, maybe."

"A Coke, please," Donovan replied.

As Caplan hurried up the stairs, stepping where it didn't squeak, Donovan pulled Resnick over to where he had been inspecting the plumbing. Kneeling beside it, Donovan said, "So the kid did a good job."

"Yeah, pretty good," Resnick replied.

"What didn't he do well?"

"The pipe looks fine," Resnick said. "But the concrete patch is a little amateurish."

"I was wondering if water didn't leak up from the ground because of that," Donovan said.

With difficulty, Resnick crouched down beside the captain and poked a gnarled finger at a crack, wide enough to drop a dime into, that radiated six inches out from the pipe. He said, "You like to be neat, but sometimes you want to make it easy to get the patch out in case something goes wrong. In basements like this that fill up with boxes right away, no one ever notices."

Donovan stood and extended a hand to help the old man up.

"What's the big deal?" Resnick asked.

"I may be moving into a house and want to make sure the basement stays dry," Donovan said.

"Like you said, groundwater could seep up through that crack. The water table is only five or six feet down. You get a good rain . . ."

"Come on," Donovan said. "I want to get my Coke, and you guys probably want to share the good news with your wives."

They went back to join the rest. Donovan checked the video camera to assure himself that it was still recording. Then he got his drink and stood around with the other men, lending his cell phone to anyone who wanted to call a spouse and making what he hoped the others assumed to be small talk.

Nicky Dollar had put on his special jacket for the occasion. It was an eye-catching thing, all rhinestones and spangles arranged into red, white, and blue stars, bars, clouds, and what appeared to be fireworks explosions. When he strode out onto the Boardwalk to greet the two detectives, the jacket caught the afternoon sun and shone as if the entirety of Times Square had been condensed into one formerly drab patch of polyester. Although on that day the man wore it over jeans and a casual shirt, the effect was blinding.

First waving as he walked, then sticking his hand way out in front of him, a kind of friendliness probe, the man announced, "Hi! I'm Nicky Dollar! Come on into Nicky Dollar's Sideshow and Freak Emporium!"

Donovan introduced Mosko and himself. The sergeant said, "You got a permit for that thing?"

"What, my jacket?" Dollar laughed.

"It's hurting my eyeballs, pal. Wanna turn down the volume?"

Those words came from a man who was wearing a T-shirt emblazoned with a photo of a B-52 bomber parked on the tarmac in front of its entire complement of bombs and missiles. The legend read

THE TERRORISTS HAVE WON THE COIN TOSS
AND HAVE ELECTED TO RECEIVE

Undeterred, Dollar stuck his thumbs under the lapels of his jacket and puffed them out to reveal, beneath, an American eagle's nest that contained an egg from which was hatching a fully armed Special Ops warrior sporting a vengeful grin. "I call this jacket 'Uncle Sam.' It's a ten, isn't it?"

"That one goes to eleven," Donovan replied, shielding his eyes. "Take if off, please."

"I never take Uncle Sam off," Dollar replied.

"You're a suspect in a murder investigation," Mosko told him.

"This ain't helping your image," Donovan translated.

"The jacket *is* hot and heavy," Dollar said. He whipped it off. It sounded like someone shaking a sheet of aluminum foil. Donovan noticed that beneath it Dollar wore the conventional attire of a certain type of Brooklyn male—three gold chains, one sporting a tiger's tooth, and a shirt with vertical metallic threads, open to the navel.

"Who am I supposed to have killed?" he asked.

"I think you know," Dollar replied.

"Victor? I read about it in the papers. Is that what you came to talk to me about?"

"Yeah," Donovan said. "Did you think we came to inspect the plumbing?"

A sly smile made its cautious way across Mosko's lips.

"I only met Victor a couple of times," Dollar protested.

"Where?" Mosko asked.

"A couple of openings. The supermarket on Neptune. The Chamber of Commerce Night at the ballpark."

"Did you have any business dealings with the man?" Donovan asked.

"Nope. He was just a guy I seen around. I'm on the circuit, you know what I mean?"

"The local Chamber of Commerce circuit," Donovan replied, nodding. "Ribbon cuttings and photo ops for the local newspaper."

"Yeah, that," Dollar replied.

"And that's how you came to know Lisa Fine," Donovan said.

Dollar brightened tremendously and said, "Yeah, Lisa! Do you know her?"

Smiling, Donovan bobbed his head up and down. He replied, "You bet I do. She's gorgeous, isn't she?"

"Absolutely," the man said, clearly beaming at having it recognized that he had been in the company of such a beautiful creature.

"She's staying at my place now," Donovan said, as another sly smile made an appearance on Mosko's face. "We were up late last night. You think she's beautiful on the Boardwalk, you should see her in candlelight."

Whatever Dollar had expected from the conversation, it wasn't that. Most likely he also failed to anticipate Donovan's taking that moment to step a pace closer, into Dollar's comfort zone. Dollar reddened and shuffled his feet, looking up and down and away from the two men, seemingly unable to speak. Then he abruptly turned away and walked a few steps back toward the safety of his freak show. He held his hands up as if imploring the gods, then put them down on his hips.

Mosko said, "Hey, pal, want me to hold your fancy jacket while you calm the fuck down?"

Dollar swiveled back to them and said, "What the fuck did you do that to me for?"

"The captain wanted to see how easy it was to piss you off," Mosko replied.

"How did I do?" an exasperated Dollar replied.

"About as good as Bush did at Yale," Donovan told him.

"You flunked," Mosko translated, figuring it was

likely that if Dollar opened a newspaper at all he never got past the comics.

"Okay, so I'm in love with that woman," he admitted. "So the fuck what? She's young and single. I'm young and single, and I ain't such a bad-looking guy. She could do a lot worse."

"I suppose," Donovan replied, looking up at the three-story facade of the sideshow. Two immense painted American flags framed the words

GOD BLESS AMERICA

COME SEE NICKY DOLLAR'S

FABULOUS SIDESHOW AND EMPORIUM

"Better me than some Hollywood asshole," Dollar argued.

Donovan replied, "More to the point, is it better you than James Victor?"

Dollar darkened for a moment, as if his brain were percolating silently within his well-coifed head. Then he said, "Yeah, to be honest, yeah. What could he have given her?"

"You mean, beyond half his fifty-million-dollar fortune, which is what *Forbes* says he's worth?" Donovan said.

"The amount of money don't matter. The guy was old. He was *forty*." Donovan silently closed his eyes and then opened them again. Dollar continued, saying, "He had a *wife*."

"They couldn't have kids," Mosko said. "He wanted a son."

"It's good to have sons," Donovan added.

"He could have adopted a kid," Dollar said. "Hey, do you think I *killed him?* Is that what we're dealing with here?"

"You tell me," Donovan said.

"Bullshit I killed him! I had nothing to do with that."

Donovan couldn't tell whether the man was honestly defiant or panicking. "Where were you Sunday between noon and one?" Donovan asked.

Dollar pointed at the door of his establishment. "Where I am every weekend day. Right in there, ringing the cash register. I was surrounded by witnesses."

"Such as who?" Mosko asked.

"Let me show you."

He led the way through the front door, pausing only to flip a switch. Instantly, what had seemed a black cavern became a brilliantly lit series of showcases. Each was like a living room with one wall removed so spectators walking down the central hall could gape past velvet ropes into the lives of Dollar's show people and freaks. None of them, Donovan noticed thankfully, appeared to be on the premises.

"Where is everyone?" Mosko asked.

"For the time being, my people only work on weekends and holidays," Dollar replied. "Once the foot traffic on the Boardwalk gets back up to where it was years ago, and the presence of the Cyclones is expected to do that, I'll open during the week. Meantime, my freaks all have other jobs."

"What's Conrad the Comic Magician do nine to five?" Donovan asked, looking at the sign introducing the first cubicle and its occupant. Among other things, the room held a small stage, a table, two chairs, a top hat hanging on a hook, and a fake window beyond which purported to be postwar Vienna.

"He's maître d' at an Italian restaurant in the city," Dollar said. "He tells jokes and does magic there, too."

"Can he make the roaches disappear?" Mosko asked.

Dollar forced a smile.

"Speaking of freaks and their regular jobs, who painted the picture of Vienna, Hitler?" Donovan asked.

Either not paying attention or not getting the comment, Dollar said, "I got the painting at a poster shop."

"We'll need contact information for people who saw you yesterday," Mosko said.

"You got it. First let me finish the tour."

The second cubicle was proclaimed as home to Captain and Mrs. Shrimp, the World's Smallest Married Couple. The set showed their living room, including a pint-sized sofa, chairs, coffee table, and other items of furniture.

"I haven't seen a nine-inch TV in years," Donovan said.

"They're midgets," Dollar explained, pointing out a photo of the two of them at their wedding. "They're not really married, though," he said. "In fact, they don't get along all that well."

"They could still be married," Mosko said.

Dollar showed the two detectives a cubicle that housed a miniature gym, complete with weight bench and free weights.

"On the left here is Mule, the World's Mightiest Man. He's a body builder. He covers himself in mineral oil and works out with weights and then poses like they do in contests. Audience members get their pictures taken with him. He picks them up and they sit on his arm, you know?"

Mosko gave a scornful look at an eight-by-ten glossy of Mule hung on one wall. "What's this jackass's real name?" he asked.

"Vinnie Carbone," Dollar replied.

Nodding, Mosko said, "Yeah, I thought I seen him around. He's an asshole."

"You got that right, detective," Dollar said. Then he added, "How about you? You want to make a couple of bucks?"

"Sure. I'll come right over Saturday night after *Shabbos*."

"Who is Abdul the Terrorist?" Donovan asked, peering into the room across the way. It contained nothing but a small stage surrounded by spotlights. A huge bullseye was painted on the back wall.

"The audiences go wild over this," Dollar said. "I got a guy and his girlfriend. They're both acupuncturists. He wears a loincloth and a turban. She dresses up in a red, white, and blue bikini and an Uncle Sam hat. They play out this scenario where 'cops' strap him to the bulls-eye and she sticks acupuncture needles into him. Each needle has an American flag flying from it. There are fifty needles—one for each state. The guy screams as she puts each needle in. The crowd goes wild."

For one of very few moments in his life, Donovan was speechless.

Shaking his head, Mosko led the way to the next attraction. "What's this?" he asked.

"On the left here is the Coney Island Pretzel. He's a contortionist. He has something like a thousand joints and can get into and out of anything. On the right is Mamie the Tattooed Lady. Every inch of her is covered with tattoos of birds. On her chest she's got the biggest parakeets you've ever seen." Dollar grinned.

"You stole that from Benny Hill," Donovan said, casting off his astonishment over Abdul the Terrorist.

Dollar said, "Hey, you got me. But you don't got me for killing Victor. Dozens of people saw me here between noon and one."

"We'll need as many names and numbers as you can supply," Donovan said.

"Come to my office."

They followed him down to the end of the corridor, passing five or six more exhibitions, each offering a different exotic treat. Soon they had gone through two more doors and were sitting in a spacious office with a view of KeySpan Park and the vacant lot beyond that soon would become the site of a high-rise apartment building.

The walls of the office were decorated almost entirely with publicity shots of freaks, sideshow performers, and other artists. There were sword swallowers, magicians, lounge singers, acrobats, contortionists, Hell's Angels, comedians, heavy metal bands, midgets, and persons with grotesque malformations of all sorts.

"Kind of reminds you of Sy Gittelson's office, doesn't it?" Donovan said.

"The Times Square show biz publicist?" Mosko replied.

"Yeah."

"I know Sy," Dollar said. "He got me Mamie the Tattooed Lady."

"We're all connected somehow," Donovan said idly,

looking out the window at the vacant lot and imagining the construction soon to engulf it.

"I need your real name," Mosko told Dollar.

"Nicholas Dalario," the man replied. "But three generations of us have gone by the name of Dollar."

"Your dad was in this line of work, too?" Mosko asked.

Dollar nodded. "So was my granddad. Right here in this neighborhood. When my dad took over after World War II, we were down the Boardwalk between the Atlantic Bar and Casino and Moe's Five Star. Then about thirty or forty years ago, when the real estate market was really depressed . . . you know, when all the low-income projects were going up and crime was through the roof . . . he bought two lots down here and moved the operation to this one." Dollar took a sheet of paper from the wall behind his desk, stuck it in the fax machine, and pressed the COPY button. A moment of whirring later, a copy came out. "These are my people's real names, numbers, and addresses," he said. "Here, I'll write in their professional names."

As he used a pencil to do so, Mosko said, "Well, if all these characters saw you here at lunchtime Sunday, you'll have no problem with us."

"With that jacket on, you think that folks don't see me?" He indicated his spangled jacket, which he had hung carefully on a hanger swinging from a nail behind the door. "I had two audience groups go through between noon and one. Hey, how did you guys get my name? From Lisa?"

"From Chloe Victor," Mosko replied.

Donovan remained silent but continued to gaze out the window.

Dollar's expression was a mixture of surprise and suspicion. "I never met her," he said.

"But you *did* send her an e-mail warning her about the affair her husband was having with Lisa Fine," Donovan said abruptly, without turning around.

Dollar hesitated, but only for a second. Then he smiled and said, "Okay, you got me on that, too. But I still didn't kill anybody."

"How'd you know about the affair?" Mosko asked.

"My cousin Eddie."

"Oh, your *cousin Eddie!*" Mosko replied. "Her neighbor who also has the hots for her."

Dollar looked first astonished, then angry. "I'll freakin' kill him. Then you can arrest me for that."

"I'm coming to think that we're gonna have to put Eddie in the Federal Asshole Relocation Program," Mosko said.

"I'll relocate his butt personally with my foot," Dollar said. "I asked him to keep an eye on her, that's all."

At that point, Donovan swung around and said, "Mr. Dollar, you told us that when your dad bought this property and moved the business down the Boardwalk thirty or forty years ago, he also bought a second lot. Is that it over there, the vacant one?"

"Yeah. That one is mine. Got to do something with it someday."

Donovan wasn't sure, but he thought he saw Mosko's jaw drop, fleetingly but perceptibly. The disclosure that Dollar had a huge financial stake in where Victor's luxury housing would be built, revealed on top of his interest in

Lisa Fine, made the sergeant the speechless one that time. Donovan and Mosko exchanged astonished looks. Then Donovan said, "You're a busy man, my friend."

"What?" Dollar asked, looking as surprised as they.

"In my line of work it's pretty common to run into guys who have *one* reason for killing someone. You, my friend, have *two*."

"Welcome to the *Guinness Book of World Criminal Records,*" Mosko told him.

Dollar turned his palms up and made a "gimme" sort of gesture.

"You guys got to help me out here," he said. "I explained to you how I couldn't have killed Victor over Lisa. And I *wouldn't* have killed anyone over a girl. I mean, come *on*, who does that?"

"People," Mosko replied. "Guys with big egos and temper problems."

"Okay, she's beautiful," Dollar said. "But she's not the only beautiful girl the Almighty . . ." Dollar made the sign of the cross over his breast.

". . . ever created. I don't want to sound like I'm bragging . . ."

"So don't," Mosko said.

"But I ain't exactly starving for attention from the opposite sex."

"Especially when you put on that jacket," Donovan said.

Dollar grabbed a silver frame off the top of his desk and showed them a photo of a striking Mediterranean beauty posing on the Boardwalk in an abbreviated bikini.

"Beautiful girl," Donovan said agreeably.

"That's Angie," Dollar said. "She used to be my fi-ancée."

"What happened?" Donovan asked.

"Ah, you know. One thing or another."

Donovan assured the man that he knew.

"So what are you talking about that I have *two* reasons to have killed Victor?" Dollar asked.

"He's saying he doesn't know," Mosko said to the captain.

"Know what?" Dollar asked.

"Have you ever met or talked to Chloe Victor?" Donovan asked.

"No. I seen her at the arts thing one time. That's it."

"Has anyone ever talked to her on your behalf?" Donovan asked.

Dollar shook his head.

"She said she doesn't even know you," Mosko said.

"She's right."

"What did you think of Victor's plan to tear down a block of Surf Avenue and put up luxury apartments?" Donovan asked.

"More power to the man," Dollar said. "It would make my property more valuable. Bring in more custom-ers. The better the economic climate in Coney Island, the better I do."

Donovan and Mosko looked at one another.

"Is the plan still a go?" Dollar asked.

"No," Donovan replied.

"Oh, *shit*," Dollar said, slamming the desk. "You know, I just can't catch a break. Can't get the girl. Can't get a little boost in my business. Can't even hire Harry the Human Hammer."

"Who?" Donovan asked.

"A guy who drives nails into boards with his forehead. The sonofabitch wanted me to pay for his medical insurance. Jeez, I mean, I was born under a bad sign. Like B. B. King said, 'If it wasn't for bad luck, I wouldn't have no luck at all.' "

"It was *Albert* King, but I get your point," Donovan said. "Hey, look, I've got news for you. I said the plan was off. I meant it was off for the Surf Avenue site. Guess where Chloe Victor wants to build?"

"You got me," Dollar replied.

Donovan pointed out the window at the vacant lot on the other side of the ballpark.

A look of shock came over Dollar's face, as if Mamie the Tattooed Lady's parakeets had just attacked the Coney Island Pretzel. It was a moment before he could speak, and then he stammered, "Here . . . on my lot? She's gonna make an offer for my lot? I mean, I was kinda hoping the Cyclones would want it for a parking lot, and so I listed it with a broker last year. Nothing happened. But this morning I got two messages to call the broker. I didn't return them because you guys were coming over."

"Return the calls," Donovan said.

"You really mean this about her wanting my lot?"

"She told me yesterday," Donovan said.

"Holy fucking shit, I'm gonna be rich!"

Donovan smiled.

Dollar high-fived the two of them, then exclaimed, "You guys got to hold on while I call my mom!"

10. ONE OF THOSE OLD-TIME NEW YORK HOMICIDES WHERE A GIRL ICES THE GUY WHO WAS PLANNING ON JILTING HER.

Donovan and Moskowitz sat on a bench beneath the Cyclone and ate takeout Chinese from a tiny shop that sat alongside the incredible clamor—bells, horns, sirens, whistles, layer upon layer of amplified music, incessant fake laughter from wildly colored plaster demons—of Astroland. The afternoon was wearing on, and foot traffic on the Boardwalk was at its highest. Brooklynites old and new ambled along, retired men and women, elderly singles in wheelchairs and on walkers with their nurses, white babies wheeled by their black nannies, young couples wearing little in the way of clothes, and the occasional uniformed officer. The beach was about half full, and all the lifeguard stands were operating. The surf was light, though, and the lifeguards seemed to have little to do beyond watching the girls—or guys, depending on gender and inclination—something they appeared to be good at.

The usual fishing boats from Sheepshead Bay were drifting along while dozens of day-trippers dipped lines into the warm water. In search of summer fluke, most of the time they hooked bergals, irritating little junk fish known for wasting the time and eating the bait of fishermen. Two oil tankers headed east up the channel into Jamaica Bay.

Mosko said, "If Dollar was faking that reaction, he

deserves to be in the movies along with Lisa."

"He's in show biz—third generation," Donovan said. "He's a carnival barker. Think of a used car salesman magnified by ten."

"This is freakin' awesome when you think of it. Dollar could have killed Victor to get the girl or so his land would be chosen as the site of the new luxury apartment building."

"That's assuming, one, he knew Chloe Victor and, two, he knew that she had her own idea where to build," Donovan said.

"Which would make it a conspiracy," Mosko said.

"We need to know if they *ever* talked," Donovan said. "I'm bothered by the e-mail thing. You get a message stating that your spouse is cheating on you and you don't reply? You don't even reply and say, 'Who the hell are you and what's your evidence?' "

Mosko nodded, glancing over at his laptop, which was perking away receiving messages via the cell modem. He said, "I would want to know who sent the message, why, and what's his proof."

"And, maybe, once that was done, to meet someplace to discuss the matter," Donovan said. The captain finished his lunch and dropped the little white container into the brown bag assigned to receive garbage. "Victor was a workaholic who was out of the office a lot," Donovan said. "Chloe could have gotten away easily for secret meetings with Dollar. And God knows there was no restriction on *his* time during the week. The sideshow only opens on the weekends."

"We should get search warrants for their phone and computer records," Mosko said.

"Do it," Donovan said. "*And* for the records of their Internet service provider. And have guys canvas every damn coffee shop between Stillwell Avenue and Kings Highway."

"They both work out," Mosko added. "I'll add gyms to the list."

Donovan nodded. "It's a stretch, but not out of the question that Dollar and Chloe could have gotten together and agreed to get rid of her husband for mutual advantage. She gets the empire. He gets rich and gets the girl. Or at least has a shot at her once Victor is out of the way. Now, Lisa didn't seem too interested in him, but you never really know. Dollar ain't exactly lacking in ego. He could have seen himself as the only alternative for her once Victor was buried."

"Everyone we've talked to but Lisa benefits from Victor's death," Mosko said. "Chloe. Caplan. Resnick and the rest of the store owners. Hennigan. Even freakin' Eddie, who no longer needs to be aggravated by seeing Victor's Porsche in front of Lisa's house."

"Eddie admitted watching Lisa, didn't he?" Donovan asked.

"Sure, but he talks the way these guys always do. You know, she was 'the hot babe who lived down the block.' He bragged that he 'knew her when.' He asked if I checked out her shower scene in that movie. I guess I'll have to rent it now and sneak it past my wife."

"That never works," Donovan advised. "Wives have amazing radar."

"Well, I think we got our suspect list pretty much done," Mosko said, adding to the garbage bag.

"Maybe," Donovan replied.

"Come on, man, there's no maybe about it. It's got to be one of those we just talked about."

"Did you ever see or read *Murder on the Orient Express?*" Donovan asked.

"Didn't you ask me that once before?"

"Did you ever answer me?"

"No, and I ain't gonna now. What's the point?"

"*All* of 'em did it," Donovan replied. "All the damn suspects turned out to have killed the bum, who richly deserved it."

"Are you saying that *all* the people on our suspect list . . . ?"

"*Your* suspect list," Donovan added.

"Don't do that to me. Go with the flow for a change. Are you suggesting that all the people on *our* suspect list would have been in on it together?"

"It could be," Donovan replied. "Everyone benefits."

"Except Lisa," Mosko said.

"Apparently."

Mosko asked what he meant.

"She doesn't *benefit* from Victor's murder, exactly, unless we're talking about one of those old-time New York homicides where a girl ices the guy who was planning on jilting her."

Mosko shook his head and said, "This is true. We checked, and she wouldn't benefit financially from the purchase of this property. I like the conspiracy thing best. With her a bystander. An innocent one."

Donovan yawned and said, "I'd like to go home. I promised Daniel I'd do something with him."

"Like what?"

"Fix something. He likes to play with my tools. I have

an old piece of Erector set we take apart and put back together. He has a good eye for what needs to be done."

Donovan leaned back on the bench and stretched out his feet, pulling them back a moment later when they were in the way of an Indian couple pushing a baby carriage. Behind him the Cyclone wooshed and creaked, taking screaming customers up and then dropping them down at speeds up to seventy miles an hour over a frame that many years old. It appeared ready to collapse at any moment. The two detectives fell silent for a time, watching a pair of F-14s fly wing-to-wing up New York Harbor and over Manhattan. The quiet was broken by a series of beeps from Mosko's laptop.

"What's that?" Donovan asked.

Mosko pulled the thing onto his lap and punched some keys.

"Priority message coming in," he said.

"What is it?"

"The FBI wants to know why you requested a copy of their report on that terrorist they shot to death near Nathan's on June sixth."

"Tell 'em I don't know why I asked," Donovan replied, closing his eyes and thinking about his son.

"Wanna hear the report?" Mosko asked.

"Give me the highlights."

Mosko said, "Okay, here goes. Let's see if I can pronounce this name. Kahlid al-Atash, twenty-eight, a Yemeni suspected of being a conduit for money sent from al-Qaeda, shot to death by FBI agents while attempting to evade capture. The report gives when and where it occurred, June sixth, Surf Avenue, etc. This guy al-Atash had been living in Paterson, New Jersey, and Flatbush here in Brooklyn, up to September tenth, 2001, when he abruptly disappeared and soon after went on the Ten Most Wanted list. It says here, the FBI does *not* know what he was doing in Coney Island. Hey, we got kosher franks. That's what he was doing here—going to Nathan's."

"Makes perfect sense to me," Donovan replied.

"Or else his stage name was Harry the Human Hammer, and he was on his way to a job interview," Mosko added.

"That too is a possibility," Donovan said.

"Al-Atash had *nothing* on him at the time of his death, it says here. No ID. No wallet. Twenty-four bucks in ones, fives, and change, a subway token, and a box cutter." Moskowitz fell silent for a pregnant pause, a rare and ominous occurrence.

Donovan opened his eyes and looked over. "What?" he asked.

"*And* he was carrying a big freakin' screwdriver," Mosko said.

Donovan looked away and out to sea, following the path of a solitary black helicopter as it moved east toward Kennedy Airport. Then he whipped out his cell phone and told Mosko, "I got to call in the screwdriver expert. We need help on this."

Once again the crime scene lights floodlit the basement of Surf Avenue News, obliterating shadows and giving even the dankest corner the look of an operating room. Two things had changed, though. Donovan had thrown a tarp over the baseball card collection and another over the spot where the chalk outline and traces of blood recalled the murder a bit too vividly for young eyes. And he had shut off the dehumidifiers that protected the baseball cards.

The store was closed again, despite the late afternoon hour, but this time Harry Caplan was content to sit and watch as Donovan carried his son down the stairs and helped him into the wheelchair that Mosko had just set up in the middle of the floor. Marcy and Lisa followed. The younger woman put a hand over her mouth to suppress a cry when she saw the tarp on the floor.

"Are you okay?" Donovan asked. She bobbed her head up and down. "You don't have to be here," he said.

"I want to know what he was doing in this place," Lisa said. Then she added, "I'll be fine."

Seeing her, Caplan said, "I remember you. You used to come in after school." Lisa nodded. "Starburst, right? A bottle of water and a package of Starburst."

"That was me."

"You must have known Victor. I'm sorry."

"Thanks."

"What should I do, Daddy?" Daniel asked brightly.

Donovan knelt beside his son's chair and showed him the extralarge screwdriver Marcy had brought from the toolbox Donovan kept in his study. "You know how you and I like to fix things?" Donovan said.

"Yeah!"

"And we use a screwdriver *a lot*."

"A lot!"

"Have we ever used this one?" Donovan asked.

"No, Daddy."

"Why?"

"It's too big."

"That's right. It's too big to fit any screw in our apartment or in Grandma's house."

"You used it to open a paint can," Daniel said.

"That's right. I used it to pry the lid off a paint can that time I had to touch up the wall in the dining room," Donovan said.

"Because I crayoned all over it," Daniel replied.

That got a laugh from the adults, and the boy laughed along.

"I remember. Now, take the screwdriver and help me out. The other day a man who has never used a screwdriver before came down here carrying one just like this. We can't figure out what he planned on doing with it. So I would like you to look around and see what you could do with a big screwdriver like this."

"Okay!"

"I came down here this morning, and I couldn't find one single screw that you could use this screwdriver on. Maybe you can find something to do with it."

"I'll try, Daddy," the boy said, taking the screwdriver from his father.

"Do anything you want with it. Almost anything. Don't stick it in light sockets or electrical outlets, right?"

"Right."

"Okay, go."

Daniel put the screwdriver in his lap and began using the wheelchair to prowl the basement looking, as little boys will do, for something to break. Donovan followed him, and after just a minute the boy had found an electrical conduit pipe running down one wall to an electrical outlet two feet off the floor.

"Here, Daddy," Daniel said, pointing.

"That's right. You could pry that pipe away from the wall. But let's not do that. Let's keep looking."

Donovan continued to follow the boy around, rejecting in turn as pry targets a separation between two boards in the stairs and the slight space between the boiler and the wall. After only a few more minutes, Daniel had brought his wheelchair to a halt at the spot where the big pipe went into the floor.

"There," Daniel announced triumphantly, pointing down at the crack in the concrete that Donovan had examined earlier.

Donovan smiled and knelt beside his son. "You're right. That concrete looks like one of the flagstones in Grandma's patio. Remember when you pried up one of the flagstones and all those funny bugs ran away?"

"They *were* funny!" the boy exclaimed.

"What else does Grandma do with those stones?" Donovan asked.

"Hides the keys," Daniel replied, delighted to have made his dad smile.

"Right," Donovan said. "She made one of those stones so that it was easy to pry up with your fingers, and she hides the house keys under it. I'm going to pry up that piece of concrete and see what's underneath. What do you think I'll find?"

"Treasure," Daniel exclaimed.

"Possibly," Donovan replied.

"Can I do it?"

"Not today. This one I have to do myself."

"You let me do it at Grandma's," Daniel protested.

"What's under rocks at Grandma's can't hurt you," Donovan said. "Let me do it this time. Now, I want you to go over against the back wall with Mommy and Lisa, okay?"

"Okay, Daddy," the boy said, resigned to it.

As he rolled in the direction of the rest of the adults, Marcy called out "William . . . ?"

"Don't worry," he replied.

"William!"

"It will be okay."

Mosko strolled up to join his boss and squatted next to him, saying quietly, "Maybe if I shield the others with my body your family will survive the blast."

"That's very thoughtful of you," Donovan replied. "But I guarantee there is no bomb in there."

"What *is* in there?" Mosko asked.

"I think you have the same idea I do," Donovan replied. "But like me, you're afraid to open your mouth."

"I'm kinda afraid to *think* about it," Mosko said.

Donovan stuck the end of the screwdriver into the crack in the concrete. With a few shoves and some wiggling, he got the distinctive section of concrete to tilt up. Mosko grabbed it and, lifting the chunk slowly up and away, whispered, "Boom."

"You got that right," Donovan said, gesturing to his friend to put the concrete aside.

There, in a hole a foot deep, was a zip-up leather case the width and height of a paperback book, about an inch thick, and protected by several plastic Baggies.

"It's okay, folks," Donovan called out. He added, "Harry, can you get me some tin foil?"

"Right away," Caplan said, hurrying up the stairs.

When several sheets of foil had been laid out on the

floor, Donovan put on vinyl gloves and carefully lifted his discovery out of the hole.

"What is it?" Marcy asked, leading the others in gathering around.

Proud as can be, Daniel rolled up next to his dad and grabbed hold of his sleeve.

"Did you find the key, Daddy?"

"Oh, yeah."

"To what?"

"I'll tell you in a minute, son," Donovan said, pulling the Baggies off the case and laying them on the foil, taking care to avoid smudging fingerprints or other evidence. He laid the case itself on the floor and began to unzip it.

"Lisa, I'm afraid this is going to be bad news," he warned.

"*Really* bad news," Mosko added.

"I'm ready," she said.

"I thought you should see the bullet you just ducked," Donovan added.

"Okay," she replied tersely.

Donovan finished unzipping the case. He opened it gently and pushed the top aside and began to inspect the contents. There were four passports, or what purported to be passports, and a thick wad of hundred-dollar bills.

"Who is *that?*" Marcy asked, bending close and looking at the passport pictures, each a slightly different view of the same young man.

"That's Kahlid al-Atash, the guy who was killed by the FBI two weeks ago near Nathan's," Donovan said. "It's clear now that he was heading here to get these so he could escape from the country. What we have here are fake Algerian, Egyptian, Saudi, and Indonesian passports.

And I would guess about ten thousand dollars in cash."

"Where's the key, Daddy?" Daniel asked.

"This *is* the key, Daniel. This is the key to how some of the bad men who attacked the World Trade Center last year got paid."

"What?" Caplan exclaimed as Lisa closed her eyes again and, slipping down to sit cross-legged on the floor, buried her face in her hands.

"I'll give you the headlines from tomorrow's paper," Donovan said. "Some of what I'm going to say is an educated guess based on some things that Chloe Victor told me and research Brian and I have been doing, but I'll bet my life I'm right. It's not generally known, but James Victor was born in Algeria of Muslim parents and adopted as an infant by an American couple. After college, he went to Algeria to find his birth parents, only to discover that both had been killed by French soldiers during the Algerian War of Independence, around 1960. He spent several years in Algeria, during which time he became radicalized and joined the Islamic fundamentalist cause. Then he came home carrying enough money to set about creating a real estate business."

"He was a mole," Mosko added.

"Exactly, planted here to act as a funding source whenever that became necessary. Three years ago he met up with a young Muslim man, Haji Nehal, a Palestinian by birth who was working at Mr. Resnick's store."

"I hired him in the spirit of peace," Resnick added, in a that's-what-I-get kind of voice.

"He fixed my plumbing," Caplan said.

"Nehal had instructions to put fake passports and money in a safe place for eventual use by al-Atash, who was sent here to help coordinate the attacks of September eleventh," Donovan continued. "Victor gave him the money, which he buried along with fake passports under the concrete patch he created in such a way that it was easily removed using a large screwdriver. The basement of Surf Avenue News was always unlocked during the day, and the owner was chronically so busy that he didn't notice what was going on downstairs. Plus, no one would think that the basement of a Jewish-owned candy store in Coney Island would hold a Muslim terrorist repository. Two weeks ago, on June sixth, al-Atash was on his way to get the fake passports and escape money when he was rudely interrupted by the FBI, whose agents shot him to death, having no idea what the hell he was doing in Coney Island. Harry, the man carried a box cutter, so I'm afraid that you would have been killed had you tried to stop him."

Caplan's fingers played at his throat nervously.

"Now, you would think that the story would end there," Donovan continued. "However, we have James Victor, who has gotten *very* comfortable in his life as a wealthy American, to the extent even of falling in love with a beautiful young actress."

Lisa didn't look up from her hands.

"Victor has been trying to buy this land for some time to make sure that no one stumbled over the cache," Donovan continued. "Plumbing *does* break down more than once, you know. So when al-Atash is killed, Victor freaks out. Now the cache will sit there until someone discovers it, probably a plumber, almost certainly *not* another radical Muslim plumber."

"I have *done* my part for international understanding,"

Resnick said. "A local kid works for me now."

"That discovery would ruin Victor," Donovan said. "It would get him put in jail and possibly send him to death row. It would end everything. We know that since June sixth Victor was in a dark mood. Then he decides to go get the cache himself so he can take it out and burn it, whatever. He borrows a big screwdriver and heads down here only to be murdered at the foot of the stairs."

"By whom?" Marcy asked.

"Brian and I thought we were closing in on the answer to that question . . ."

"Until a couple of minutes ago," Mosko said.

Leaving the pouch on the floor, Donovan stood and said, "So, we accomplished *something* today, though not what we came to Coney Island for. We know how one of the uncaught September eleventh terrorists was planning on getting out of the country. And we know why Victor was so obsessed with buying this land. I'd say that this is an important piece of the World Trade Center puzzle." Breaking into a smile, Donovan added, "Who wants to be on Larry King tonight?"

Shocked, the others looked at one another. "You?" Caplan suggested, after a time.

"Homey don't do that," Donovan replied, shaking his head. "You do it, Harry. Your wife will be *so* proud of you. She'll be married to a famous man. And think of all the handshakes you'll get at the next meeting of the Coney Island Committee for Common Sense."

"Well," Caplan said, drawing out the word, "Larry King *is* a Jewish boy from Brooklyn, so . . ."

"You're the man for the job," Donovan said.

"Pilcrow's gonna *love* this," Mosko said. "This will get him off our backs forever."

"I was thinking of him as a way to keep the five thousand reporters this news will draw away from us while we figure out who killed Victor."

"Who's Pilcrow?" Caplan asked.

"Deputy Inspector Paul Pilcrow is my boss, and he's always complaining that I get the wrong kind of publicity," Donovan said. "Sergeant Moskowitz is right. Pilcrow and his cadre of PR people and yes-men will eat this up. He *loves* to display evidence for reporters. Brian, call Howard and get his evidence team down here again."

"Yo, boss," Mosko replied.

"I'm calling Pilcrow."

Donovan took out his cell phone and walked away as he made the call. "Deputy Inspector Pilcrow, please . . . Captain Donovan . . . Yes, it's important. Actually, it's *very* important. Pull him out of the meeting . . . If he's in with the mayor and commissioner, it's all the more reason for him to talk to me. They will want to be in on this, too."

Marcy came over, guiding Daniel's wheelchair. She put her arm around her husband.

"Bureaucracy," Donovan said in an aside. Then he resumed the call. "Paul . . . Bill Donovan . . . Look, I need you in Coney Island right now, and I need you to bring your PR guys . . . No, I did not punch out a reporter . . . No, I did *not* solve the murder of James Victor, not yet, anyway. This is much bigger, *much* bigger. It involves the World Trade Center investigation . . . a big break, and . . ."

Donovan held the phone away from his ear to avoid the flurry of surprise and dismay that Pilcrow was pouring into the phone. Then Donovan put the instrument back to his lips and said, "Paul, stop yabbering and get your black ass to Brooklyn!" Donovan clicked off the phone and smiled at his wife. "Don't worry, honey," he said. "Brian and I just became unfireable."

"I wouldn't mind having you home full time," Marcy said.

"This is what I do," Donovan said, sweeping his arm around the crime scene.

"You can do it part time as a private person," she replied. "Remember Christmas time, at that party? The commissioner dangled a consultancy deal in front of you."

Donovan nodded, but in a perfunctory sort of way, as if he really hadn't heard a word.

Marcy continued undeterred. "He said, since you and I had so much to do helping Daniel with his issues, maybe you would want to retire as chief of special investigations, keep your gun, badge, and rank, and work as a consultant . . . pick your cases, work when you were needed and wanted to."

"Yeah, 'captain emeritus,' it sounds like a character on *Star Trek*." Donovan knelt beside his son and said, "But *you*, you are the real star!"

"Can I be on TV, Daddy?" Daniel asked.

11. DONOVAN AND MOSKO AUTOGRAPH A PIZZA BOX.

···

As it turned out, the little boy—the wheelchair-bound son of the illustrious detective—*was* on *Larry King Live* along with, and over the many objections of, his father. They joined Pilcrow, the commissioner of the NYPD, the mayor of the City of New York, the deputy director of the FBI in charge of the World Trade Center investigation, and Harry Caplan and Brian Moskowitz in displaying how creative detective work by local law enforcement—with a little help from an adorable, handicapped child—could result in major breaks in hideous international crime.

Despite his objections, expressed in a torrent of pleas, demands, threats, shouts, waved fists, and offers to take the commissioner up on the consultancy deal *right then* so he could stay home with his wife and child, Donovan spent the balance of that week shaking hands, giving interviews, raising money for the families of World Trade Center victims, and appearing on too many TV shows to count. Events had slipped way beyond his control, and he quickly found himself with such celebrity that total strangers began stopping him on the street and in the lobby of his apartment building to shake hands. After a few days of it, Donovan began to understand why celebrities had bodyguards and big fences that surrounded stone houses with strong doors. The toughest part, he felt, was when doctors and assorted other actual or alleged medical practitioners began calling with offers to cure Daniel, to help him walk. At first the Donovans were excited by the appearance of possibilities that previously hadn't occurred to them. Soon, though, purveyors of magnet therapy and almond-pit oil began calling, and Daniel's lineup of *real* doctors hated that turn of events as much as his mom and dad did.

In the interim, the James Victor murder case proceeded with Mosko at the helm, reporting to his boss in more or less constant cell phone conversations—one of them occurring during a live interview with Brian Williams, much to the amusement of the MSNBC news anchor. The now-solicitous FBI confirmed most of the details of Donovan's telling of the Victor saga. It wasn't difficult to trace the buried money back to Victor, and the leather case revealed several fingerprints from Haji Nehal, who immediately replaced al-Atash on the Ten Most Wanted list.

Chloe Victor went into seclusion. The shock of recent revelations had overwhelmed her stoicism. She did, however, stick to her pledge to cancel the purchase of the Surf Avenue property.

Harry Caplan's store was closed for two days while the FBI sent in its own forensics team to duplicate Howard Bonaci's work. Despite the new solicitousness, if they found anything extra, they were disinclined to share it.

Lisa Fine stayed at Donovan's apartment until Friday. The first night following the discovery of the cache she locked herself in Donovan's study, burning up the phone lines to her buddy in California and crying. But the next morning and the two after that she took kung fu with Marcy, and by the end of the week she was beginning to keep up, sort of, with the much more advanced martial artist and had regained her confidence. She had begun to talk eagerly about the start of filming in the fall and was ready to go back to Coney Island, unafraid to be alone. But first there was a stop.

After Mosko picked up Donovan and Lisa and made a stop at the Twin Donuts on Broadway, he continued uptown to 125th Street. Then he hung a right and drove down Harlem's main drag, past the Apollo Theater and former President Clinton's office and across the Triboro Bridge to Queens. Soon they all stood inside the Ford conversion van dealer while Donovan took proud possession of a bright red wheelchair-accessible van. While the captain did the paperwork, Mosko had his laptop set to receive reports via the cell modem, and Lisa was bringing work in the repair bays and on the showroom floor to a screeching halt. Her beauty had returned, shining out from one of the several new outfits she had bought on Broadway. She kept signing autographs and posing for pictures with the men who worked at the dealership and their friends up and down the block. They stood around three deep waiting for the opportunity to make small talk with her and, thoroughly misunderstanding the circumstances of her arrival, casting jealous glances at Mosko and his Corvette.

An hour later, Donovan and Mosko said good-bye to her outside the office of the Coney Island Council on the Arts. It was a wonderful June Friday, with a cloudless sky and temperatures predicted to top out in the upper seventies. Donovan had pulled the van to the curb behind the Corvette and joined Mosko and Lisa for his farewell bear hug.

"*Thank you* for everything," she said, after giving him an extra squeeze.

"I'm glad to help," he replied. "How are your bruises?"

"Healing," she said. "They'll be gone before shooting starts, and, hell, if they aren't there's always makeup. You don't see Angelina Jolie's tattoos in her films."

"You're not going back to L.A. right away, are you?" Donovan asked.

"Actually, I am . . . at least for a while. I have to be queen of the Mermaid Parade and ride on a float. It's being held on Sunday this year. But I'm leaving that evening."

"Is that like being in the Rose Bowl Parade?" Donovan asked.

"Not exactly," Mosko replied with a sly smile.

"Have you ever been to the Mermaid Parade?" she asked.

"No," Donovan said.

"It's more Mardi Gras than Rose Bowl," Mosko explained.

Lisa said, "There are a lot of amateur floats and half-naked men and women. I'll be a mermaid, of course, wearing a tail. I'm going upstairs now to see what kind of outfit I can throw together."

"Marcy and Daniel want to see the parade," Donovan said.

"Then you'll be there! I can get you on the float. You're a celebrity now. Both Daniel *and* you."

"We'll pass, thanks," Donovan said.

"Maybe Marcy would want to strap on a tail and ride with me," Lisa said.

Donovan shook his head. "My impression is that mermaid fantasies aren't African American experiences."

"How about you?" she asked Mosko.

"I don't look so good in a tail," he replied.

"I don't mean *that*," she laughed. "I mean, you could ride on the float with me."

"Yeah, well, we'll see about that."

"Have it your way," she said. "But William, be sure to bring Daniel to the parade, though. It's really colorful, there's a lot of music, and afterwards everyone goes to the beach."

"Okay," Donovan said.

"I guess I'll have to wear dark panty hose under my tail to cover up the damage your wife did to my butt," Lisa said, laughing.

Donovan told her he was sure she would look marvelous in her tail.

"Here's what I insist on, though," she continued. "You'll be in the reviewing stand along with the borough president and . . ."

"Not more politicians! I did my part the past two days."

"The reviewing stand is wheelchair accessible," she said.

"Okay," Donovan replied. "We'll show up and see what happens. What time on Sunday evening is your flight out?"

"Ten-forty-one," she replied.

Donovan smiled warmly, leaned forward, and gave her a kiss on the cheek. "Daniel likes you," he said.

"And he's a beautiful little boy. Kiss him for me when

you get home with his wonderful new toy." She patted the side of the van.

"I will," Donovan replied, then watched as she waved good-bye to Mosko and disappeared into the building.

"Classy babe," Mosko said.

"Yeah," Donovan replied.

"Nice ass, too."

"I didn't notice. Did you arrange for the surveillance?"

"Yeah, you got it. Undercover surveillance, twenty-four/seven until she steps onto the plane back to la-la-land. What I don't know is why."

"Simple," Donovan replied. "Other than the killer, she was the last one to have contact with Victor. You forget that there's still at least one terrorist out there—Nehal, the guy who buried the money and fake passports in Harry's basement."

Mosko clapped his boss on the back and said, "Which brings me to my analysis of who killed Victor."

"Let's hear it," Donovan replied, turning and strolling down the block with Mosko at his side.

"Forget . . . just freakin' flat-out forget about all the suspects we've listed to date," Mosko said.

"I've already forgotten most of their names," Donovan replied.

"Well, what can I say? You're getting to the age where that happens."

Donovan gave him the finger while continuing to stroll in the direction of a tiny pizza parlor that stood in the middle of the block.

"Here's how I see it," Mosko went on. "All of our Coney Island suspects have alibis or wouldn't profit from

Victor's death in any way that we can unearth. This I can tell you with absolute certainty following a search of heaven *and* earth. Lisa made the calls she said she made and no more. Chloe Victor collaborated with nobody and had secret meetings at coffee shops with nobody else. Caplan and Hennigan are local schlubs. Nicky Dollar is, well, Nicky Dollar, but he ain't no murderer. As for Eddie, we're still struggling to get information on him. When a guy cashes his paychecks at the *cambiamos cheques* place and pays his bills using money orders, it's kind of hard to trace what he does. So that leaves us with the freakin' Arabs or whatever the hell they are. Nehal buried the cache in Harry's basement a couple of years ago, and at some point either he or Victor gave instructions to al-Atash as to where it was and how to dig it up: Bring a big goddam screwdriver and pry up the chunk of concrete sitting on top of it. Then September eleventh goes down and the heat goes up. The feds are rounding up every single guy who has a mustache and knows how to spell 'Mecca.' Earlier this month al-Atash gets iced by the feds as he walks down Surf Avenue, screwdriver in hand. And Nehal is sitting in some fleabag motel down the road from the flight training school in Florida thinking, 'I gotta get outta here!' Because he knows there's ten grand in cash, traceable to him, in the basement of Harry's store. And he knows that *Victor* knows and might be expected to go after the stash himself, you know, to hide his involvement."

"Which Victor did," Donovan added.

"Yeah," Mosko said, proud that his boss appeared to be agreeing with him. "So look, Nehal takes the Greyhound to New York, or maybe he was here all the time and now is living in a boardinghouse on Northern Boulevard or Atlantic Avenue with the rest of the Arabs . . ." This time Mosko pronounced it "*A*-rabs." ". . . and he goes for the cash and runs into Victor. Or better yet, *they arrange to go together.*"

"Nice thought," Donovan said. "I like that."

"The reason being to cover one another, so each one knows the other doesn't have an advantage, whatever. And they have to do it on a Sunday."

Donovan smiled and nodded.

"Why, you ask?" Mosko said.

"Did I ask?"

"I'm telling you anyway," Mosko continued. "Because they *gotta* do it on a Sunday. During the week, Harry isn't that busy and might notice what was going on in the basement. Saturday is *Shabbos*. Harry is closed. Nighttime? Well, maybe, but there are a lot of police patrols cruising Surf because of the new ballpark being so close to the projects and the subway, and cops notice *everything* that goes on at night. You know, the old odds thing."

"There are, like, a hundred times fewer civilians than during the day but the same number of cops, so the odds of running into a cop are much higher," Donovan said.

"You're pretty sharp, you know that?" Mosko said. "Anyway, that leaves two Sundays since al-Atash was killed, last Sunday and the one before. Let's suppose that the Sunday before there wasn't enough time, they didn't get the chance to talk, the bus got a flat in South Carolina and was late getting into New York, whatever. So Nehal and Victor decide to go for it last Sunday, when there are a gazillion people on the beach and the street, customers four deep at the counter, and Godzilla could sneak into that basement without being noticed. Victor goes first, screwdriver in hand. Nehal goes second, grabs the first heavy item he sees . . ."

"As fate would have it, a bronze replica of Ebbets Field," Donovan said.

". . . and beats Victor's brains in with it," Mosko said proudly.

"Then why didn't Nehal take the money and run?" Donovan asked.

"I haven't worked that part out yet," Mosko replied. "Maybe he freaked out and ran. Maybe he tried and couldn't get the screwdriver out from under the corpse. Maybe he heard a noise?"

"Like what?" Donovan asked.

"Like a squeak from that step on the stairs," Mosko said.

Shaking his head, Donovan said, "No good. I went over the videotape. The stair doesn't squeak every time."

"Oh," Mosko replied, a bit thrown off. "Hey, I don't know yet why Nehal . . . if it was him at all . . . didn't finish the job. Give me time to work out the details, okay?"

"I think you're onto something with the Nehal angle," Donovan said, giving Mosko a playful punch on the arm.

"Victor was murdered because he was a mole," Mosko said, "not over real estate and *not* because of his love life."

Donovan stopped in front of the pizza parlor and looked around. He walked to the gutter and looked in it, then peered down at the sidewalk, then went to the middle of the street and looked back at where he had left a puzzled Mosko. Donovan went back to his friend and said, "This is where I saw the hot dog cart on Sunday."

"What, you're hungry *again?* We just had breakfast."

"I'm thinking," Donovan replied, staring down at the sidewalk once more.

"What are you *looking for?*" Mosko asked.

Donovan headed toward the pizza parlor. Before he could reach the door, the owner came bounding out, his sauce-stained white apron flapping, his hand outstretched. "You guys are the cops!" he exclaimed.

"Guilty as charged," Donovan replied.

"You were on TV the other night. What you did was great! Now we know how the bastards got money to live on."

"I guess so," Donovan said.

"I want to shake your hands. Do you mind? I don't got pizza sauce on my hand."

"Glad to meet you," Donovan replied, doing as he was asked.

"I'm Andy, and this is my shop."

"Bill Donovan."

"And you're the other guy," the pizza man said to Mosko.

"That's me," Mosko replied. "And that's what I'm having put on my tombstone—'He was the other guy.' How ya doin', pal?" Mosko grabbed the fellow's hand.

"You gotta be from Brooklyn," Andy said.

"Nowhere else."

"If you ask me, whoever killed that guy Victor should get a freakin' medal."

"That's why we're looking for him," Donovan said brightly. "I got something I want to give him real bad."

"What are you guys doing here? You guys want a slice? The problem is the oven is just getting hot and it will take me a while."

Donovan shook his head, saying, "We just had breakfast. What I want to ask you about—I was here on Sunday with my family, and there was a hot dog cart right out by the curb here." Donovan pointed at the spot.

"Yeah, I talked to the guy," Andy said.

"I ask because he might, you know, be taking business away from you, and I was sure you noticed him."

"I got all worked up the first time I saw him," Andy said. "But then I figured out he was only selling hot dogs, gyros, and pretzels, and I don't sell those. Sodas, okay, he was selling sodas. But there was plenty of business that day, and he seemed like an okay guy."

"Describe him," the captain said.

"I don't know, man . . . forty-something, kind of on the heavy side, and got a ratty-looking beard."

"Did he have an accent?" Donovan asked.

"Yeah, he was foreign," Andy said.

"Any idea where from?" Mosko asked.

"What do I know? I sell pizza. Everyone is foreign these days. I can tell you this, he wasn't from, you know, the regular places like Ireland and England and France. Germany? Nah. No way he was a *paisan*, so Italy is out. Greek? I only know the Greeks at the diner on Flatbush Avenue."

"The Floridian. I know 'em, too," Mosko said.

Andy continued, saying, "He wasn't Russian. I know because I got a lot of them come in here. Not Chinese or Korean or any of those things. I never met any Serbians or anything like that."

"There's been a lot of people on TV in the past year who come from. Afghanistan," Donovan said.

The pizza man's eyes widened, and he said, "You know, that could be. He sounded like those guys on TV. Is he one of the terrorists?"

"I don't know," Donovan replied.

"Jeez, he seemed okay to talk to."

"Hitler loved children and dogs," Donovan replied.

"He was kind of funny. On his cart he had this sign that was pretty funny once he explained it to me."

It was the turn of Donovan's eyes to widen.

"It said something about Buddha and . . ."

Donovan used both hands to draw an imaginary sign in the air. Then he added, "Said Buddha to the hot dog vendor, 'Make me one with everything.'"

"Mojadidi," Mosko exclaimed.

"The one and only," Donovan replied.

The captain took a small photo from his jacket pocket and showed it to the store owner. "Is this the guy?" Donovan asked.

"Yeah, that's him! You know him?"

"I had a run-in with the man a few years ago," Donovan said.

"The last time I saw him he was going home to fight the Taliban," Donovan replied.

"He could have worked a little harder and a lot faster," Mosko said.

Donovan added, "I lost track of the man and could only imagine him off in the mountains with his rifle gunning down fanatics."

"Maybe his job wasn't done until lunchtime Sunday," Mosko said.

Smiling, Donovan rapped his friend on the chest one more time and said, "You d'*man.*"

"We gotta find this guy," Mosko said.

"What time did he take off on Sunday?" Donovan asked the store owner.

"That was the funny thing," Andy replied. "Here on one of the biggest Sundays of the year he suddenly shuts down, hooks his cart to his car, and takes off like a shot."

"What time?" Donovan asked again.

"I was still warming up the oven, so it was before noon. I would say eleven-thirty, maybe quarter to twelve."

"Did anything lead up to it?" Donovan asked.

The man shook his head. "I was getting ready to open, so I don't know. Maybe he got a call on his cell phone or something."

"He had a cell phone?" Mosko said.

"He seemed to be on it a lot," Andy replied.

"Let's check that," Donovan said. "Mojadidi had a cell phone the last time I saw him. There was a lot of cell phone use going on around all those inaccessible mountains in Afghanistan, which astonishes me because I lose the signal when I go to Chinatown for lunch."

"I'll check the cell phone records," Mosko replied. "But you know, the license bureau has no record of a licensed hot dog vendor on this block, which matches what you said before. A block from Nathan's, hey."

"The lines were plenty long at Nathan's," Donovan said. "Besides, Didi wasn't here to sell hot dogs anymore than he was parked on Fifth Avenue a couple of years back. He was keeping an eye on someone."

"And being parked a little down the block from Lisa's office . . ." Mosko said.

"Would be one way to watch her. She takes off. He follows her."

"But he needed someone watching Victor and/or Lisa's house. He would have needed at least one accomplice. But who?"

The pizza man seemed a little uncomfortable being in on that information, as if such knowledge might make him a target as well. So he began edging toward his door and finally said, "You guys . . . I got to open, and . . ."

Donovan placed a comradely hand on the man's arm and said, "We shouldn't have gone shooting our mouths off in front of you like that. I can trust you, right?"

"Yeah, *yeah!* I love my country, y'know."

"So do we, friend," Mosko said.

"Any time you want to stop in, I would be honored."

"I think I'll bring the wife and kids around for a pie sometime," Mosko said.

"On *me*," Andy insisted. "Hey, wait a second . . ." He ducked into the store, emerging a moment later with a pizza box and a felt pen. "Sign this for me, would ya?"

Donovan and Mosko obligingly signed the cover of the pizza box, inscribing their names on either side of the drawing of the pie crust lofted by the fat, smiling chef with the pencil mustache. In time, the pizza box cover would be framed by small American flags and put in a place of honor on the wall of the pizzeria near the Boardwalk. There it would remain basically forever, or for years anyway, until it grew stained with olive oil, turned yellow, and fell into a tub of sauce, after which it would be tucked away on a shelf.

Walking back to where they parked, Donovan said, "Any accomplice would have to know when Victor made his move toward the candy store. And that leaves us with . . ."

"Blondie upstairs," Mosko replied, hooking a thumb in the direction of the Coney Island Council on the Arts.

"Five minutes ago you thought she was the most beautiful and wonderful creature God ever graced the planet with," Donovan said. "Now she's 'Blondie up-stairs?' "

"Fortunes change rapidly amidst the fog of war," Mosko replied, using an expression Donovan had uttered years before and forgotten.

"We also have to think of Eddie," Donovan said.

"That's right. He could have dropped a dime on Victor, no problem."

"We need to know everything about him, including telephone records."

"I'll take care of it," Mosko replied.

"We need records of every call made by every one of 'em over the past few weeks," Donovan said. "Fortunately, in the current patriotic climate all you have to do is say the words 'World Trade Center' to a judge and you got a court order, no questions asked. Did you know? Put Scott Jamison, Blondie's L.A. pal, on the list . . . everyone with a possible reason to kill Victor. I want to know every time they dialed the phone."

"Can do," Mosko replied.

"I guess it's possible that Victor's name was on a list of sympathetic men of Muslim descent that turned up when the CIA searched an al-Qaeda base."

"And Mojadidi got it," Mosko said.

"And decided to return to the Big Apple to take him out."

"Who just happened to be threatening to shoot you, explaining your fondness for the bum."

"That *did* warm the cockles of my heart a degree or two," Donovan conceded.

"And you forgave him for pegging a shot at you a few days earlier, in the garage where he stored his goddam hot dog cart."

Donovan smiled and said, "This time, when we locate the garage he's using *now, you* can be the one to go in after him."

"Thanks."

Donovan looked at his watch and said, "It could have happened like this. Didi is here, keeping an eye on Lisa Fine. His spy is watching her house. Her house and office are the two places you're most likely to find her, right?"

Mosko nodded. "She's a celebrity and can't just hang at the bowling alley," he said.

"Didi gets the call that Victor has arrived in Coney Island and is at her house . . . on the way to pick up the stash. If al-Qaeda kept records of moles, they probably also kept records of stashes. Or, at least, they knew there was one around here someplace. So around eleven-thirty, eleven-forty-five give or take, he gets a call and quickly packs up the cart and drives . . . to where?"

"He puts it on a side street someplace," Mosko said.

"He finds a parking spot in Coney Island close to noon on a summer Sunday?" Donovan asked. "He finds *two* . . . one for the car and another for the cart?"

"Oh," Mosko replied.

"He drives it a bit farther away . . . a dozen or so

blocks up into Brooklyn . . . and leaves the cart in an industrial area. Then he drives back to Coney Island to Lisa's house. He watches Victor get into his Porsche. Follows him to Surf Avenue. Sneaks behind him into the store and follows him into the basement. Didi is good at stealth."

"And beats his head in," Mosko added.

"Yeah," Donovan replied, but without enthusiasm.

"What's the matter?" Mosko asked.

"A professional soldier comes all the way from Afghanistan to kill someone and doesn't bring a weapon?"

"Customs has been a *bit* more careful lately."

"There are gun shops in Brooklyn and Long Island," Donovan replied. "He would have arrived at the store armed. He wouldn't need to pick up a sculpture of Ebbets Field to kill someone with."

"Yeah, well, I don't know, he could have," Mosko said.

The sergeant opened the passenger's door of his Corvette and used a whisk broom to clear out doughnut crumbs.

"When am I gonna be able to get you to clean up after yourself?' " he asked.

"When am I gonna be able to get you to ask how Didi knew about Lisa?" Donovan replied.

Mosko straightened up, tossed the whisk broom onto the floor of his car, and shut the door. "How did he know?"

"There are only four people that I can think of who could have told him—Chloe Victor, Lisa, Nicky Dollar, and my old buddy from Pamiristan."

"Mdivani," Mosko said, exhaling a gush of air and relaxing his chest muscles in a sigh.

Donovan nodded, adding, "The border of Pamiristan is forty or fifty miles from Mojadidi's mountain in Afghanistan. Forty or fifty *miles!* That's closer than it is to my mother's house."

"Where the keys are under the rock," Mosko added.

"Okay, so there's no Long Island Expressway . . . probably a blessing. There have been weekends when I could have made better time on a donkey. And you know something else? Were you there when Mdivani said, 'Whatever happened to that Bamayani?' "

Mosko couldn't recall.

"Nowhere in the papers a couple of years ago was it mentioned *where* in Afghanistan Didi came from. And I sure didn't say."

"But Mdivani knew."

"That's right," Donovan said. "And I also find it interesting that, out of nowhere basically, Mdivani asked if I had any idea what happened to him."

"Afghanistan *has* been in the news this past year," Mosko said.

"Nonetheless . . ."

"Mdivani was trying to find out if you were onto the return of Yama Mojadidi to America," Mosko said.

"He also wanted to know if I was involved in the World Trade Center investigation," Donovan said.

"He was pumping you for facts," Mosko said. "Running into you that day may have been accidental, but he figured you were in town and would have come 'round to see him anyway."

"I am *really* pissed," Donovan said. "The only thing

that gets me madder than being lied to is being underestimated."

"How do you want to proceed?"

"You go back and talk to Mr. Personality at the sideshow. Find out if he knows more than he's been telling us. Impress on the sonofabitch that all we have to do is tell the feds that he is a suspect in their investigation and he is fucking disappeared! No second warning. No call to an attorney. No Alan Dershowitz to bail his rhinestone-studded ass out of jail."

"That could get his attention," Mosko agreed.

"If he knows anything about Mojadidi, he better admit it," Donovan said.

"Where are *you* off to?" Mosko asked.

"All of a sudden I got Georgia on my mind."

12. "ARE YOU TIRED OF BEING FUCKED OVER BY THE TIRED, THE POOR, THE HUDDLED MASSES?"

Even at noon on a Friday, the Gemini was full of smoke and static. So many cigars and cigarettes went up in flames on the average night that a permanent pall of smoke hung midway between dance floor and ceiling. The spotlights had to cut through it on their way to the stage, lending to the smoke layer an unearthly glow that reminded Donovan of an early morning fog over a graveyard.

Three paste-white women in skintight minidresses—red, white, and blue, of course, those being the colors of even obscure corners of New York City those days—ran through their act. Accompanied by a keyboard player and a drum machine, they sang "Stop! In the Name of Love" in Russian, which Donovan felt was extremely weird. As they sang, their poorly crafted early sixties haircuts flounced in the smoky air.

Mdivani sat at his usual table, drinking one of his cups of coffee and watching them. A woman, Russian by the look of her, sat nearby pulling at a small bottle of Georgian mineral water, the sort with sediment in the bottom, and doodling in a school composition book. She may have been in her early twenties but looked like a teenager, an impression augmented by a vast expanse of midriff broken only by a gold navel ring.

Donovan strode up and planted himself in front of the table. Mdivani began to spring to his feet, holding both arms out in front of him for his welcome-old-friend bear hug. But Donovan stopped him by raising his own hands—his shield in one and two business cards in the other. One card was from the deputy director of the FBI, and the other bore the name of Jack Dooley, assistant director of the New York regional office of the Immigration and Naturalization Service.

"My old friend, what is this?" Mdivani asked.

Donovan wasn't sure whether the man was genuinely bewildered or had been taking acting lessons. "Sit down!" Donovan commanded.

Mdivani sat down. The girl beside him looked up, her eyes gleaming with suspense and perhaps fear. She seemed shocked to hear someone treat a powerful man like her boss . . . or whatever he was to her . . . in such a way.

"Green card," Donovan said, putting away his shield

and tapping a fingertip on the table next to the steaming cup of liquored-up espresso.

"What?" Mdivani replied. The Georgian had become unmistakably rattled.

"I said, 'Let's see your green card. Your immigration papers. I want them on the table and I want them now!"

"I . . . I . . ."

Donovan heard footfalls and turned slightly to catch a glimpse of the shaved-headed muscleman who had come up behind, to a distance of ten feet. In a move practiced over thirty-plus years and honed to a fine art, Donovan swept his revolver out of his shoulder holster and wheeled on the man.

The girl screamed. The man jumped back. The band stopped playing, and the Russian Supremes flounced off the stage, squealing in terror.

"You want something with me, kid?" Donovan snarled. " 'Cause if you don't, you can go back to cleaning the toilets."

The goon and his boss exchanged glances. After a bare second or two, Mdivani waved the man away.

Donovan put the gun back and returned his attention to Mdivani. "I asked to see your papers," the captain repeated.

"I do not . . . have them with me . . . they are in my office . . . in my apartment, I mean."

Donovan slapped the business cards down on the table and forced Mdivani to look at them. Then the captain took out his cell phone and dialed a number. Then he said, "Jack? Bill Donovan here . . . Yeah, the same . . . Wife and child are fine. Same with yours? . . . Good, good . . . No, I'm not part of the formal investigation. It fell into my lap . . ."

Mdivani tried to get up again and made gestures to interrupt the captain. Donovan used an accusing figure to motion him back into his seat, then continued speaking into the phone. "You want a part of this? . . . Great. Look, I got a guy here who's a suspect in the World Trade Center investigation, and . . ."

"No!" Mdivani shrieked, jumping up so suddenly his knees hit the table. Everything on it crashed to the floor. "No! Please! I'm sorry! I should have told you! I apologize!"

Donovan glared at the man for a moment, then said quietly into the phone, "False alarm. I'll talk to you later."

Donovan closed the cell phone and returned it to its belt holder.

Mdivani sat down, breathing so hard and fast he was in danger of hyperventilating.

"Get outta here," Donovan said to the girl, who scrambled off, nearly tripping over her fallen bottle of mineral water.

Donovan looked around on all sides to make sure the room was clear. There were two waiters hovering near the front door, staring at the scene. Donovan snarled, "Go across the street to the Zodiac and have a *wodka*. On him!" He nodded at the hapless Mdivani and then watched in silence until the waiters were gone.

Then he turned back to the club owner, who held his hands out imploringly, saying, "I was afraid he would kill me."

"Mojadidi," Donovan replied.

"Yes. He is a tough and dangerous man."

"And what am *I?*" Donovan grumbled.

"You . . . I guess I do not know you as well as I thought. To me you are a gentleman who let Mojadidi go even after he shot at you. Where I came from, it is unimaginable that you did not kill him."

"I didn't kill him because I didn't have to," Donovan said. "That may have changed."

"The man is a mujahideen," Mdivani said. "He killed dozens of Taliban and al-Qaeda."

"Which is what I had in mind when I let Jack Dooley deport him years before," Donovan said. "It turned out to be necessary to kill Taliban. He only should have done more of it. Now, when did you talk to him and what did he say? Exactly."

"Won't you sit down and have a drink with me?" Mdivani said.

"No, and the Uncle Ivan act has worn out. Just stick to business."

"Mojadidi came to me here, right here, twenty-four hours after the FBI shot that terrorist to death on Surf Avenue."

"Continue," Donovan said.

"We knew each other years ago, when he was leader of a mujahideen group fighting the Russians. As a Georgian I had no argument with that, you understand."

Donovan said that he understood.

"I was . . . at that time, I was merely the manager of a Soviet tractor factory in Pamiristan, which as you know borders Afghanistan on the north. But given my feelings for the swinelike Russians, I was to some extent acting as an independent entrepreneur."

"You sold them guns," Donovan translated.

Mdivani shook his head. "That is not so," he replied. "But I did help with their armored vehicles. You see, many tractor parts can be adapted for other purposes."

"What happened two weeks ago?" Donovan asked.

"He walked in, with a very determined look on his face, and shocked me almost to death, you can imagine. I had no idea if he was dead or alive. Anything was possible, given the events of the past year in Afghanistan and here. Mojadidi told me the following story. He is, as you know, what the American press has come to call a tribal warlord, part of the Northern Alliance against the Taliban. His group was one of those that took Kunduz. After the fighting was over, Mojadidi was going through an al-Qaeda command bunker when he discovered records alluding to the terrorist operations in America and the men running them. Two names stuck out: al-Atash and James Victor. So Mojadidi decided to go to America to hunt them down."

"Why not just give the names to the CIA?" Donovan asked.

"Years ago, as a young man, al-Atash had gone to Afghanistan to volunteer in the fight against the Russians. He wound up fighting with Mojadidi's group . . . or rather, he was assigned to look after Mojadidi's daughter while the big man was off in battle. Well, al-Atash deserted his post—ran off to begin terrorist training. In consequence of that, the girl strayed from safety and was killed."

Donovan nodded gravely. "I can imagine the rest," he said.

"Of *course* you can," Mdivani replied, clearly grateful to have given Donovan useful information that satisfied him. "Mojadidi is determined to avenge the death of his daughter by killing everyone associated with al-Atash. When he heard that al-Atash was in Coney Island, where Victor operated, Mojadidi flew straight here to finish the job—by killing Victor."

Donovan's muscles relaxed, and he let out a sigh. Seeing it, Mdivani smiled. He said, "See, I am helpful to you as always."

"Don't get too friendly," Donovan snapped, scooping up the business cards and returning them to his pocket.

"Mojadidi knew that I was here and would be able to help him as well," Mdivani continued. "Now, he did not *tell* me that he was here to kill Victor, but I knew. And I thought, the man . . . Victor . . . is a terrorist. If I am part of eliminating him this will be a good thing. I am saving the FBI bullets, I thought."

Donovan made a grunting sort of sound.

"So I told him how to get to Victor without knocking on his door. By watching the girl, Lisa Fine."

"He had to have someone working with him," Donovan said.

"That is something I do not know. Whatever arrangements he made, they were his own."

"Where is he staying?" Donovan asked.

"Another unknown."

"You didn't ask him?"

"Mojadidi said, 'I will find a place.' "

"Do you have any idea how he got into the country?" Donovan asked. "Do you know when he arrived and on what airline?"

Mdivani shook his head. "I only know that he said he

flew in from Karachi. And the date, of course. June seventh."

"What name was he using?"

Mdivani shook his head.

"What passport?"

Mdivani turned his hands up. "You have it all," he said. "I have given you everything."

Donovan straightened his jacket, then looked around. Then he reached down and got the bottle of water and put it back on the table. A large pool of sugar, vodka, and coffee was beginning to congeal on the dance floor.

"Sorry about the mess," Donovan said.

"You have embarrassed me in front of my people," Mdivani replied.

"You'll get over it," Donovan said. "You can tell them that I'm one of those brutal American policemen that they've been warned about."

The captain turned and walked out of the club and into the afternoon air under the elevated railroad tracks in Brighton Beach. When he got into the van, he dialed the same number he called before, got the answering machine again, and said, "Hi, honey, it's me. Ignore the previous message. I was pulling someone's chain. Hey, I'm here on Brighton Beach Avenue and could bring home some fruit if you want. Oh, I picked up the van, and it's sensational. I'm going to stop at Toys 'Я' Us on the way home and buy a toy van like it for Daniel. He'll love that."

Then Donovan drove a block or two down and double-parked long enough to fill up two bags with fruit, vegetables, and bagels.

. . .

The afternoon was winding down as Donovan parked the van midway down an ordinary industrial block on the outskirts of Bensonhurst. The block was full of square warehouses and light manufacturing buildings marked by signs indicating that therein were makers of awnings, metal shelving, coat hangers, TV tables, restaurant supplies, and bowling shoes. One largish boxy structure of the sort with windows browned out by decades of exhaust and grime was identified as Sal's South Brooklyn Commercial Parking. Mosko was parked in front of it, doing what he called "Brooklyn undercover." That meant double-parking the 'Vette with both doors open and the radio blasting while he beat out the rhythm on the dashboard with one hand and talked on his cell phone.

Donovan parked the van right behind him. He took off his jacket, removed his shoulder holster, put his revolver in his pants pocket, and opened the top several buttons of his shirt and turned up the collar. Then he got out of the van and hurried up to slip into the passenger's side of the 'Vette. He switched off the radio in the midst of a raging rock song.

"Hey," Mosko objected.

"I want to be able to talk," Donovan said.

"That's my music."

"What *was* that, heavy metal?"

"That's Drowning Pool, my new band. Hard rock, heavy metal. The lifeblood of the U-nited States, boss. Too bad you didn't go slam dancing at CBGB with me years ago."

"I cry myself to sleep every night over that," Donovan replied.

Mosko noticed the Captain's new look. With a sly

smile, he said, "So what's this, you trying to look like a *cujine?*"

Donovan shifted his weight uncomfortably.

"You got to take the undershirt off before unbuttoning the two top buttons of the shirt," Mosko continued. "Or else you look like a dork. Face it, you couldn't look Brooklyn if you got an olive oil injection. You is what you is, Cap—an Irish cop. *Cujines* don't wear khakis."

"I'm half English," Donovan protested.

"Maybe that explains your vocabulary and your taste in food," Mosko replied.

"What happened with Nicky Dollar?" Donovan snarled.

"My opinion? The guy is a dumb butt, but all-American. He would soil his polyester if anyone came up and announced they were from Afghanistan."

"Then he had nothing else to add?"

"Not a thing. He's in love with that girl, boss. Can't stop thinking about her. Now, if his alibis check out, we can forget about him."

"Look into his background all the same," Donovan said. "See if there are any criminal associations. I think it's really hard for someone in the freak show business . . . you know, sleazy entertainment . . . to live out his life squeaky clean."

"I'll check with the OCTF," Mosko replied, referring to the Organized Crime Task Force.

"Just for the hell of it, run backgrounds on his employees," Donovan said.

"All the freaks were accounted for at the time of the murder," Mosko said.

Donovan grunted.

Mosko made notes while Donovan filled him in on the encounter with Mdivani. Then, as they sat in front of the garage for half an hour, Mosko made calls to get the search apparatus of the NYPD and related agencies in high gear. Everyone was to be on alert for Yama Mojadidi. In an attempt to prevent him from escaping, all airports, train stations, bus terminals, and car rental agencies were to be notified and put under observation. The man's assorted residences from the old case would be watched.

When Mosko was through giving orders, he put away his phone and said, "We'll get him. *Somebody* will get him, us or the FBI or whoever."

"Uhm hmm," Donovan replied.

"Hey, come on. Let's show a little optimism here."

"The man is a master at blending in," Donovan said. "He got into the country without anyone knowing. He'll get out of it."

"Not without what I'm gonna show you," Mosko replied.

After a quick look around to make sure no one was watching, Mosko led the way into the garage. He turned a key in a lock, and the sliding door rose under electric power, revealing a dark cavern that smelled of mold, oil, and cold fat.

"You've checked this place out, right?" Donovan said. "I ask 'cause the last time I went into a garage looking for Mojadidi I got shot at and wound up with my face pressed against the floor along with the fossilized bubble gum and dead flies."

"We're cool. I walked over to the owner's and got a key and was in there before."

"Tell me about the owner," Donovan said.

199

"He's an ex-GI named Sal who has a Rambo poster on his office wall, so what can I say?" Mosko replied.

"He doesn't sound like a risk," Donovan said.

"He runs the place by himself but isn't here a lot. The deal is you pay your monthly rent and get a key to the front door. You come and go when you want."

"Sal trusts them to behave?" Donovan asked. "He trusts them to close up after themselves and all?"

"Well, the door closes and locks by itself, and you have to open it again with a key to get out."

"A clear violation of the fire code."

"Nah," Mosko replied. "There's a side door with a crash bar on it. But to get a vehicle out, you need a key."

"There are mostly cars in here?" Donovan asked, squinting to see.

Mosko shook his head. "Mostly pushcarts of different kinds—hot dog, ice cream, pretzel, falafel, you name it. There are also some big refrigerators to store your stuff in overnight. Sal serves most of the street vendors you see in downtown Brooklyn, Coney Island, Brighton Beach, and along the Belt Parkway near Gravesend where all the kite flying goes on every weekend."

"And the customers don't steal from one another?" Donovan asked.

"If Sal catches them, he throws them out," Mosko replied.

"How's he catch them if he's not here?" Donovan asked.

Mosko placed a hand on his boss's shoulder and said, smiling, "He's got a security camera running."

Donovan exclaimed, "God *bless* guys named Sal with Rambo posters on their walls! Did it pick up anything?"

"You bet. Come on, I'll show you."

Mosko led the way into the blackness, pausing just long enough to hit a switch on the wall alongside the door. "Time delay," he explained. "Shuts itself off after fifteen minutes."

The overhead lights revealed a veritable fleet of food service carts—not one of them exactly licensed by the Council on Fat-Free Dining—and the accumulated grime of decades. Donovan got the feeling that it would be a long time before he bought another hot dog from a sidewalk vendor.

Mosko led Donovan down the broad central aisle until he pointed out one cart in particular.

"Oh, yeah," Donovan said. "It's déjà vu all over again."

The tall aluminum pushcart was exactly as the captain recalled it—colorful due to the red, blue, and yellow signs advertising pretzels, hot dogs, hot sausages, sodas, and ice cream snacks of several kinds. There was also an ALLAH IS GREAT bumper sticker and the exact sign that first caught Donovan's eyes a handful of years back on a wintry Christmas-season morning outside FAO Schwarz.

SAID BUDDHA TO THE HOT DOG VENDOR "MAKE ME ONE WITH EVERYTHING"

"We found the cart an hour or two ago and have had it under constant surveillance," Mosko said. "When you and I drive off, there will be other guys front and back waiting for Mojadidi to return."

"Good."

"And he *will* return. Look at this."

Slipping on vinyl gloves and crouching low, Mosko reached under the back of the cart—just below the compartment holding ice cream sandwiches and Moon Pies, down a bit from the hand-lettered sign reading HALAL—and tugged on something. Donovan heard the sound of Velcro coming apart. Then the sergeant stood and showed the captain a plastic case the size of a videotape cassette box.

"We pulled good, clean prints off this and e-mailed them to the database. Mojadidi's name came right up. And there's more yet." Mosko opened the case and displayed the contents proudly. Inside were two fake passports, both showing the same recent photo of the Afghan but identifying him, under different names, as a businessman from Pamiristan.

"Pamiristan," Donovan sighed.

"Yeah, I thought you'd get a kick out of that. Also, we tracked down the flight info. Mojadidi took a flight on a Tupelov . . ."

"Speaking of courage," Donovan added, referring to the Russian-made jetliners with the increasingly famous tendency to experience midair meltdowns.

". . . from Pamiristan to Moscow and caught a connecting flight to JFK. Not counting a borscht break in Moscow, he was in the air ten hours, landing in the desolate outer reaches of the reprehensible borough of Queens . . ."

Smiling, Donovan added, "Adjacent to Canarsie."

". . . at seven-fourteen in the morning on June seventh," Mosko concluded. "He hauled ass to get here."

"The day after al-Atash was gunned down."

"The address he gave immigration at the airport was . . . get this . . . remember the falling-down dive next to the Sunnyside railroad yards?"

"With the Mount Kilimanjaro of old tires right beside?" Donovan said. "You gotta be kidding me. That's the same address he gave us years ago."

"And he was gone by the time we got there," Mosko added.

"I don't believe Mojadidi had the balls to use the same phony address twice," Donovan said.

"The neighborhood has come up a little since he left. Maybe he's not as smart as you think."

"No, he's pretty sharp. Got to be to stay alive as long as he has. Think of it—survived the Russians, the Taliban, the war, and random tribal violence, not to mention tangling with you and me."

"Is tough the same thing as smart?" Mosko asked.

"No, but tough and lucky can be a hard combo to beat," Donovan said. "What's that photo under the passports?"

Mosko pulled out a snapshot of a pretty young woman standing in front of the Great Buddhas of Bamiyan. These monumental rock sculptures, carved a millennium ago into the side of an Afghan mountain, had been destroyed by the Taliban a few months before war broke out.

"Remember her?" Donovan asked. "That's Mojadidi's daughter, the one who was killed in the fighting with the Russians."

Mosko remembered.

"This isn't the original photo, it's a copy," Donovan said. "Still, he left it here. Why?"

"He's traveling light at the moment," Mosko offered.

"And he doesn't want to have his real name get out if he's caught."

"Oh, really? Yama Mojadidi gets picked up by a cop in New York City and nobody can figure out who the fuck he is? The bum could identify himself as Huckleberry Finn and the Afghan name still would pop up on any cop computer. It's not like we never heard of the guy. His prints are on file. *I* would know he was here in less time than it takes to say 'Kabulshit.' In fact . . ."

"You were wondering the other day," Mosko interjected.

"His name flashed across my frontal lobes the second I saw that hot dog cart disappear when it did," Donovan replied. "A hot dog cart is a *great* cover. Nobody pays the slightest attention to the owner."

Mosko scrutinized the photo, the fake IDs, and the cart with Donovan's bullet hole in it. "He knows that if he kills James Victor, who funds terrorists, you will get involved in the case. He also knows that you *let him go* once before."

"Exactly what I was thinking, bro'. Mojadidi *wants* us to know that he did it, so he signed his name to the crime. He used his old hot dog cart as cover. He used a fake address that we have been to before. And just to drive the point home, *and* to remind me of the tragic loss that prompted me to let him go the first time, he leaves a copy of the photo of Mehle, his beloved daughter, killed in the fighting with the Russians."

"But he didn't leave the original," Mosko said.

"No. A copy. The original he keeps next to his heart."

"Do you feel a little manipulated?" Mosko asked.

"A *little?*" Donovan replied.

"Wait till you see the security tape."

A few minutes later they sat inside what passed for an office in the back of the garage. A metal folding chair was pushed partly under a mustard-colored table that had no doubt been pulled, Donovan thought, from someone's curbside garbage not long after it was made in the 1970s. The mustard color, the hue of kitchen appliances produced during the disco decade, had been burned in spots by errant irons and torn here and there as the mold of the ages caused the veneer to lift up. Atop the table sat an assortment of papers plus a phone, an answering machine, a VCR, and a monitor. The latter equipment was connected to wires that were stuck to the plaster wall with duct tape, running up past the vintage Rambo poster to disappear into a mouse-sized hole near the ceiling.

The two detectives stood watching the monitor as it displayed a black-and-white video of the cycle of life in the parking garage. Donovan had his hands jammed into his pants pockets and wore an expression that hovered between dejection, disappointment, and rage.

"Here we go, here we go," Mosko said, tapping him on the arm to snap him out of his reverie.

"What?" the captain said.

"Watch. Here."

Mosko tapped the screen as it showed a burly man of fifty or so with a mustache push his cart into its parking space and fiddle around with it. "The time code on the tape says this happened at two-oh-seven on Sunday afternoon."

"After the murders," Donovan said.

"Yeah, which fits with the parking ticket he got. Did I tell you about that?" Donovan shook his head. "Remember how Son of Sam got caught?" Mosko asked.

"A guy from Yonkers gets a parking ticket near where a Son of Sam murder goes down in deep South Brooklyn—which is, like, *forever* away from home—late at night."

"A rental car taken out using a name on one of the phony passports we found hidden below the cart got a ticket at ten to one Sunday afternoon while parked in a bus stop on Surf Avenue in front of this stand where you can get your picture taken sitting in a gigantic easy chair. This is a block from the candy store."

"At the time of the murder, or a little after," Donovan added. His dejection was fading, replaced by rising anger.

Speaking with that air of finality reserved for royalty and justices of the Supreme Court, Mosko said, "Mojadidi came to Coney Island to kill Victor. He went after Victor at his most vulnerable moment—when he was moving around incognito so as to meet up with his girlfriend. Mojadidi followed Victor down to that basement and killed him. Now, Mojadidi would prefer not to be caught at all, but if he is he would like to be caught by you. Why? You let him go once before. He's sure you will do it again, especially since there's a war on and he just eliminated a terrorist. He probably thinks of himself as a hero. End of story. Curtain comes down. Play taps. Say goodnight, Gracie."

"Goodnight, Gracie," Donovan said dully, gazing up at the look of iron vengeance in Rambo's eyes.

"Yo," Mosko said, rapping a knuckle on the monitor.

Donovan looked down to see Mojadidi finish with his cart, walk up to the camera, and give it a salute.

Feeling, once again, a deep despair in the pit of his

stomach, Donovan turned and walked out of the office, to the far wall, and out the back door. There he stood, hands on hips, breathing the fresh air and feeling much as he did the day the World Trade Center came down—old, tired, worn out, fucked over.

When Mosko joined him, the sergeant said, "You okay?"

Shaking his head, Donovan said, "I did something for civil rights in this country. I fought against an unjust war. I became a cop to do some good and be a good example for all the cops who don't do so good. I tried real hard not to be one of those old-line Irish cops . . . yeah, like my father . . . who had no concern for suspects' rights and were expert at beating confessions out of 'em on the way to the station house. I *really* didn't want to be one of those guys. So I try to be nice and to understand people's problems. I allow them their idiosyncrasies. I don't judge."

"You get screwed," Mosko added.

Donovan nodded, continuing, "You're right about me. I like people, and I like colorful people in particular. So I always 'adopt' one."

The captain made quotation marks in the air, but using his middle fingers.

"Who has it been so far?" he went on. "Andrea Jones . . . this was before you joined the squad. She tried to kill me. Michael Avignon, let's not forget *him*, he sheltered a killer. Katy Lucca, who was pretty entertaining, I have to admit, before she set me up to be shot at. Mdivani lied to me. And Mojadidi . . . he was doing some good things elsewhere in the world, so I let him get away with stuff that would have caused my dad to beat the crap out of

207

him en route to the precinct house on 126th and then send him up the river for twenty years."

"Do you see an analogy for America here?" Mosko asked.

Donovan said, "I suppose so."

"Are you tired of being fucked over by the tired, the poor, the huddled masses we extend helping hands to?" Mosko asked.

"I don't agree with everything you just said," Donovan snapped, whirling on his friend and stabbing a finger at his inflated chest.

"Do you agree with enough of it to go get this bastard?"

"Let's go get him," Donovan said.

13. ONLY THE DREAD KNOW BROOKLYN.

The hand-lettered FLATS FIXED sign that Donovan recalled as adorning the fake-stone facade of the run-down building adjacent to the Long Island Rail Road yards in Sunnyside was gone, replaced by a modern placard reading COMING SOON—LUXURY TOWNHOUSES. The mountain of tires that once stood next to the building was gone, replaced by a fenced-off construction site, the gate to which held a similar sign. The building itself, which a few years ago was posted with eviction notices but still occupied by a few desperate souls, was solidly boarded up, with expensive plywood no doubt installed by the local developer, hoping to cash in on the surge in Manhattan rents. That spike, at least the size of the mountain of tires Donovan recalled, had driven up the demand for apartments of any kind in the outer boroughs. Sunnyside, with its wonderful Manhattan views and one-subway-stop proximity, was only the latest neighborhood to go into full-tilt upgrade mode. The captain had found himself amused several months earlier by a newspaper notice of the existence in adjacent Long Island City, not so long ago a redoubt of mafia car-stripping shops, of an arts movement.

Now Donovan was sitting in a takeout Chinese restaurant, called the Wing Lee Jade Palace, that had little to recommend it beyond clean line-of-sight to the Sunnyside address Mojadidi had used. It was evening edging toward night on another spectacular June weekend. Donovan and Marcy had spent much of Saturday taking Daniel for rides in his new red van, beaming as parents do as their beloved little boy cackled with glee at the arrival of a great big toy.

He quickly learned to use the wheelchair lift, and with great glee he got his chair into its place, switched on the VCR, started a Barney tape, and, like a billionaire in the back of his stretch, ordered his mom and dad to drive him to McDonald's. Exhausted at the end of the afternoon, Daniel accepted the inevitability of his father going to work that night. But he had the promise of the whole family going back to Coney Island the next day to go into brand-new KeySpan Park and sit in the reviewing stand with his nanny and mom while the Mermaid Parade marched by. Daniel's excitement was partly fueled by the knowledge that "Aunt Lisa" would be queen, proudly displaying herself in mermaid costume.

Sitting in the Wing Lee Jade Palace, dressed down in jeans and his old suede jacket, Donovan watched with amusement the surveillance set up around Mojadidi's purported address. One corner was occupied by a beat-up old car that gave the impression of having been a casualty of the stunt driving in *The Dukes of Hazzard*. A second vehicle, a "Con Edison" van, was parked in midstreet alongside a manhole cover. Though Donovan couldn't see them, he knew that two of his men were on the Long Island Rail Road tracks posing as inspectors. Clearly, it had been a long time since so much official attention was paid to that block.

It was just seven, and the sun was beginning to set behind the spires of midtown just across the East River. Customers were coming in and out of the restaurant at the rate of one every ten or twelve minutes. The smells from the kitchen vaulted the battered Formica service desk, as did the babble of Mandarin and the clatter of kitchen utensils. The most basic cost analysis, Donovan was sure, would prove it impossible for the amount of business to support the ten to fifteen employees who appeared to be working at the place unless they were all either family, paid in free room and board, or immigrant slave labor, illegals whose tiny wages went largely to the smugglers who brought them to these fair shores. The latter was how things often worked in New York City's East Asian restaurants. Donovan couldn't be sure which it was at the Wing Lee Jade Palace; possibly both.

Mosko pulled up in front in his Corvette and swung the door open, smoothly reaching for his wallet as he climbed out. He was to casual eyes another guy whose woman had dispatched him to pick up dinner.

"You're good at that," Donovan said as his friend plunked himself down at the table and grabbed the copy of the *Daily News* that, Donovan found, was an inevitable feature of the landscape at takeout Chinese restaurants.

"You taught me," Mosko replied. "It's the little things that help a cop on surveillance become invisible—reaching for the wallet, checking out a parking spot, stopping dead in your tracks to stare at some babe's ass."

Donovan thanked him for the compliment, then asked, "Is everything in place?"

"Yeah. All the guys are where they should be. If Mojadidi so much as shows up in the neighborhood, we'll be all over him."

"This is good," Donovan replied.

"One thing we got to watch out for, though."

"What's that?"

"When we put out a bulletin on Mojadidi, the FBI chimed in by sticking him on their Ten Most Wanted list," Mosko said. "Which means you can forget about his preferring to be caught by you if he gets caught at all. Now he's desperate to get out of the country and can't be relied on to say, 'Oh, hi, Bill, I guess you got me,' if you corner him."

"Wonderful," Donovan said.

"Another thing. Remember you asked me to check and see if he had a cell phone?" Donovan remembered. "Well, he does, and guess who he made a lot of calls to in the week before the murder?"

"Eddie," Donovan replied.

"You got it," Mosko said.

"Have somebody pick him up. The charge is conspiracy to commit murder."

"Some other news came in," Mosko said. "Nicky Dollar's employees all back up his story. He was there the whole time the murder went down, either on the Board-walk braying like a jackass to get people into his freak show or else giving them guided tours inside."

"I'm not surprised," Donovan replied.

"They also alibi one another. The Coney Island Pret-zel couldn't even go around the bend without someone taking notice. And their backgrounds are okay. They're working freaks, nothing more. Moreover, Dollar's phone records show nothing illuminating. Neither do the com-puter records of the Victors or Lisa Fine. And we had guys visiting all the coffee shops that Chloe Victor might have stopped in for a secret meeting with Victor. They found nothing. What are you doing? Eating or what?"

"Nope. I'm saving the calories for tomorrow. I want to have a dog and a beer at the ballpark. I figure this is an essential lesson for a son on what it means to be an American."

"Gotcha," Mosko replied. "So look, there are two places I think Mojadidi might show his face. One is around here along this strip of stores, and the other is over at the entrance to the subway. I vote for the subway."

"Why?"

"The trains are running every seven minutes this time of day. He could take off and be in Manhattan as quick as that."

Mosko slammed his palm on the table, spilling Don-ovan's tea and earning himself a stern look from the young Chinese woman with the blue-streaked black hair behind the counter.

"Don't worry about it," he called over to her, and she went back to stuffing packets of soy sauce into a white paper bag.

Then Mosko turned back to Donovan and said, "From over by the subway he could also cut across the railroad yards. There's a hole in the chain link fence."

"And get run over by the express to Fire Island," Donovan said.

"And lose any vehicular pursuit. Of course, our guys on the tracks would nab him."

"If *they* haven't been run over," Donovan said.

"Which surveillance site do you want to drop in on?" Mosko asked.

"Neither. I'm staying around here."

"Have it your way. I'm going over to the Con Ed truck, but I'm going on foot. The car is a little conspicuous for me to be putting around the 'hood in it."

"Whatever," Donovan said.

Mosko opened his left fist, at which time Donovan noticed that he had been clutching his car keys in it. He had been holding them tight enough to leave an impression in his palm. Stiffening while forcing the words out into the soy-scented evening air, Mosko said, "Take my keys, and if you gotta move my car . . ."

"Why should I have to move your car?" Donovan asked.

"I'm in the bus stop," Mosko explained.

"The bus can go around."

"It's a narrow street, and you know how I feel about scratches. If you gotta move it, move it. But don't drive it."

Sopping up some spilled tea with a napkin, Donovan said, "Move it but don't drive it. Okay. Got that."

"You drive a stick, right?"

"*Yes*, I drive a *stick*. I learned to drive on a Model A Ford tractor out at my aunt's place."

"Running into chipmunks don't leave scratches," Mosko replied.

"Gimme the keys," Donovan growled, snatching them.

"I mean it, man. My car is a sacred object to me."

"Get to work," Donovan replied, pointing to the door.

When Mosko had gone, Donovan finished what remained of his tea and tossed the container into the trash. Then he looked over at the young woman behind the counter and said, "He can't help himself. He was born that way."

"Very nice," she said, flashing a gigantic, uncomprehending smile.

Donovan went out onto the sidewalk. The long shadows of the setting sun had been replaced by the damp, gray dark, a city night sliced by the rumbling of the subway and the neon glare from signs in the windows of the small stores on the block. Ancient neon signs, fly-specked in the dust and grease of too many years without a cleaning, hung from wires seemingly too flimsy for the task. Neon, Donovan mused, had become quaint, like Granny's quilt, a reminder of decades past when tubes glowed in radios and in windows and that glow was thought wonderful by some and cold by many more. In a city awash in mercury vapor lamps and towering LCD screens, a neon Budweiser sign glowing in a deli window seemed old and warm as burnished brass.

Donovan scrutinized the block, which held the Chinese restaurant and a bodega, dry cleaner, cobbler, pizzeria, check-cashing store . . . CAMBIAMOS CHEQUES flashed in yellow neon . . . and a takeout chicken place. That part of Queens was built before the arrival of the grid that staked out the rest of the borough, and the block upon which Donovan stood was at an off-angle to the thoroughfare where the surveillance was. The block had the look of a sad old penny that someone had tried to polish but in the end dropped into the gutter.

Most of the stores were of no interest to him. The chicken place stood out, however. Most of the signs in the window were mundane—a takeout menu taped to the glass, a neon 7-Up sign, and two shirt cardboards on which were hand-lettered the names of specials. But it was another notice that caught the Captain's attention. A third shirt cardboard bore a single word—HALAL.

The sign was an alert to the observation of the Muslim dietary laws; Donovan called halal "Arab kosher." It bore a resemblance to the sign taped to the side of Mojadidi's cart, as if lettered in Magic Marker by the same hand.

Customers walked in and out, going to and from yellow cabs double-parked along the block. Donovan reflected upon the stereotype that held that New York City cabbies in the early twenty-first century were largely Middle Eastern. Indeed, on that evening several of the cabs bore distinctive silver bumper stickers reading ALLAH IS GREAT in English and Arabic.

Three newspaper vending machines were chained to a bus stop sign down the block a bit. Two of the machines offered free copies of throwaway publications, the *Village Voice* and a brochure offering free courses for would-be writers. The latter yellow machines were everywhere in

New York City, prompting Donovan to wonder why so many people would aspire to a profession destined to keep them broke permanently. The third machine sold copies of the *Daily News*.

As a cabbie approached en route to the restaurant, Donovan fed a single quarter into the two-quarter machine and tugged at the door, which refused to open and did so loudly enough to attract the man's attention. The captain slammed the side of the box with his hand.

"Piece of shit," Donovan swore at the box.

"You put money in it?" the cabbie asked, betraying an accent devolving from somewhere in the Fertile Crescent.

"Yeah," Donovan replied.

"You put in two quarters?" the man asked.

"I put in two quarters," Donovan replied.

"Put again."

"What am I, made of money here?" the captain replied, but he fished in his pocket for two coins nonetheless.

Surreptitiously, he fed two nickels into the machine and pulled on the handle again. When nothing happened but the refusal of a metal lock, Donovan slammed the machine a second time.

"You got to kick it," the cabbie said, now deeply into the New Yorker's habit of butting in on nearly everything. "I here all the time. You got to put in two quarters and kick it just as you pull handle."

Grumbling, Donovan got two quarters from his pocket and fed them into the slot. As he yanked the handle he kicked the box. This time the door sprang open and a cascade of extra change spilled out of the coin return and onto the sidewalk.

"You win lottery!" the cabbie exclaimed as Donovan removed his copy of the newspaper and retrieved the coins.

"This is my lucky day," Donovan replied. "Now I can afford to eat. My buddy told me about this place." The captain nodded in the direction of the storefront chicken restaurant and said, "Is it any good?"

"This good, yes, very good," the cabbie replied.

"You going in there?" Donovan asked. He deftly used the paper both to point at the restaurant and to hide his face from those inside as the two men walked into the chicken joint, to all eyes a happy guy with his cabbie buddy. Donovan thus remained undetected for the crucial five seconds it took to spot Mojadidi.

He was standing halfway behind the cash register, talking to a cook, who was clearly an acquaintance, and glancing occasionally out the window and at the surveillance site. A dozen or more customers, men exclusively, sat around arguing in Arabic and English and smoking ferociously.

Donovan pulled his Smith & Wesson and caught Mojadidi's eyes as the Afghan used a fork to clear shish kebab chunks off a skewer and onto a mound of rice.

"Hey, yo," Donovan said in his best Brian Moskowitz Brooklyn accent, "make me one with everything."

A sudden anguished and angry look gave Mojadidi's otherwise round face the momentary appearance of the jagged hole left in the Afghan mountainside after the Taliban blew up the Great Buddhas of Bamiyan. It didn't last. "Donovan," Mojadidi muttered, dropping down behind the register just before the captain yelled, "Police! Freeze!" Customers scattered.

When the Afghan burst back up he brought the cash register with him, overturning it and the yellow counter atop which it sat onto Donovan. The captain fell backward, scrambling to get his knees out from under it and crashing over a two-person table. Rice, onions, tomatoes, lamb, cucumber, and tzadziki sauce flew in all directions. Flat on his back and pushing away from the overturned register with his feet, Donovan saw Mojadidi scoop up a large carving knife and whirl around.

Donovan pulled the trigger twice, putting twin holes in the wall near where it met the ceiling and showering plaster down onto a commercial microwave. Mojadidi rushed toward the door, slipping in the spilled food and knocking over a table on his own, and then was on the pavement as Donovan made it to his feet and followed.

One of the handful of cabs double-parked outside had been left alone, its motor running, while the owner bought dinner that now was splashed across the floor. An American flag hung from the radio antenna, and an ALLAH IS GREAT sticker shared the rear bumper with one reading I LOVE NY.

Mojadidi hurled himself into the cab and took off with a squeal of rubber. Donovan made it to the curb about the same time as the cab's owner.

"My cab!" the man exclaimed.

"My ass he's getting away again," Donovan swore to the evening air, now perfumed by burning rubber.

Out of the corner of his eye, he could see that the men on his surveillance a block or more away had taken interest in the proceedings.

"Hack number?" Donovan yelled at the distraught cabbie.

"What?" the man stammered.

"I'm a cop! What's your hack number?"

The man yelled it out, and Donovan nodded and replied, "I'll be in touch." Then he took off at a run for the red Corvette.

Donovan jammed himself behind the wheel and twisted the key in the ignition, and the engine roared. As the car swayed from side to side with the power of it, Donovan pushed the stick into first gear and put the car into a Brooklyn U-turn. "I'm glad he taught me that," he said to the steering wheel as he raced out of the narrow side street and onto Hunters Point Avenue.

Donovan ran the light and roared around a white truck that was lingering near the corner while its driver left off a delivery of Mrs. Wagner's Pies. As he did, he saw the yellow cab turn left on Twenty-first Street. Donovan's men were running over from the surveillance. One of them had already arrived. Brian Moskowitz stood square in the middle of the street, his fifty-inch chest puffed out in anger, holding up his hand like a traffic cop. Grimacing, Donovan slammed on the brake and brought the Corvette to a screeching halt just in front of Mosko's knees.

As Donovan jumped out from behind the wheel, Mosko reached out and flicked a wet leaf off the immaculately polished hood. "You got some freakin' nerve, you know that?" he snarled.

"Get your Irish-Jewish ass behind the wheel and drive," Donovan yelled, racing around the car and yanking open the passenger's door.

Getting behind the wheel, Mosko said, "If I find *one* scratch!"

"Drive!" Donovan yelled.

Half a second later, the car took off again, leaving twin ribbons of rubber on the dark and pockmarked asphalt of Hunters Point Avenue.

"Left on Twenty-first," Donovan said, and Mosko roared around the corner in time for them to see Mojadidi making a right—a rather leisurely one, Donovan thought—onto the Long Island Expressway service road.

"That him?" Mosko asked.

"Yellow cab with a flag on the antenna," Donovan said.

"He's heading for the ramp onto the LIE. He's going into the city. We'll lose him if he does."

"He's not going into the city," Donovan replied, watching with satisfaction as Mojadidi, a block and a half ahead, made a left onto Eleventh Street. "He's going for the Pulaski Bridge."

"Into Brooklyn," Mosko said. "If the sonofabitch goes into Brooklyn, we got him. Nobody gets away from me in Brooklyn."

Mosko turned the corner onto Eleventh and let out a whoop when he saw the cab drive over the bulge of the Pulaski Bridge where it crossed Newtown Creek from Queens into Brooklyn.

"This asshole is gonna dread going to my home turf," Mosko said.

"Only the dread know Brooklyn," Donovan replied.

Mosko let out another whoop as he ran a red light and swept over the bridge and onto McGuinness Boulevard into Brooklyn. The cab was halfway down through the neighborhood of Greenpoint and moving cautiously, like a drunk does when he wants to go unnoticed.

"Either this guy doesn't see us, or doesn't expect to see such a hot car on his tail, or doesn't care," Mosko said.

"He's spent most of his life in the mountains of Afghanistan," Donovan said. "Driving city streets has got to be a bit strange and take up most of the fucker's random access memory. For *anyone*, finding a sensible route through Brooklyn is halfway impossible."

"We like our driving to come with challenges," Mosko said. "You see those commercials where some guy gets off by driving through the desert full-tilt? Well, we get off chasing some asshole through Greenpoint."

He pronounced it "Greenpernt," in the old Brooklyn fashion.

"So what happened before?" Mosko asked. "We heard two shots."

"I found him in the Arab chicken joint. He just gave us the phony address so he could hang out nearby and see if we were paying attention. He grabbed a knife, and I got off two rounds at him."

"You missed," Mosko said.

"The first time we met he missed me. This time I missed him. That makes us even."

"You don't owe him nothing," Mosko said.

"What I owe the world is to put this prick out of the misery he and his buddies have been inflicting on it with their medieval religious antagonisms and Stone Age tribal rivalries," Donovan said. "A plague on all their huts and caves. If Mojadidi lives another two hours, I'm gonna hand him over to the federal prosecutor and be outside the death chamber to pull the switch personally."

"I thought you were opposed to the death penalty," Mosko said.

"I was on September tenth," Donovan replied, slipping his cell phone into the cradle and punching in some numbers. As Mosko drove through the Brooklyn neighborhoods of Greenpoint and Williamsburg, past the odd mix of Hasidic Jews, African Americans, West Indians, and artistic types who no longer could afford the supposedly affordable artistic parts of Manhattan, Donovan called off the Sunnyside surveillance and asked some of his men to follow them to Brooklyn.

"To the garage," Mosko said, joining in what had become a conference call conducted over the car's loudspeakers.

Donovan said, "I want some guys at the garage. But I also want backup on Brighton Beach Avenue. I'm pretty sure that Mojadidi is on his way to see Mdivani at the club. Here's what's happening. Mojadidi set up two phony deals for us to find. One is the Sunnyside address, so he can see if we're onto him. The other is the garage in Brooklyn. He set that up—photos, fake passports, and all—knowing the first thing I would look for is the garage where he keeps his damned cart. He expected that I would obsess on it and sit there watching while he leans on his old pal Mdivani to get him out of the country."

Several murmurs of agreement came over the airwaves.

Mosko asked, "You want a surveillance on Mdivani's club?"

"No," Donovan replied. "But I would like to have a perimeter around it."

"That's the Gemini on Brighton Beach Avenue near the intersection of Brighton Court," Mosko announced. "Keep it loose and stay hidden once you get there, which will be after us unless any of you got immediate access to a chopper. I don't want anyone going into the club except me."

Mosko looked over, thought a moment, then said, "The captain likes to sneak a beer when nobody's looking."

Donovan made an obscene gesture, then announced, "I just gave him the finger, guys." That brought a number of cheers. "One of you guys sitting on the garage should run over to Ocean Parkway and see if you can pick up Mojadidi. Yellow cab with a big American flag."

Mosko picked up the thread and said, "You don't see that many yellow cabs this deep in Brooklyn. Most people use local car services. So it shouldn't be too hard."

Donovan listened vaguely as Mosko gave more instructions and the Corvette slipped through downtown Brooklyn, up onto the Prospect Expressway, and continued on its way toward the sea.

At one point, a voice came over the speakers, saying, "Yellow cab, U.S. flag on the antenna, southbound Ocean Parkway near Church."

"Are there any others in sight?" Mosko asked.

"Nope" was the reply.

"Stay on him. We're falling back."

"You got it."

When Mosko returned his attention to Donovan, he said, "From Ocean Parkway, if he goes to the end and turns left, he's in Brighton Beach. If he turns right before

223

we get there, he's going to the garage. Either way we got him."

Donovan said, "He'll turn left toward the club. Hell, man, it's *Saturday night!*"

"Ten bucks on the garage," Mosko insisted.

Reaching for the cell phone cradle one more time, Donovan said, "I know the perfect man to hold the bet."

He punched up some numbers. Before long the car speakers resounded with a phone ringing, then the sound of a young woman's voice, heavily accented, saying, "Gemini."

"This is Captain Donovan. Get me Mdivani."

A short silence was followed by "Who is this?"

"The troglodytic American policeman you've been hearing about. Put Mdivani on the line *now.*"

It wasn't long before the club owner answered. His voice was terrified, as betrayed by nervous laughter. "So . . . you want to humiliate me some more," he said.

"I'm calling to save your status as a future American citizen and possibly your life," Donovan replied.

"What is it?"

"I'm following Mojadidi. He stole a cab and is on his way to you."

"My God," Mdivani said. The nervous laughter was gone.

"No deity can help you now," Donovan said. "Only me. Here's what I want you to do."

"Okay."

"Where is your office in the club?"

"On the second floor."

"Has Mojadidi been there?" Donovan asked.

"Yes."

"How many entrances?"

"Two. One from the hallway leading to the restrooms. The other from the alley . . . there is an outside stairs. I keep the alley door open sometimes to help get rid of the smoke."

"Now, Mojadidi wants you to help him get out of the country. Why is that?"

Clearing his throat, Mdivani said, "Well, ah, under certain circumstances and considering he is a comrade-in-arms in the war against terrorism . . ."

"Enough," Donovan said. "I got it. I want you to sit in your office and wait for him. Get rid of your amateur bodyguard—he'll only fuck things up. Get rid of guns. Mojadidi only has a knife."

The unease was palpable even over the phone. Mdivani said, "I am getting on in years, and my warrior days . . ."

"Which days were those?" Donovan asked.

". . . are behind me. I cannot disarm a man with a knife."

"You won't have to. Just go along with him. Get a drink for yourself . . ."

"I will definitely do that," Mdivani said.

". . . and offer one to him as well. Talk to the man. This is something you do very well. You do exactly what I say, and not only will you stay alive, I'll talk to Immigration and see if I can help you out."

"You are not so bad after all," Mdivani replied.

"When he arrives, do your normal schtick—hug him, clap him on the back, ask how things are going, offer him a drink, then go down to the bar right away and get it.

If he doesn't want a drink, go get one for yourself. Then don't come back up."

"I will need a drink," Mdivani said.

"Do you have one now?" Donovan asked.

"What do you think?"

"Get rid of it."

"Now I think you really *are* a brutal American policeman," Mdivani said.

"And get rid of any bottles you may have in your office. Give yourself an excuse to get out of there. Mojadidi will expect this of you," Donovan said.

"Where are you?" the Georgian asked.

"On Ocean Parkway about a minute behind him," Donovan said.

"Does he know you and I talked?"

"Not unless you told him."

Mdivani said, "If Mojadidi thinks I told you about him, he will kill me."

"I plan to get to him first," Donovan said. "Now go and do what I told you."

When the phone went dead, Mosko said, "We could just call in the local cops and nab this guy right here on the road."

Donovan shook his head slowly and with feeling. "This is personal," he said.

"There will be lots of people in that club at this time on a Saturday night."

"They'll be downstairs," Donovan replied.

"This is *really* personal with you, isn't it?" Mosko said.

Donovan nodded.

The Special Investigations detective who had been pulled off the garage surveillance soon picked up the yellow cab with the prominently displayed American flag. Mosko let the red Corvette fall several blocks behind, a sizable gap considering Ocean Parkway's long blocks. Donovan fell silent and let Mosko run things. He gazed out the window at the Hasidic families, clad in black like his mood that night, strolling up and down the twin malls that ran the distance of the six-lane-wide boulevard in its leisurely walk to the sea.

In an earlier century and deep in the mist of history, someone laid out Brooklyn somewhat along the lines of the plan of Paris, with several broad thoroughfares, such as Eastern and Ocean parkways and Fourth and Flatbush avenues, radiating from the hub of the central city. The good intentions didn't entirely work out in other parts of the borough, but Ocean Parkway retained a laconic gentility, with marble mansions and massive houses of worship.

Donovan's silent thoughts ended abruptly when Mosko put the car into an abrupt left-hand turn onto Brighton Beach Avenue, where the elevated subway tracks cast rusty shadows over a dozen or so tiny blocks of fruit stands, grocery stores, and clubs. Russian and other Eastern European women roamed the piles of fruit, which sold at bargain prices but always seemed to go bad within a few days, pushing foldaway shopping carts that had been lined with black plastic garbage bags. A few children straggled along despite the hour, hanging on to their mothers while gaping up at the train rumbling to a ground-shaking halt overhead.

Over the car speakers, a voice said, "He's gone down Brighton Court and ditched the cab by a hydrant. He's going down the alley behind the Gemini. He looks in a hurry."

Donovan said, "Watch the alley. Brian is going to keep an eye on the front door of the club. When more guys arrive, you and Brian switch."

"Got it, boss" was the reply.

"Form a perimeter," Donovan continued. "Let people in and out, but keep a watch for the suspect. If he tries to run and gets past me, grab him."

"Got it," someone said.

"As far as I know, he's only got a knife—a kitchen carving knife—but stay awake."

"You bet."

As Mosko drove the several blocks, he issued a number of orders, related to perimeter formation, to the Special Investigations detectives rapidly closing on the scene. Meanwhile, Donovan looked out the window at the Saturday-evening pedestrians and shoppers, nearly all of them recent immigrants from the other side of the globe. He wondered if they were getting what they expected from their young experiences in the New World.

Mosko turned onto Brighton Court and pulled up alongside the cab. As Donovan got out of the car, the detective who had been watching the club hurried over, saying, "He went up the back stairs, like you thought he would."

"I'll be up front," Mosko said, taking off in that direction.

The side street was dark and quiet. Though they were less than two blocks from the Boardwalk, Donovan could barely see its lights. There were few seaside attractions in Brighton Beach like those in Coney Island despite the two communities being barely a bagel's throw apart. The only light and bustle was on Brighton Beach Avenue, with its shops, clubs, and elevated rail line—the Q train, the Broadway express that began in Manhattan near the glitter of Central Park South and the elegance of Carnegie Hall and rumbled through midtown and lower Manhattan and Brooklyn to culminate in Brighton Beach and Coney Island. Down the side street, lined with old apartment buildings whose fronts had grown somber with time and grime, shadows grew deep and black.

A lone hundred-watt bulb yellowed in its metal cage, barely lighting the way down the alley to the stairs and the Dumpster at the bottom. Something furry, dark, and furtive scurried between the Dumpster and a brick wall sodden with the ceaseless dripping of an old faucet. Donovan's Smith & Wesson found its way into his hand as he walked silently into the alley, looking up and around.

As he drew nearer to the stairway, Donovan moved next to the wall, then slid along it. At the foot of the stairs he could hear a mix of sounds. Through the brick came the thumping of a band . . . the bass and drums, anyway . . . playing a laconic beat. Donovan couldn't identify the tune or hear the inevitable dolled-up singer, but he could imagine the packed club and the smells of tobacco and vodka and the whisk of women's nylons as their owners danced with thighs pressed together by skintight evening dresses.

He stepped on the bottom iron step and paused when he heard men's voices. Donovan could make out both Mdivani and Mojadidi arguing loudly—in Russian, unfortunately. *Hadn't thought of that possibility*, Donovan grumbled to himself. *I really am getting soft.*

He started up the stairs. Halfway up he paused again. The tone of the voices had changed. Mdivani sounded softer, his usual jocular self. And whatever he was saying, Mojadidi's tone had become less frantic. After the initial flurry of words, he sounded calmer, a man buying into a plan of action that he found acceptable.

Donovan wondered about the route that Mdivani promised the Afghan warrior would get him out of the country and back to his native mountains.

Then Donovan heard the creak of a chair being gotten out of, followed by footsteps crossing the floor. Mdivani asked a question in Russian; Donovan was sure it was the offer of a drink. Mojadidi said, "Nyet," and the captain heard a door open, admitting a blast of nightclub music. The tune Donovan had been unable to identify was "Up, Up, and Away," sung, of course, in Russian. The door closed again, and the song mercifully disappeared.

Donovan took a deep breath, exhaled, and dashed up the stairs, taking them two at a time. The door had been left open halfway. He kicked it all the way open. It smashed against the wall with the force of a flash grenade.

The Afghan had been standing with his back to the door, hands on hips. He whirled.

"Police! Freeze!" Donovan shouted, to no avail.

As the man turned, he swept something off the desk. Donovan saw a glittering object.

Mojadidi spun and raised his knife. Donovan aimed at his middle and pulled the trigger once. The Smith & Wesson sounded like a cannon in the small office and echoed in the brick alley beyond.

Mojadidi's face registered something—a flickering shock—but he kept coming, bellowing, charging like a bull and swinging the knife in a broad arc. Donovan's thoughts raced to Marcy and her exercises . . . *step inside, grab, pivot, throw.* He stepped inside the arc of the blade, grabbed Mojadidi's shirtfront and felt hot blood on his fingers, then pivoted and used the man's own momentum to hurl him out the door. The Afghan hit the stairway rail with a grunt and a wail of rusty metal giving way.

Donovan threw a punch, an old-fashioned American right hand, that caught Mojadidi in the face just as a cough of blood came up from the bullet hole in his lung. Mojadidi was thrown backward, taking the rail with him. He plunged ten feet and landed flat on his back on top of the Dumpster, then rolled off onto the cold, wet asphalt of the alley.

Donovan ran down the stairs after him. Mosko and the other detective were coming around the corner, guns drawn.

When Donovan reached Mojadidi, the man was lying on his back, panting out gobs of blood and staring wide-eyed into the Brighton Beach night.

The captain crouched over him, fist raised, ready to strike again. He said, "You're under arrest for the attempted murder of a police officer and the murder of James Victor."

"Didn't kill Victor," Mojadidi sputtered.

Donovan fell silent, thinking.

Mosko crouched on the other side of the Afghan. "What'd he say?" Mosko asked.

"Came to kill Victor but too late," Mojadidi said.

"Convince me," Donovan replied.

In the background, the other detective ordered an ambulance.

"Saw killer come up from basement," Mojadidi said between spurts of blood. "Had bloody gloves. Went down. Confirmed Victor dead."

"Do you believe this guy?" Mosko asked.

"Who killed Victor?" Donovan asked.

Mojadidi was fading in and out as he began to slide into shock. Donovan grabbed him by the shirt and pulled his head up off the pavement.

"Who?" Donovan shouted.

"Blond hair," Mojadidi gasped.

"There are *two*," Mosko shouted.

"Blond," the Afghan replied. Then his eyes shut and he went off into shock and disappeared.

"Damn," Donovan swore, lowering the man's head back down onto the asphalt.

The captain stood, stepped away, straightened his jacket, and let the tide of NYPD follow-up wash over him. Sirens came from all over. Lights swirled in the night; soon there were more than on the Tilt-A-Whirl in Astroland not so very far away. Radio sounds filled Brighton Beach, drowning out all else.

Mosko said, "Which blonde, Lisa or Chloe?"

"I don't know," Donovan replied, looking around for the inevitable reappearance of Mdivani. The club owner yet again had redeemed himself in Donovan's eyes.

It wasn't long in coming. Mdivani came down the stairs, carrying his trademark coffee cup stuffed with espresso, sugar, and vodka. He gaped at the inert form of the mujahid and the growing number of policemen hovering over him. Joining Donovan in leaning against the far alley wall, Mdivani said, "Holy shit, my friend."

Donovan made a noise that sounded like "mmmmm."

"Is he dead?"

"Not yet, but if he lives, his warrior days are over and he's in jail for trying to kill me—years ago and today."

"Just as well," Mdivani replied.

"All these guys should go back to tending their herds, growing their poppies, or whatever they do when they aren't slaughtering one another," Donovan said.

Mdivani took a sip of his drink and said, "I have no proof, but in Mojadidi's case I believe that poppies were involved."

Donovan looked over at the Georgian. "So if he dies, no loss, eh?"

"No loss," Mdivani said.

"Gimme a hit off that," Donovan said, reaching for the cup.

14. "MOMMY TOLD ME THAT AUNT LISA HAS SOMEBODY'S SECRET," DANIEL SAID.

The next-to-last Sunday afternoon in June was cloudless and brilliant. The beach at Coney Island was packed. Hardly a grain of sand was visible between blankets. Splashers and waders were three deep at the edge of a gentle surf.

On the Boardwalk, in Astroland, and on the streets surrounding KeySpan Park, hardly a square foot went unaccounted for. The Wonder Wheel and the Cyclone took thrill seekers far above the crowd and then dropped them back down again, screaming, at seventy miles an hour.

The Tilt-A-Whirl spun children around shrieking in the combination of fear and joy that children and not-quite-developed men so enjoy, and crowds pressed into KeySpan Park. There they would sit in the sun and sea breezes and enjoy the day's events: the kickoff of the annual Mermaid Parade, a flyover and aerial acrobatic show by the U.S. Navy's Blue Angels, and the feature ball game in which the league champion Brooklyn Cyclones would face off against the Mahoning Valley Scrappers.

Mary O'Connor, Donovan's cousin from Ireland and Daniel's nanny, lowered the lift and let the proud little boy wheel himself out of the sparkling new red van and into the KeySpan Park lot. The spot they found was auspicious—against the Boardwalk and smack at the base of Brooklyn's Eiffel Tower, the Parachute Drop.

"See, Daddy, I can get off the lift myself," Daniel said happily, just before his chair rolled up against the formidable legs of Brian Moskowitz.

The sergeant stood, arms folded, protecting the driver's side of his Corvette. He said, "Hiya, kid. Watch out for the paint."

"Hi, Uncle Brian!" the boy replied as Mosko bent over to engulf him in a beefy hug that left him momentarily hidden from sight.

Donovan came around the van, freshly shaved and looking rested by a satisfying night's sleep. He had on his white-on-blue NYPD T-shirt and jeans and also, to help in getting through the crowds, a blue NYPD jacket that had SPECIAL INVESTIGATIONS displayed in bright yellow on the back. So did Moskowitz.

Following the news that they had arrested an Afghan warlord, thought to be a drug merchant, who came to the United States to wage war, Donovan and Mosko had received a last-minute invitation to ride in the Mermaid Parade and receive the applause of a grateful Coney Island. They chose to ride with the queen of the parade, Lisa Fine, on the float designed for her atop a squat Emergency Services van. That would give them a bird's-eye view of the parade and of the crowds gathered to watch and, not least, access to Lisa.

As the Donovans unloaded their own van—tumbling out came three L. L. Bean bags full of towels, goodies, toys, and other supplies—Mosko said, "I've been coming to this every year since they started in 1983. It's the official opening of the high summer in Coney Island. What happens is a couple hundred people dress up for the day and have a ball. The girls dress like mermaids . . . tails on their bottom, or, y'know, whatever passes for a tail, and nothing or almost nothing on top. Band-Aids, Post-it Notes, that sort of thing. The guys dress up like pirates, Neptunes, whatever. They put together floats that I guess you would say are a bit informal. Like strapping beach chairs to the roofs of their Camaros and throwing a bunch of clam-shells and seaweed around. Then they assemble at the ball-park, put music on speakers, and start drinking."

These activities had already begun. Donovan looked over the scruffy collection of half-naked women and beer-swilling men arranging themselves atop a motley collection of falling-down cars and trucks while music roared. "This sounds like the softball games at 106th and Riverside," Donovan said.

"The organizers pick a king and queen," Mosko continued. "This year's queen is Lisa, of course. She'll be riding up in front of everyone, but I think that's safe. Our surveillance didn't catch so much as a mosquito going near her. Now, as for the king of the parade, I don't know who that is. Sometimes they pick him on the spot. Some guy who looks drunk enough or outrageous enough."

"I know who it is," Donovan replied.

"Who?" Mosko asked.

"You'll be surprised."

"Okay, well, fine. I love them surprises. So, once the parade is assembled, it goes into the ballpark and around the field, passing the reviewing stand behind first base. It goes by the field boxes, where your family will be sitting, and then out of the park and along Surf Avenue to Astroland, which is the only facility around here that is weird enough to make the parade participants look normal. The parade wraps up at Astroland, and then everyone goes to the beach and continues getting drunk. One day the whole thing will be on an episode of *Wild On*."

"What's *Wild On?*" Donovan asked.

"As if you don't know. So look, our pal Nicky Dollar is emceeing the parade. We'll get to see him in action."

Donovan grunted.

Marcy dropped two of the Bean bags at Mosko's feet, gave him a hug and a kiss, and said, "Help carry, okay?"

"You got it, Mrs. D.," Mosko said jauntily.

Donovan said, "Honey, I think we ought to leave the bags in the van and pick them up after the parade is over."

She looked around at the parking lot and the ballpark, then past the towering spire of the Parachute Jump and to the Boardwalk. A wheelchair-friendly wooden ramp ran from the base of the Parachute Jump up to the Boardwalk.

"I guess you're right," she replied, then helped Mosko put the bags back in the van.

"Are you going to be in the parade, Daddy?" Daniel asked.

"Yes, I am," Donovan replied.

"Will you ride with Aunt Lisa?"

"Yes. I need to talk to her about something."

"Will Uncle Brian be in the parade, too?"

"You bet, kid," Mosko replied.

"Can I be in the parade, too?" the little boy asked.

"Next year, son," Donovan said. "This time Uncle Brian and I will be working."

The boy thought for a moment, then said, "Daddy . . . is Aunt Lisa in trouble?"

"Why do you think that Aunt Lisa may be in trouble?" Donovan asked, kneeling beside his son and looking at him as if he were the Oracle at Delphi.

"Mommy said that Aunt Lisa has somebody's secret," Daniel said.

"What?" Donovan asked.

Marcy looked at her son.

"Mommy called Aunt Lisa 'Miss Victoria's Secret,' so I thought maybe she was in trouble."

"Daniel," Marcy laughed, blushing. "I didn't say that."

"Yes you did, Mommy," Daniel said with a giggle.

"The kid sees and hears all, like his old man," Mosko said.

"I better get Daniel out of here before he gives anything else away," Marcy said.

Donovan checked his watch and looked over at the back end of the line of parade vehicles, which was a few dozen paces away. That was close to the adjacent Abe

Stark Sports and Recreation Center, named after the Depression-era Brooklyn clothing store owner who parlayed his famous HIT SIGN, WIN SUIT sign in Ebbets Field into a political career. Colorfully dressed bodies primped alongside and on top of their "floats." They bustled around with a lot of urgency, in contrast to the hordes of beachgoers who moved along slowly, bearing assorted party gear, and the Cyclones fans, who walked into the park carrying little more than their hopes for another winning season.

"Uncle Brian and I have to go," Donovan said to his son. "Now, I want you, Mommy, and Cousin Mary to go into the ballpark and wave to me when you see me go by in the parade, okay?"

"Okay," the boy said agreeably.

"Be careful," Marcy said, kissing him.

"Always," Donovan replied.

When the two detectives got to the line of cars, they found mermaids of all ages, heights, and shapes. They wore as many different breast coverings as could be imagined, from generic bikini tops to, in fact, Post-it Notes. There were tails that included Halloween outfits, homemade fabric tubes that had been dyed a goldfish color, and filmy veils. For the most part, the men were pirates, sailors, and a drunken assortment of Neptunes. Life rings abounded, as did tridents—one with two beer cans and a salami impaled on its points—along with blaring music and a stunning supply of beer. The several men in Hell's Angels outfits appeared to *be* Hell's Angels, attracted, Donovan felt, not by the rites of summer so much as by the women and by the free beer that was supplied by the many bars that paid for the floats and contributed contestants and other revelers.

The EMS van on which the queen's "throne" sat brought up the *end* of the line of vehicles. It was covered with fish netting, cork floats, life rings, plastic fish and crabs and lobsters, excelsior draped to mimic seaweed, and shells. The van itself was a squat mobile intensive care unit, and atop it were strapped two wicker wing chairs—thrones for the king and queen. Both chairs were painted gold, that being the color of the day for most of what wasn't ocean blue or sea green.

Lisa Fine stood by the back of the van, wearing a white terrycloth robe and signing autographs. Around her in addition to fans were two or three parade organizers, all wearing white T-shirts reading

MERMAID PARADE COMMITTEE
WE'RE THE SOBER ONES

Standing nearby was Nicky Dollar, resplendent and nearly blinding in full regalia: sequined jacket, gold lamé shirt and pants, an Uncle Sam top hat, and a drum major's baton that had been painted red, white, and blue. He greeted Donovan and Mosko with open arms and the kind of naked enthusiasm that comes from either complete innocence or a severely warped criminal mind. "Hey, my favorite ossifers," he proclaimed, shaking both their hands nearly in unison.

"Hiya," Mosko replied, as Donovan grunted hello.

"How do you like the whole deal?" Dollar asked, proudly holding his jacket open and displaying himself, an electric peacock, to the parking lot.

"Out-fucking-rageous," Mosko said.

"You look like Liberace on Halloween," Donovan said, smiling.

"Nah, I'm Uncle Sam, Coney Island style," Dollar said, apparently insult-proof that day.

"So you emcee the whole thing?" Donovan asked.

"You got it, Captain. I introduce everyone, call off the names of the participants, and celebrate the king and queen of the Mermaid Parade. And here she is . . ." He waved their attention toward Lisa, who had dispensed with the admirers. They walked over to her.

"Hi, William," she said, giving Donovan a hug and a kiss on the cheek.

"Hey," he replied.

"Brian," she said, repeating the greeting.

"*Qué pasa*, babe?" he said.

"What a great day," she said. "And how great it is that you guys could join me."

"Wouldn't miss it," Donovan replied.

"Five minutes before we get going," Dollar announced, ostentatiously checking a gold-toned pocket watch that swung at the end of a gold chain. He reached over to Lisa, gently grabbed her shoulder, and said, "Hey, you go out there and knock 'em dead."

She smiled and removed his hand from her shoulder. "Behave," she said.

"Man, I don't get no respect," Dollar said. "No matter how nice I try to be, I can't get to first base with this doll."

"You want to get to first base?" she asked, nodding in the direction of the ballpark. "Sit on the front bumper and I'll drive you to first base."

"Sheesh," Dollar replied. To the two detectives he said, "Would you tell her that she could do a lot worse than me?"

"This is absolutely true," Donovan said.

"Yeah, right," Lisa replied.

Donovan noticed a change in her. Now in her element—about to go on a stage of sorts—she was firmer and more in command than before. Of course, losing a loved one and being accused of his murder could have caused the ego deflation apparent in the past week, Donovan realized. Now she showed a hard edge.

"I guess that's life," Dollar said. He pointed up the line of parade vehicles and added, "I got to grab my microphone and get to work. About the *king* of the Mermaid Parade, would you crown him, sugar?"

"Sure," she replied. In a conciliatory tone, she added, "See you later, Nicky."

He left with a smile on his face.

Mosko looked around for the king Dollar said would be anointed that day but saw no likely candidates. Beyond other parade participants, there were only a few gawking teenage boys, who kept their distance.

Donovan smiled, looked down, and shuffled his feet on the pavement.

Lisa stepped up to Mosko, grabbed his jacket, and ran the zipper down.

"Hey," he said.

"I want to see the T-shirt du jour," she replied. It read

BROOKLYN—CENTER OF THE FREAKIN' UNIVERSE

"That's the G-rated version," Donovan said.

"Thank God," she replied.

"What gives?" Mosko asked.

"Congratulations, Your Majesty," Donovan said.

"You're king of the Mermaid Parade," Lisa said, grabbing Mosko's hand and pumping it.

A hesitant smile worked its way onto his face, and after a moment's reflection, he said, "No shit!"

"You d'*man*," Donovan added.

"I wish the guys from the gym were here," Mosko said.

"Some of 'em no doubt are."

"How come I'm king?" Mosko asked.

She shrugged. "Two hero cops, one of them from Brooklyn . . . it's a no-brainer."

"*He* normally gets most of the attention," Mosko said, tilting his head in the direction of his boss.

"He's from *the city*," she replied. "He doesn't even *like* Brooklyn."

"Not true," Donovan replied. "Like somebody . . . Mel Brooks, maybe . . . said, 'Brooklyn is a great place to be *from*.'"

Mosko uttered an oath.

"Come on, guys," Lisa said. "Get up on the truck and help me put on my tail."

They followed her in climbing up the back of the truck and edging along the low ceiling to where the twin wing chairs were strapped. She sat on the edge of the left-hand chair and unzipped a soft leather Gucci traveling bag, to one handle of which were affixed airport baggage handling tags bearing the codes LAX and JFK.

Lisa pulled out a resplendent gold tail, made like chain

mail but lighter, with thousands of overlapping gold scales sewn onto a fabric base. Unlike the assortment of amateur tails seen on other women who were preparing for the start of the parade, Lisa's was professionally made, pure Hollywood. It was blinding in the afternoon sun, like Nicky Dollar's outfit.

"Whoa," Mosko said, upon seeing it.

"Nice tail," Donovan added.

Lisa parted her robe, kicked off her sandals, and stuck her feet into the tail. "This is the actual tail that Darryl Hannah's body double wore in *Splash*. Cool, isn't it?"

Both Donovan and Mosko agreed that it was very cool indeed.

"Help me here," Lisa said, standing and wiggling into the shimmering gold stocking, pulling it up her body. The two men supported her as she pulled the skintight costume up her thighs and then, abruptly, stopped. She tapped Donovan on the chest and directed his eyes to her derriere, visible despite the meager efforts of a filmy bikini bottom. "Look at that," she commanded.

"If you insist," Donovan said agreeably.

"Nice butt," Mosko added.

"I predict an Academy Award," Donovan said.

"I meant look at the bruise," Lisa said, stabbing a just-manicured finger at a fig-shaped black-and-blue mark. She added, "Thank your wife for that."

The bruise was just below a tiny tag that Donovan could see read VICTORIA'S SECRET. He laughed. "Marcy is here," he added. "So is the whole family."

"Oh, good. I'll wave."

Donovan added, "Chloe Victor is here, too, in the

owner's box. This is good because Brian and I need to talk to her."

"We need to talk to the two of you real bad," Mosko said.

"I'll wave to her, too," Lisa said. She wiggled her hips—a bit more than was necessary for the purpose of tail application, Donovan thought—and pulled the tail up until it covered the bikini bottom. She snapped it into place. "There," she said.

Donovan heard a rumbling off to the east, a deep roar that grew fast. He looked over just in time to see the Blue Angels come roaring up along the beach and its 1.1 million sun worshipers. Flying a tight V formation, the Navy jets burst over Coney Island, trailing white smoke. Then two of them banked left over the ocean, a third climbed nearly straight up, and the other two banked right, curving around the 250-foot-high Parachute Jump like lariats around a hitching post. The crowd roared nearly as loudly as the planes.

"Look at that," Mosko exclaimed.

"Look at *these*," Lisa shouted, casting off the robe and sticking out her chest. The bikini top was gauzy, matching the bottom.

Donovan applauded politely, using the tips of his fingers.

"God save the queen's," Mosko said.

The half dozen pirates and Neptunes standing nearby whooped.

Nicky Dollar's voice came over speakers. He said, "Ladies and gentleman, start your engines."

As the vehicles started up and the participants cheered, Lisa pushed Mosko down into his chair and then sat beside him. Remaining on his feet, Donovan took up a position next to her.

Lisa reached down to the tail and, with a little effort and a frown, detached two scales. She gave one to each detective and then turned to begin waving at the crowd, which grew as the parade left the parking lot and drove into the packed baseball stadium. "There," she told Donovan and Mosko, looking back quickly. "Now you can tell all the boys at the office that you got a piece of tail from Lisa Fine."

The two detectives exchanged glances. They were the sort of glances men give one another after having been dissed by a surly cocktail waitress. Then Donovan said, "We have to talk."

"So you said," she replied, her smile broadening as the end of the parade swept into KeySpan Park and the crowd jumped to its feet cheering.

"Can you wave, smile, and talk at the same time?" Donovan asked.

"I'm an actress," she replied, suddenly smiling even more as she shouted, "Hi," and waved at someone in the crowd at the stadium entrance.

Donovan heard Nicky Dollar, his voice now booming over the stadium's public address system, saying, "Ladies and gentlemen, let's give a big Coney Island welcome to the queen of the Mermaid Parade, an international motion picture star, born right here in Coney Island, Lisa Fine!"

The audience cheered wildly, partly because of Lisa and partly because the Blue Angels were making another pass. This time they flew in vertical formation, stacked like layers in a cake above the beach and Boardwalk.

"I could get used to this," Mosko said, doing a good job of smiling and waving himself.

Dollar said, "In a moment, we'll get to meet Matilda, the famous armed hang glider that Lisa flies in her hit TV series, *Ladyhawk.*"

"Surprised?" she asked Donovan.

He shook his head. But she might not have seen that, so he added, "I heard last night about Matilda coming in from L.A."

She flicked her head in his direction, then back to the crowd.

The procession had begun to arc around the infield. The parade route led from left field past third base, behind home plate, and up to the reviewing stand, which was near first base.

Dollar said, "Let's give another big Coney Island welcome to the two hero cops you've been hearing about this week. Bill Donovan and Brian Moskowitz of the NYPD Special Investigations Unit were the guys who cracked a big chunk of the attack-on-America investigation right here in Coney Island earlier this week, and last night in Brighton Beach they nailed an Afghan hood who had come to this land of the free to commit murder."

The roar was frightening.

Dollar continued, "We're in a forgiving mood on this glorious day and will forgive Captain Donovan for living in Manhattan."

There were laughs and a few silly boos.

"But Sergeant Moskowitz is a proud Brooklyn boy, and today we honor him as king of the Mermaid Parade."

Again there was a roar. Mosko stood, punched the air,

then sat back down as the procession continued its slow rumble around the ballpark.

Lisa looked up at Donovan and said, "That man you caught last night . . . did he kill James?"

"No," Donovan said.

She stopped smiling, at least for a moment. "No?"

"But he saw the one who did," Donovan replied.

"Who?" she asked hesitantly. She looked around, as if the killer—or more cops, Donovan thought—might be nearby, in the crowd. When Donovan wasn't forthcoming with an answer to her question, she sighed and said, "Look, I'm sorry if I came off a little hard before."

"You're not hard," Donovan said. "And you have the bruise to prove it."

"I want to get back on track with my career. I'm going back to L.A. tonight. Scott is there for me."

"Actually," Donovan said, "Scott is *there*." Donovan pointed to the top of the Parachute Jump, where a hang glider, painted like a hawk, was unfurled and poised to launch into the summertime.

Lisa looked up, then looked back at the captain. "How did you . . . ?"

"Know that your boyfriend was coming to Coney Island, glider and tail in tow?"

"Yes, but Scott is *not* my boyfriend, exactly. I slept with him three times when there was nothing on TV. Come *on*."

"Have you explained to him that he's not your boyfriend?"

"Not exactly. But hey, he's my stunt coordinator and friend."

"Who refuses to set foot in New York City, you told me."

"He made an exception to bring in the stuff I needed for the parade and also to help me pack and go home," she replied.

"Who never comes to New York City but seems to regard the Bay Ridge Comfort Inn as his favorite hotel."

"He was there *once*," she replied. "A year ago, on my birthday."

"Twice," Donovan said. "Did you know that ever since September eleventh the feds keep track of everyone who takes a transcontinental flight—especially when they buy first class tickets at the last minute, paying cash?"

"Oh," Lisa replied.

Donovan felt she was about to say something else, but the words were lost in the roar when the Blue Angels flew by a third time, this pass in an inverted V formation. Again, everyone oohed, aahed, and cheered.

The end of the parade with the float bearing the king, queen, and Donovan came to a halt in front of the reviewing stand. Abruptly, Nicky Dollar ran back, clambered halfway up onto the hood of the van, and took Lisa's hand. Then he announced to the crowd, "Hey guys, guess what? I finally made it to first base with Lisa Fine."

There was another roar and a lot of laughter.

"You're too freakin' much, pal," Mosko said.

"Never give up," Dollar replied, his mike momentarily off.

Mosko took the sequin Lisa had given him, showed it to Dollar, then tucked it into the man's shirt pocket.

Brightening, Dollar said, "Does that mean I can say that I . . . ?"

"Yeah, how did I know you'd jump right on that one? One day I'm gonna have a ball telling my grandchildren about you."

"Got to get back to work," Dollar said, jumping down to the gravel of the warning track and switching his mike back on to continue his spiel.

Donovan heard a tiny voice yell, "Daddy!" He turned and waved at his son.

"Hiya, Killer," Mosko shouted.

Lisa's smile was gone, replaced by a dazed and confused look.

Mosko reached over and patted her on the tail. "Smile, Your Majesty."

The smile snapped back onto her face.

As Nicky Dollar went about the business of emceeing the awards ceremony, Donovan said, "You were about to say something."

"Oh," Lisa replied. "Did you say that Scott was here *twice* before?"

Donovan nodded. "A year ago on your birthday. Then last weekend. He took a morning flight out of LAX, got into JFK around dinnertime, and took a cab straight to the Comfort Inn in Bay Ridge. He did the whole thing under the name Robert Houdin, fake ID and all."

"Who's Robert Houdin?" she asked.

"The legendary magician Harry Houdini named himself after. A *great* escape artist. Too bad your boyfriend isn't as good."

"Scott isn't my . . . oh, never mind. And he wasn't in New York last weekend. I told you I called him at home."

"I have your phone records," Donovan said. "*And* his. You called him at this number."

Donovan held up his cell phone. The display showed a number in the 818 area code, which included Studio City, California.

"That's the number," Lisa said.

"That's his cell phone," Donovan said.

"He doesn't *have* a regular phone. He uses the cell all the time. But he told me he was in bed watching TV."

"He probably was. They have pretty good TVs at the Comfort Inn."

"Are you telling me that Scott . . . ?"

"Murdered James?" Donovan asked.

"That's what the man's telling you," Mosko said.

"Remember that photo you kept on top of your TV, the one with two adorable blond kids in Hollywood? About six this morning, a detective showed a copy of that photo to the man we caught last night, as he was about to go into the operating room so doctors could fix the bullet hole I made in his lung. He positively identified Scott as the man he saw coming out of the basement of Surf Avenue News dripping blood."

No longer smiling at all, Lisa looked into Donovan's eyes and said only, "Scott . . ."

"Sorry," Donovan told her.

"If you will pardon my French," Mosko added, "your track record with men sucks. Frankly, I would give Nicky Dollar a second look. We ran a background check on him, and he's clean as the driven snow. A little over the top, but hey, don't you have something to do with a little thing called 'Hollywood?' "

"How do you contact Scott today?" Donovan asked.

"Cell phone," she replied, in a stunned sort of voice. "He's got a headset."

With that, Donovan pressed the TALK button on his phone. A few seconds later he heard a click and the words "Hi, honey."

"Hi, sweetie," Donovan replied.

Following a brief and tense silence, Jamison asked, "Who's this?"

"What, you can't hear the PA system up there in the stratosphere?" Donovan said. "This is Captain Bill Donovan of the NYPD. Look down . . . over here, by first base . . . I'm the tall, distinguished man standing on top of the truck next to Ladyhawk."

Donovan's eyes followed the ladder, enclosed in a yellow iron lattice, that ran straight up the north face of the tower. He thought he saw a man looking down from beneath the fluttering hang glider but later would conclude that he probably imagined it.

"Yeah, that's me," Donovan said. "I want to talk to you about the murder of James Victor. So fold your wings and prance down the yellow iron steps."

Perhaps to offer an example, Donovan climbed down from the top of the van. As he did so, Lisa began to cry. Mosko stood, waving to get Nicky Dollar's attention. When he got it, he yelled, "Get over here! She needs you."

The emcee came over on the run and, fairly leaping up onto the van, asked, "What's the matter?"

"Details later," Mosko said. "Right now we gotta take the hang glider out of the show. Sorry."

"Oh," Dollar said. His eyes flicked between the golden bird-of-prey glider atop the Parachute Jump, the sobbing girl, and the glint of sun off the gold badge that Donovan had just affixed to his jacket's breast pocket. *"Oh!"* Dollar added.

"Take care of her," Mosko said. "She's a good kid."

Lisa's body was wracked with spasms of crying, giving Donovan a creepy feeling. One thing few men want to see, he realized, is a naked . . . or half-naked . . . woman crying. He looked up at her and said, "I'm sorry. I truly am." But she probably couldn't hear him.

"What do I tell the crowd?" Dollar asked.

"You're in show biz," Mosko said. "Make up a story."

Dollar smiled and, after a nanosecond or two, said into the microphone, "Ladies and gentlemen, it seems that our queen is overcome with emotion from seeing so many loving Brooklyn hearts come to welcome her. Let's give her a second while I help the judges hand out the award for Best Float."

Tired of the silence from atop the Parachute Jump, Donovan spoke again into his cell phone. "Are you still with me, kid? If so, fold your wings and climb back down."

The phone remained silent, but Donovan swore he could detect anger, fear, and maybe a trace of resignation. Then a voice said, "Fuck you, man."

And with a flourish and a flapping of fabric that Donovan felt he could hear, the hang glider launched into the midday air.

The crowd, which had not yet caught on to what was happening, pointed, smiled, and waved.

"How *about* this guy?" Mosko said.

"Get your royal butt off the throne," Donovan said.

Mosko hopped off the hood of the van. He straightened his jacket.

Donovan spoke into the cell phone again as the hang glider began a broad, sweeping arc over the stadium to continuing applause. "That's right, stick to the script. Circle the stadium once and then land. You get down here and we'll go someplace and talk."

There was more silence. Toward the end of his turn, Jamison's voice said, "Fuck *you!*" The hang glider veered away, heading toward the Boardwalk and the beach.

"Where do you think you're going?" Donovan said. "It may have escaped your attention, but you're in the City of New York. This ain't California, where you can fly behind some mountain and escape."

There was silence from Jamison, but Donovan heard Nicky Dollar announce, "That's better! Ladies and gentleman, how's that for a smile? I tell ya, is she a star or *what?*"

There was more applause. Dollar continued, "We were gonna show you a landing by Lisa's famous hang glider, Matilda, but it looks like she's heading back to L.A."

The audience laughed.

"Well, there's no accounting for taste. Who would want California when there's Coney Island?"

The applause was loud and sustained as the parade resumed. Meanwhile, Jamison flew away from the stadium and over the Boardwalk.

Donovan spoke into the phone. "You can't get away. There's cops all around." He turned to Mosko and said, "Prove it."

Mosko got out his own phone, and shortly thereafter

there were sirens. Unmarked and patrol cars that had been holding back switched on lights and sirens in side streets all around KeySpan Park. An NYPD helicopter that had just swept over from its base on Floyd Bennett Field off to the east banked over the Boardwalk and stopped there, pointedly going no further. A blue-striped white police boat could be seen racing up the channel, tossing foam from her bow.

Donovan and Mosko ran out of the ballpark, up the wooden ramp near Daniel's red van, and onto the Boardwalk. Crowds parted for the two men with badges and cell phones.

The hang glider was circling the beach, riding a thermal of hot air that rose off the sun-baked sand and the sun-soaked bodies lying upon it. Jamison was gaining altitude in preparation for a try at escape . . . but to where?

Donovan told him, "You ain't goin' nowhere, kid. You want to try reaching that spit of land across the channel? That's Breezy Point. It's where the cops and firemen you've heard so much about live. Have a ball. And I'll tell you what—you want to try to make Manhattan? How about the Bronx and Staten Island, too?"

Mosko smiled.

If Jamison heard the captain's words, he didn't say. He appeared to be focused on gaining altitude and figuring out where to go. It was unclear whether he ever heard the booming amplified voice that came from the police chopper, either. It said, "Glider pilot! You have entered a restricted flight zone! Land immediately!"

The chopper itself began a fast descent, coming straight down at Donovan and Mosko and the folks around them, some of whom ran away screaming. Random bits of napkin and hot dog wrapper blew away from the helicopter blast. Donovan and Mosko, hair flying, clothes fluttering, whipped their heads to the east as the incredible roar they had heard three times before that sunny afternoon reappeared, growing like a nearing storm.

"Holy mother of God," Mosko swore as the Blue Angels came roaring up over the beach on their final and most spectacular run, spewing red, white, and blue smoke, flying upside down under computer control.

Donovan and Mosko watched in stunned awe as the fighter jets roared right over the glider, missing it by yards but sucking it up violently. The Hollywood bird of prey was swallowed by the red, white, and blue smoke and shredded by the jet blasts. The hawk had become a sparrow caught in the talons of an eagle.

Screaming, the million-plus people on the beach scrambled up and stared as Jamison plummeted four hundred feet, a body flailing amidst twisted pipes and tattered fabric.

The Blue Angels continued on their way, finishing their run and roaring off, crossing New York Harbor and vanishing above the wilds of Jersey.

Donovan and Mosko ran down the nearest ramp to the beach and fought their way to the surf as lifeguards pulled Jamison's body onto the sand. Donovan looked down at the dyed blond hair, the lifeless eyes staring up from the salt water and the seaweed. A sand crab scuttled by, maybe the same one the captain caught for his son the Sunday before.

"Would you kill and be killed over a woman?" he asked Mosko.

"I would kill to protect my wife," the sergeant replied.

"So would I, but that's not what I'm asking."

"You want to know if I would throw it all away over a blond babe who only touched me when she didn't wanna watch *Touched by an Angel?* No way, José."

"Lisa slept with him three times when there was nothing on TV, and he thought it was love forever," Donovan said. "That's the problem with these kids today—they don't know how to have casual sex."

A lifeguard looked at Donovan and said, "Who was this guy, officer?"

"In the end, nobody," Donovan replied. He turned to walk back to his family and the hot dog and beer he had promised himself the night before.

15. A BLACK CHICK LAWYER AND HER BLACK-SHEEP COP HUSBAND.

It was a leafy block of brownstones where each tree was surrounded by a miniature white wrought-iron fence and the sounds of the city were a stone's throw away, on the corner of the avenue.

On that avenue there were shops and restaurants and the occasional bar filled, since this was the West Village, with heartbreakingly beautiful young women and handsome, fashionably unshaven young men, as well as any number of folks for whom gender was of no apparent consequence—all of whom gave the impression of being movie extras on a break between takes. On the side street where the Donovans soon would live, there was the kind of tree-lined brownstone tranquility that most New Yorkers only *see* in movies.

Donovan and Mosko sat on the steps with bottles of beer in their hands—Kaliber for the captain and Guinness for Mosko—and a big bag of popcorn between them. The sergeant had just arrived, bearing the beer and his laptop, which he set up atop one of the white concrete lions—miniatures of the famous lions that guard the entrance to the New York Public Library—that bracketed the front door.

Marcy was inside doing something or other in preparation for moving in. Daniel was rolling up and down the sidewalk to the corner of the avenue and back, laughing, with Mary in hot pursuit.

Donovan hadn't shaved that day. Drinking beer on the stoop in old clothes, he looked like one of the construction guys they'd hired to make the building wheelchair friendly. He did not look *anything* like the owner and consequently drew a few disparaging glances from passing neighbors-to-be. This was much to Mosko's amusement, and after watching for a while he said, "Some of the local aristocracy is acting like Hunter Thompson is moving in next door."

"They should have seen me a few years ago," Donovan grunted.

"I got to tell you, man . . . no matter how much money or how many houses and cars you guys have, you'll always be a black chick lawyer and her black-sheep cop husband," Mosko continued.

"With a kid in a wheelchair. Damn, only the Irish nanny looks like a normal person."

Mosko said something like "mmmm" into his bottle

while having a swig. Then he grabbed a fistful of pop-corn.

"We'll *really* be popular after they get a load of the parking spot," Donovan added. He had prevailed upon the city to declare the parking spot in front of his new home a "special reserved handicapped zone" to accommodate Daniel's van. Since parking spots in the West Village were as rare as orchids on the moon, Donovan anticipated a little resentment.

"So you got some mafia construction guys putting in wheelchair ramps," Mosko said.

"I wouldn't call them *mafia* construction guys."

"Do you know for sure they're not?"

Donovan shook his head.

"Want me to find out?" Mosko asked.

"Nah. They're going a good job, whoever they are," Donovan said. "We also have them putting in a physical therapy room in the basement. You know, for Daniel's therapist. We're not giving up on a cure."

"Do the doctors know what's wrong?" Mosko asked.

Donovan patted the several sheets of printout that stuck out of his pants pocket. "The latest thought involves synapses . . . nerve connections . . . in the lower spinal cord. The official diagnosis is 'diplegia of the legs,' which sounds fancy but really doesn't say anything except that his legs are paralyzed and they don't know why."

"Poor little guy," Mosko said.

"Daniel is the happiest kid I ever saw," Donovan said, a tear arising nonetheless. "He's really a happy, optimistic little critter. Kind of a chipmunk, you know. Anyway, we're looking into stem cell research . . . the Christopher Reeve stuff. Researching this or going to doctors is what

I do when I'm not running around the city with you. Or freaking out the neighbors," Donovan added, in reaction to an old woman who gave him the hairy eyeball while toddling past alongside her miniature poodle.

"In Brooklyn they line up to shake your hand and ask you to sign pizza boxes," Mosko said. "Here in the city you're just a guy drinking beer on the front stoop and lowering property values."

"I didn't get into this line of work to become famous and sign autographs, even on pizza boxes," Donovan said. "I did it because I thought I could help out in the world."

"How much *does* this place go for in the open market?" Mosko asked. He hooked his thumb over his shoulder at the house.

"You don't want to know," Donovan said.

"I want to know."

"No you don't."

Mosko said, "C'mon."

"About five and a half," Donovan replied, lowering his voice as if in embarrassment.

"Five and a half what?" Mosko asked.

"Five and a half what-the-hell-do-you-think," Donovan said.

"Jeez," the sergeant exclaimed.

"Do I look any different?" Donovan asked, somewhat snappily.

Mosko smiled and gave his friend a backhand slap on the upper arm. Donovan would feel it three days later, though he never would admit as much.

"I heard that was one hell of a right hand you threw that knocked Mojadidi through the railing and down on top of the Dumpster," Mosko said. "I take back what I said about you getting soft."

"Thanks," Donovan replied.

"Anyway, I brought news along with the beer. The DA has decided to go after Mojadidi on two counts of attempted murder of a police officer and one of fleeing to avoid prosecution. Plus the sonofabitch has a problem with the feds concerning traveling under a false passport and entering the country illegally. Not to mention the fact that the Army boys in Afghanistan have taken an interest in finding out just what Mojadidi grows up there in the mountains. I take it you're not willing to let him go this time."

"What, so he can change sides and move to Florida for flight training?" Donovan replied.

"The one we *did* get is Eddie," Mosko said proudly.

"Tell me."

"You were right about him being Mojadidi's ear. We found out he got a chunk of money the Wednesday before the murder and was flashing it around the bar on Neptune where he goes to watch Islanders games. *And* there were a lot of calls to Eddie's house from Mojadidi's cell phone."

"Charge him with conspiracy to commit murder," Donovan said. "It doesn't matter that Didi didn't kill Victor. He *intended to* and enlisted Eddie's help. At least this *will* help get him to leave Lisa alone. Not that she has to worry about him anymore, since she packed and went home to L.A."

"Nicky and her didn't hit it off, I guess," Mosko said.

"He took her to dinner, and they had a nice time," Donovan said.

"That's it?"

"Yeah," Donovan said.

"There must have been something good on TV."

"No doubt."

"The FBI is still looking for Nehal," Mosko continued. "They're focusing now on Detroit."

"They may never find him," Donovan said. "I'm sure that Victor wasn't the only sleeper agent in this great big land of ours. There's sure to be another escape-money Muslim like Victor in Detroit. Nehal will get passage to Toronto and disappear."

"Well," Mosko said, "we did what we could. We helped out in the world."

"I'm tired of this war," Donovan said, taking a hit off his Kaliber. "I want the kind of life I had before."

"You miss the old West Side, and you haven't even moved off it yet," Mosko said.

"I miss what the West Side was when I was younger. Marcy is right—the old turf is too expensive now for interesting people to live there. The artists and intellectuals who don't happen to be rich have moved to Greenpoint and Williamsburg. And I really *do* need a place where Daniel can get around in his chair by himself. You know . . . go into the garden by himself, hit the pavement by himself . . . in a few years he's gonna want to roll up to the bodega for an Eskimo Pie."

Mosko looked over fondly at Donovan and waggled his bottle in a toast. "You're a really good guy, you know that?"

"Thanks," Donovan replied, picking up a pebble and bouncing it off one of the concrete lions—the one without the laptop on it. Then he added, "Those things have got to go."

"I know this place on Ralph Avenue where you can get really cool concrete flamingos," Mosko said.

"Sounds good to me," Donovan replied.

"Me and the boys are planning on coming around and giving you a housewarming party. We'll fill the joint up with beer cans and Doritos and pizza boxes and make you feel just like the old days when you were a bachelor and the only thing you had to worry about was keeping enough ice in the fridge."

Donovan stood and stretched. Sensing closure, Mosko joined him.

"Want to see where we're building the physical therapy room?" Donovan asked.

"Why not?"

"I'm also having the gym equipment you guys gave me for my fiftieth put in there," Donovan said. "Maybe you and Daniel and me can work out together sometime."

"That's a deal," Mosko replied, picking up his laptop and handing the bag of popcorn to Donovan.

A proud homeowner, Donovan said, "Come let me show you my basement." And he led the way into the brownstone.